UNBOUND TRUST

DIANA CASTILLEJA

Purple Sword Publications
Tucson, Arizona

This is a work of fiction. Names, places, characters, and events are fictitious in every regard. Any similarities to actual events and persons, living or dead, is purely coincidental. Any trademarks, service marks, product names, or named features are assumed to be the property of their respective owners, and are used only for reference. There is no implied endorsement if any of these terms are used.

UNBOUND TRUST
Copyright © 2014 DIANA CASTILLEJA
ISBN 978-1-61292-121-1
ISBN 10: 1612921213

Cover Art Designed by Anastasia Rabiyah
Edited by Shoshana Hurwitz and Traci Markou

Published by Purple Sword Publications, LLC
Tucson, Arizona, USA
www.PurpleSword.com

Chapter One

"He's beautiful, Delilah," Brooke said, leaning over the tinted wood crib where her six-month-old nephew slept without a care in the world. A disorderly wave of black hair flowed over his head. The baby resembled a sweet cherub in his fluffy white jumper. Brooke's first thought was that looks could be deceiving, knowing what kind of child her older brother had been. All four of the brothers and sisters had some story to scare their mother gray. "I'm sorry I wasn't here for the big moment."

"Don't worry about it," Delilah replied. Standing several inches shorter than the new mama, Brooke peered up at her sister-in-law. "Roman kept himself together long enough to get me to the hospital. Then," Delilah said with remembered humor, her eyes twinkling, "he had my permission to fall apart."

Brooke's finger drifted to smooth the rich cap of hair covering Adrian's crown. The sensation reminded her of soft down, silken and delicate. Her brother and his wife were a very lucky and blessed couple. Brooke asked curiously, "There weren't any problems at the hospital, then?"

Delilah shook her head. "The blood samples didn't show anything."

Brooke exhaled in quiet relief. "I've always wondered. We were born at home, and needless to say, we stay away from doctors and needles and avid curiosity."

Sunshine brightened the baby's room from the large windows flanking the outer wall, washing the room in light and warmth. The room was filled with an impossible-to-miss gentle happiness, making Brooke's own urges seem to be right in front of her.

"From what I can tell, talking to your dad and Roman, the changes happen after puberty. Isn't that when you started training for it?"

Brooke inched away from the crib, where she'd been admiring her nephew. Delilah draped a thin blanket over the baby for his nap. "Yeah. It sounds right. I guess we're a little spoiled with Selene in the family. Our own doctor."

"Sure doesn't hurt anything, that's for sure," Delilah remarked with an answering smirk. "Speaking of the dynamic duo, are they back yet?" Delilah asked as they left the baby's room, walking into the living room together.

"No. St. Marten doesn't have a prayer. Something else I missed while I was in Belgium with Aunt Jerry—their wedding," Brooke replied with a regretful sigh. "I swear, if she hadn't needed me so much, I would have been here in a heartbeat. Their wedding and Adrian's wonderful arrival."

"I have pictures. Do you want to see them?" Delilah offered.

"I'd love to." Brooke was amazed at the woman Roman had found for his wife. Delilah was a gracious, generous woman. She stood inches taller than Brooke and looked fabulous for recently having had a baby.

Brooke had noticed her blue eyes first, a shade darker than sky blue. They were beautifully framed by black hair. What shocked Brooke more was that Delilah had taken their family secret and had made it her own.

When Brooke had arrived the day before in

Oregon, intent on finding her sister, she'd discovered that Selene was on her honeymoon. Being out of the country had put Brooke out of contact with the rest of the family, and she'd missed all the good stuff. After calling Morgan and Roman, Brooke came to crash with Roman in Wyoming. Plus, she got to see her first nephew. Dead asleep, he was a charmer.

"I'm sure once they get home, Selene will be only too happy to tell you about Bram." Delilah turned the photo pages at a slow pace. "He's exactly what that doctor needed," she told Brooke with amusement.

"Is that him?" Brooke asked, examining a picture of a tall man in a tuxedo.

"That's him. Not bad for a doctor," Delilah said, smiling in apparent memory of the wedding, her fingers dancing over the various pictures. "Really nice guy too."

"I'm sure he is if Selene found him. She's very gentle," Brooke said.

Delilah's brow flickered in surprise. "Gentle? Her?" She laughed again, but not unkindly. "Your sister will face anything. That doesn't equate to gentle with me."

"Reminds me of someone, but I wonder who?" Roman's teasing bass made the women snap up from the picture album on Delilah's lap. "Hi, Babs." He bent and gave Delilah a quick kiss. "Hello, beautiful," Roman said in a purr.

Brooke giggled behind tight lips. It was good seeing her brother so in love. "Hi, Roman. Get everything in town?" Brooke asked as he straightened from kissing Delilah. Married life and fatherhood agreed with him, if his adoring expression was anything to believe. "Yeah, I'll have Adrian's playground done in no time," he informed them.

Delilah rolled her eyes. "Roman, he can barely roll

over."

"That's why I'm starting now. I might have it done by the time he graduates," he said, laughing with a rich, happy sound. He ran a hand over his midnight black hair, disturbing the thickness with his absent gesture. "I'll be around back. Just holler if you need me."

"All right," Delilah replied.

Brooke continued to peruse the photos in the packed album. Selene's wedding had been beautiful. Her dress flowed like a mythical creation of satin, lace, and sheer gauze that sparkled as though it were sewn from the stars, glinting in the daylight. She had made a stunning bride.

Brooke struggled with her own fears with both her sister's and brother's happiness so right in front of her. *Two down, two to go.*

"She was gorgeous, wasn't she?" Brooke managed to say through a raw throat a moment later.

"Yeah." Delilah sighed. "Your parents have the most incredible house. I wouldn't be surprised to see all of you married there."

Brooke shook her head regretfully. "I doubt it. Morgan probably; he's still gorgeous. Especially with those eyes. Me," she told her wistfully, "I'm an old maid. Thirty-one sucks."

Side by side, Delilah bumped Brooke's shoulder with her own. "Hey, I hit thirty this year."

"Nice try. You're hitched and a new mom. But it's not a big deal. I'm not trying. Selene found Bram on the trails by chance when she was studying. That was fate with a capital F. The closest I get to a male form is the checkout boy at my grocery store."

Delilah stared at Brooke, a concerned frown cinching her brow. "I haven't known you long, but is there something you want to talk about?"

Brooke covered up her lonely misery with an

absent rush of words. "Just the usual. I'm over thirty. I feel that urge. I'm lonely. I'm surrounded by people who've found what I feel I'm missing." Brooke drew a deep, steadying breath. No sense in being maudlin this early in her visit. "Sorry, I've been on a pity party for over a month now. I don't know why," she explained sheepishly.

Delilah leaned toward her. "Would you be offended if I looked? Maybe I could see something on the horizon for you."

Brooke openly studied the guilelessness in the brunette's blue gaze. "A week ago, I'd have jumped at the chance. For some reason, being home messes with me. Thanks, but no. I'll take my lumps like a big girl."

Delilah offered an understanding smile. "I know. It's hard, and you've got a lot to catch up on." Delilah's attention shifted toward the nursery when Adrian began to cry. "Here, look some more. Let me go see what the prince is upset about."

Brooke moved the album over to her lap as Delilah swept from the couch and aimed for her son's room. There were pictures of her parents and the house where Brooke and the others had been raised. In Brooke's mind, there was nothing like northern Minnesota, beautiful with trees and unbelievable snowfalls during the cold winters. Christmases had been a blast with snowball fights and sledding to die for. There were pictures of Roman and Delilah, with Adrian bundled up like a miniature snowman in a cute powder-blue outfit in their arms. Delilah appeared almost normal in height compared to Roman, and Roman's expression was absolutely, gloriously happy in the picture.

There were more photos of Selene, her blonde hair curled at the ends, standing with people or standing alone holding a huge bouquet of tiger lilies. Brooke's finger traced the photo. She flipped the page slowly, regretfully. She was really sorry she had missed it.

The next photo she found was of Selene and Bram. He was a very handsome guy. Thick brown hair and an aura of happiness in every picture. They were a perfect match also. Brooke could almost feel the strength of their bond in the picture at her fingertips. The way he held her close, a possessive and protective hand on her slim waist. There were a few photos of when Delilah had captured him unaware, with an adoring gaze, staring at her sister. The blatant ease of his emotions brought up that poignant ache in her one more time. Alone, it was harder to dismiss the nagging emptiness to the background of her mind.

Where was her mate? When was she going to find the man who would hold her and cherish her?

Brooke felt so old.

The sisters shared the blonde hair, although Brooke's was a bit darker, more honeyed. It was their most obvious shared gene, which came from their mother. Selene and Morgan were both born with those incredible storm-gray eyes while Brooke and Roman had the near-obsidian black stare of their father.

Most people thought she wore contacts because they were so dark. Hers were several shades lighter than true black, but against her blonde hair, they came across much bolder. It was an intimidating combination with Roman's black hair. Brooke didn't believe she could say the same. The difference was too startling, too contrasting, to be considered beautiful.

Brooke hadn't been blessed with the looks, either. Morgan got that entire gene, the rat. Roman was as tall as could be and built to tackle a bear. Selene was of medium height but had the smarts.

Brooke, well, was simply Brooke; Babs to her brothers, as in babbling brook. It was meant with love, she knew it, but some days she could just smack them senseless. And since she'd arrived home, she'd been bombarded by this incredible sense of melancholy. As though something was just out of reach. Brooke knew she really wasn't old, but over barely a year's time, two of her siblings had found their mates. That made her feel old.

Brooke's fingers continued to follow the photos of family and friends. She found one near the bottom of a page of Bram and another man, arms locked around each other in friendship. They wore broad grins, laughter making both attractive. Both men were tall, with solid shoulders and similar expressions. There was something playful about the pair. Maybe they were best friends, she mused. She squinted and found herself giggling at the picture. The other guy was giving Bram rabbit ears! Two fingers poked up over Bram's head, and he was completely oblivious to it. She laughed a little harder now, seeing the mischief aside from their joviality. Someone got Bram at his wedding.

"Sorry. He rolled over and couldn't find reverse," Delilah said, sitting next to Brooke once more. "What's so funny?"

"This." Brooke pointed to the picture.

"Oh, that's Mitch. He's a crack-up." Delilah squinted too. "I never noticed that before," she said, chuckling deeply with Brooke. "That stinker."

"Who is he?" Brooke asked, curious.

"Bram's younger brother. He's a firefighter in St. Louis."

"I should have known," Brooke murmured, noticing the resemblance easily now. Her finger traced the photo with absent sweeps.

"Yeah, he's a great guy too. I guess their family had good male genes or something," Delilah told her. "Their mom is sweet. She married an architect not too long ago who she'd been dating, Bram found Selene, and Mitch is single."

"Wow, you keep up on the family pretty well." Brooke turned the page, wondering if she'd find any more of Mitch. He was cute.

"Between diapers and feedings, I also counsel the Senate, and I've developed a new surgery to give men brains," Delilah intoned with an airy toss of her hair.

"In other words, what else is there to do?" Brooke asked, teasing her sister-in-law.

"Something like that," Delilah said, smiling glibly. "I'm not complaining, but it's quiet out here. I've slowed down a lot. I'm glad you came by here first."

"Me too. I love Aunt Jerry, but she's eccentric. She's doing better now with her garden up to par, but let me tell you, when she became depressed last year, I thought I'd be the one to run her through. I'm glad she pulled out of it. She's a tough woman, hardy." Brooke flipped another page, stopping unconsciously. "I missed talking about normal stuff. I love herbs and flowers, but Aunt Jerry turned it into an extreme sport."

"How?" Delilah asked with a perplexed stare.

"I guess it was how she worked her way out of her depression. She literally started from scratch and renamed everything. And I mean everything, from parsley to hummingbirds. At first I thought she'd gone off the deep end, until I began to recognize a few of the names. She renamed everything to match the old-world language forms, before Latin, then I had to learn them so I knew what I was doing. I don't know when I'll ever need it, but if you want archaic language for a witch's brew, I'm your gal."

"Incredible," Delilah murmured. "I had no idea people still... Well, actually that's not true. I guess I did. I mean, look at your family. Look at me, for that matter. We're everywhere, aren't we?" Delilah asked, bending closer to keep her voice lowered.

"All over the place," Brooke replied in agreement. "But we're outnumbered. I don't want to recreate the Salem Witch Trials with what I know."

"Me neither," Delilah' responded.

"Del! Can you give me a hand?" Roman's brusque shout was quite clear in the midday stillness of the house.

"He's going to wake up Adrian! Time to beat him up again." She rose from her perched seat on the couch, saying, "Stay put. Could you get me if Adrian wakes up?"

"Sure," Brooke replied, wanting to wander over more of the photos. She listened as Delilah left, muttering under her breath about flipping him again. Brooke didn't even want to ask.

The album had closed over her hand while she and Delilah had sat talking, but she opened it when Delilah left. She found another one of Mitch, standing with an older couple. His mother and her new husband, she guessed. He'd tilted his head toward his mother, who stood probably eight inches shorter than her son. His mother wore an easy smile, a mirror image of her son's, with her graying hair twisted up in a doubled braid. Brooke wondered where their father was.

The last picture she found of Mitch was his best. He was by himself, propped on a shoulder against a tree, with his arms crossed over his tuxedo-covered chest and his gaze following something out of sight. He wore a relaxed, laughing grin, the sunlight hitting his brown hair through the sifting leaves of the tree. The picture was carefree, innocent. He possessed his own charm in the curve of his mouth, in the coiled lounging of his body.

Yep, he was cute all right.

Brooke continued through the rest of the album,

catching flashes of her childhood home. She was extremely happy for both Roman and Selene. She shouldn't feel so let down because she was alone. When she'd agreed to help Aunt Jerry, she knew it would be a long road for her and a longer one for her aunt, but she'd missed so much over the last year and a half, like somehow she'd missed her chance. She honestly didn't know what that chance was or what she'd missed out on.

If she had a biological clock, it was the equivalent to a ticking time bomb now, but she wasn't going to have sex, not to have a child, alone. She believed in marriage and love and family. It was probably why there was a tightness in her chest being with her brother. He had what she wanted.

She knew the problems and obstacles she faced when it came to finding the one man who would be everything to her. Somehow Roman and Selene had surpassed them. Somehow their mates had accepted their family's secret. Her father had always said it was different for everyone, every generation. Brooke didn't know if she could take the chance to reveal herself. She wasn't a bountiful beauty to capture a man's attention. She wasn't a model of courageous strength to attract a strong mate. She was just herself—a woman who could recite the herb dictionary backward in two languages. A woman who really wanted children. A woman who was tired of being lonely, who wanted someone to hold her hand on long walks, who could hear her in the depths of the wilderness and not be terrified.

She wanted someone she could trust with her secret. She wanted someone to fill the growing void inside her. She wanted to find her mate.

Unconsciously her hand returned to a page of the photo album. Her gaze fell on Mitch, against the tree.

If she didn't have anyone right now, she could dream, and maybe someday she'd find her mate, or he would find her.

She'd told Delilah the truth. She'd been absorbed with Aunt Jerry. Brooke needed time to focus or to let the Fates have their wicked way with her. Digging into the future now wouldn't be productive. She closed the album with a heartfelt sigh. Maybe it was time to start looking around her, though. After all, there were men in Wyoming and Oregon. Maybe one of them was her mate. She couldn't have a family without one. Not the way she wanted one.

She'd been on a few dates, but not with anyone who set her world on fire, no one she felt compelled to include in her circle, no one she wanted to trust with what she was.

She stood, putting the album on the bookcase from where she'd seen Delilah pull it off. Brooke's gaze wandered over photos of Delilah and Roman on their wedding day, others with Adrian.

This was what Brooke wanted. She didn't have any clue how to get it or if she was going to have to continue to be patient. Since her urges had been getting stronger, it made patience a hard-to-find commodity. She could do this, one day at a time.

When she heard Adrian whimper, she strolled to his room. Not every emergency required a mama. *Sometimes an aunt could fill the bill,* she thought with a smile.

Chapter Two

"Hey, Mitch, you still heading out on vacation this week?"

Mitch tipped up from where he and Mack were watching TV on the upper floor of the firehouse, relaxing lazily on the large, abused couch. "Yeah, Bram should be home, and I wanted to talk to him about some stuff." Mitch studied his crew chief as Tory sauntered over and rested with a thigh against the arm of the couch.

"You're not thinking about leaving us, are you?" Tory asked in his usual straightforward manner.

"Nah," Mitch said with an unconcerned shrug. "But there's some great property up there. I thought I might make an investment for later."

Tory coughed a laugh. "For retirement?"

"Yeah, sure. I don't plan on keeping your asses out of trouble for the rest of my life," he retorted with a laid-back grin. "When I went up there for those fires a few months ago, before his wedding, the views were incredible. Have you ever flown over Yellowstone or the Tetons?"

Tory scratched his head. "No, can't say that I have."

"What about you, Mack? You ever been up there?" Mitch asked, turning the other way.

The muscled blond next to him shook his head. "Nope. Not even close. The farthest west I've been is Dallas."

"That's a ripe area for forest fires," Tory added.

"I know. I can't help but get kind of nervous because both Bram and his brother-in-law live in a hot zone," Mitch said, running a palm over his neck.

Mack made kissy noises next to him. Mitch punched his arm.

"Knock it off," Tory said gruffly, but Mitch couldn't miss the weight of Tory's watchful gaze on him. "Come to the office, Mitch."

"Mitch is in trouble," Mack sang in a high falsetto.

"You're next, Branson," Tory said in a growl. Mack shut up and started watching TV again.

Mitch followed Tory downstairs, wondering what was going on. His vacation had been pre-approved over two months ago, not long after those corridor fires he'd been sent to do the flyovers on.

He loved what he did, and he wasn't contemplating any intention of bailing on his crew, his other family: Tory, Mack, Eli, Big, and himself.

Tory was their leader. Mitch respected him after serving with him for more than nine years at the same house on the same trucks. Mack Branson was similar to Mitch: well-trained, calm, and collected.

Eli worked the water, and Big did anything needing strength: wall bashing, door crashing, and ladder.

They'd worked out their system over the years and performed with precision when called into service. Mitch knew of no reason to want to change it.

He entered the commander's office behind Tory, hearing a terse voice in response say "Shut the door."

Tory was a little older than the rest of the crew, around forty, but he was as fit as a man of twenty-five. He issued the orders, but he worked as hard as any man on his team. No man was an island on his crew. That was one of the things Mitch really respected about his crew chief.

Tory gave Mitch a signal to sit down. "I won't bust your balls over this. I know you've been restless since you were called out to do the flying drops. I guess what I'm saying here..." Tory coughed, glancing down, then raised his knowing gaze once more, not hiding his concern. "...is that if you decide you're leaving, don't leave me hanging."

Mitch sat in stunned quiet. One leg was propped over a knee, but it dropped with a rather shocked slap. "I'm not going anywhere, Tory. I went, I liked what I saw. I can be close to my brother if I do get something out that way. That's it."

Tory gave Mitch an assessing stare. "What about your mother?"

Mitch met his gaze unflinchingly. "She's in good hands. Harold treats her damned well," he remarked. "Look, Tory, if you have something to say, just spill it."

Tory didn't blink an eye. "All right. I believe you." Mitch noticed as tension seemed to disappear from Tory's shoulders as he relaxed beneath his uniform-blue T-shirt. "I guess I'm concerned. You're like a son to me, Mitch. You've been here the longest, and I got to watch you take your training. You love to fly, and you've been scratching your ass since you got back trying to figure out how to make it all work."

He'd been that obvious? "Yeah, I guess I have, but I'm not leaving. I haven't been on a real vacation since I came on board. Bram's wedding doesn't count. I was gone for three whole days."

Tory leaped to his feet unexpectedly and thrust out his hand. "Enjoy your time, Benedetti. Be back in two weeks, or I'll come looking for you."

Mitch smiled, clasping his chief's hand in a firm grip. "I will, and you won't have to."

* * * *

Mitch couldn't restrain the relaxed smile he wore as he drove from the Bend Airport to Bram and Selene's cottage. With his window rolled down, he inhaled a deep draught of clean air. Nothing like it in St. Louis, or anywhere. In that, he could agree completely with his older brother.

Bram was the codirector at Bend Medical Center along with his now wife, Selene. They were a remarkable team and absolutely, completely made for one another.

He couldn't grasp how his brother, Bram, the solid and quiet one, had become tied up in a kidnapping and shootout. As he'd heard it, Selene and her brother Morgan had been trying to expose a poacher, but it had turned into a huge fiasco with the police department.

The poacher turned out to be one of the deputies. He, in turn, had kidnapped Rebecca, Bram's ex-wife. She had made an unannounced visit, trying to play her guilt card with Bram over their divorce.

The whole situation turned weird after that. The deputy who had kidnapped Rebecca wanted to trade for Selene, which made no sense to Mitch about what the man had wanted with his sister-in-law. Bram had been shot during the rescue. Rebecca claimed she'd been led from the camp where the poacher had hidden her, saved by a dark wolf.

Mitch snorted in definite disbelief. Wolves didn't live out here. Even he knew that. He knew most of the wild ones he'd heard reported were near the Yellowstone protected lands. The wolves couldn't understand what being on protected lands meant to them, but it did mean they weren't living this far west. It had probably been nothing but a large German shepherd or some other type of rescue dog. It had been raining in thick sheets and dark as black ink from the stories Mitch had heard about the whole episode.

Rebecca had obviously suffered during her ordeal. The deputy had held her for more than two and a half days at a minimal survival camp out in the wilderness. It was sheer luck that Bram had found her and was then able to stop the poacher before anyone was killed.

There had been some very deep concern for his brother for a while, though. Bram had spiked a fever during his recovery from the bullet he'd *stepped in front of*. It had been touch and go for a couple of days, but he was completely recovered now and going full steam ahead. If Mitch's notes were right, they should have returned from St. Marten last week. He guessed that should have been enough time before showing up on their doorstep. That's what family did, and he was talented at being a nuisance. He grinned with devilish enjoyment at seeing his brother again.

Yet, even with the anticipation of seeing them, as much as he hated to admit it, Tory was right. He had been feeling restless, but it wasn't a reason for him to bail on the firehouse or the crew. Yes, he liked flying. Nothing compared to the adrenaline rush of meeting the fire head-on, flying over it, and using the best of his abilities and training to serve that purpose: to make a mark, to hit the fire where it would do the most good, to save the forests, the wildlife, and the people. That was what he had trained for, but there wasn't one thing on his horizon to make him not want to return home. The firehouse was his home; the crew was his family. Mitch wasn't about to give any of it up.

With, at most, half of his attention on where he was going, he traveled the highway ahead to the first turn he needed when his thoughts derailed. Mitch slowed his rented Jeep as he focused into the tree line with a dread-filled stare. He pulled up behind the wrecked car, buried windshield deep into the trees. He parked a safe distance away, automatically reaching for his phone on his belt, but remembered he'd packed it. Damn airline regulations!

"Hello?" he called out as he cautiously hurried to the driver's side. He couldn't smell any gas, which by the car's condition was a miracle. The car was an average-sized, dark blue sedan and as he neared, he discovered the top of a blonde head. "Hey, can you hear me?"

The air bag had deflated and she appeared unconscious, slumped against the steering wheel. He jerked on the door, metal grinding with the tugging pressure of the fender being shoved up against the door. "Can you hear me?" he asked again as he searched for a pulse. He found it, strongly thrumming beneath pale skin. Relief was a quickly controlled emotion. He did a quick inventory and noted her legs, jammed tight under the wheel and dash. "Damn it!"

Mitch raced for his Jeep. Tearing through his luggage, he yanked out his phone and turned it on, cursing impatiently as it found a signal. Calling for help as he neared the car again, she moaned. The woman's voice was thin, pained. He knelt down. "Can you talk? I'm going to call the hospital and get you some help." He pushed her hair out of the way, searching for signs of distress. Except for her pulse throbbing in the column of her neck, he couldn't discern anything more yet.

He was shocked to hear her argue. "No. Hospital," she gasped on a low moan. "Call. Selene. Sister," she said, sounding stronger than he would have thought possible, even if she was dazed and uncomfortable.

"You've got to be kidding." This woman needed a hospital. He had no way of knowing if she had internal injuries or something more than he could find on his own without removing her from the wreckage, and that had to be done carefully because of the collapsed dash. Her head lolled in his direction, and her eyes opened. Not gray like his sister-in-law's, not even blue for being a blonde, but the deepest coffee black eyes he'd ever encountered.

She licked her lips. "Call Selene. No hospital." She gave him the number on pain-filled, breathy bursts, stunned she'd managed it at all before her eyes slid shut to pass out once more. He would call Selene. She was only a few miles farther up the road. Mitch knew she'd want to know what had happened if this was her sister. Then he would call the hospital.

She answered right away. "Selene, this is Mitch," he rattled off hurriedly. "I know you weren't expecting me, but I found your sister, or she says she's your sister."

"Brooke?" she cried, immediately worried. "What happened? Where is she? She was supposed to be here almost an hour ago."

Mitch explained what he had found and her sister's condition to Selene. "I was going to call the hospital next. She may need X-rays."

"No, don't call anyone. I'll come and get her." Selene hung up before Mitch could argue. He held his phone out and stared at it. Don't call anyone? Were they all nuts? Brooke groaned next to him and he shifted on his haunches to see her better, forgetting everything else but trying to help her.

"Hang in there. I'm going to sit you up," he explained, keeping his tone low and soothing. He stretched across her slack form to undo her seat belt. He ran trained hands over her body, searching. He didn't feel any prominent breaks in her upper body, but he couldn't reach her legs buried under the frame of the car. No telling if she needed help there. He found bruises on her arms where the bag had ruptured the plastic of the wheel compartment. She had a solid bruise on her forehead, but that was all he was able to find.

He heard Selene's Cherokee pull up with a sliding grind of roadside, then her fast-running steps. "Let me take a look," she ordered quickly. Mitch made room as Selene did an educated check on her sister's vitals. "Thank God. Nothing serious."

"What about her legs? We need a lift to pull the dash off her," he pointed out.

"Brooke, Babs, honey, can you hear me?" Selene said next to her sister's ear. Brooke moaned incoherently. "Can you feel your legs? Can you move them?"

Mitch watched her lips move but couldn't hear her himself while standing over Selene's shoulder.

"Good. Mitch, could you get my medical bag? It's on the backseat," she said with a calm assurance, motioning with a toss of her chin toward her vehicle. Mitch was impressed as he turned at a run. If she was this composed with her own sister, her patients would have a doctor of steel.

When he returned, he stopped behind her, shocked to find Brooke lying on the ground next to the car door. "How did she get out?" Selene crouched next to her, running her palms over Brooke's legs.

"I helped her twist," she replied without emotion. "But she's out again. Can you hold her? I'll take her to the cabin, and she can rest there."

"Selene, doesn't she need to go to the hospital?" He knew he sounded as bewildered as he felt.

"No, she'll be fine. After she wakes up, she can tell us what happened." Selene accepted her bag and took Brooke's blood pressure, swabbing an antiseptic wipe to clean the bruise on her forehead. A small break in the skin seemed to be the worst of the damage. "At least she doesn't need any stitches."

"But what if something's broken?" he asked her.

"There isn't," Selene reassured him. "Pick her up, and I'll call Bram in a few minutes. He was due off this afternoon anyway."

"Will my Jeep be all right?" He tossed a meaningful glance at the red 4x4 he'd rented.

"Yeah, you and Bram can pick it up in an hour or so when he comes home. We don't have strippers out here," she told him.

He shook his head as he knelt, gathering Brooke's limp form. "How does a country girl know chop shop lingo?" He cradled her petite form in his hold, standing straight. "What does she weigh? She's light."

"Probably one-twenty. You're just strong," she teased even as she kept a sharp eye on her sister. "And I lived in California when I studied. You learn all kinds of things that aren't educational on campus." He hefted himself up into her vehicle, careful of Brooke in his arms.

Selene made the drive as fast as the road seemed to allow without too many bumps. She opened his door, then the front door of the house. "Take her to the guest room. I'm going to call Bram and let him know you're both here."

Mitch did as she asked. No hospital, but if Selene the doctor knew it wasn't necessary, then there wasn't anyone better.

Mitch made Brooke comfortable, taking off her sandals and tossing a blanket over legs of creamy, pale skin in peach-colored shorts. She looked restful, fairly pretty, even with an egg-sized bruise on her forehead.

He left her sleeping on the bed to join Selene in the kitchen at the front of the cabin. "I wonder what happened."

"I have no idea. Brooke is a very careful driver."

Selene offered him a drink, sipping at her own tea. "The car is history."

"She must have been going fast, but that was the turn," he said, worry behind the wreck dimming the relaxed pleasure he'd been enjoying on the drive. "I guess we'll have to be patient."

"I'm not well known for patience either," she agreed with a commiserating smile. "Bram will be here in about twenty minutes. Are you hungry?"

Mitch rubbed his stomach. "I could eat."

"Yeah, let me twist your arm," she retorted with an easy, short laugh. Mitch offered his help, but she pushed him out. "Go stare at a wall somewhere."

"Yes, ma'am," he said with a wink. Mitch ambled down the hall to wash his hands and decided to slip a peeked glance into the spare room to check on the woman resting on the bed. *Well, that's what I get for showing up unannounced,* he thought. He'd have to get a hotel room. Not a problem. He didn't stay in the doorway long when he found her unmoved from where he'd left her.

He strolled to the living room, deciding to hang out until his brother showed up, then he'd get his Jeep and return to town to check into a hotel somewhere.

The paintings on the wall above and around the fireplace were awe inspiring. He couldn't help but study them. Their detail was no less than museum quality. Several were wolves in striking oil colors and elegant scrollwork frames. One of the paintings depicted a whole pack, six all together.

There were others, a beautiful pale one standing alone, another which was as dark as a sooty night. There were others placed along the wall. Tilting in his study, he realized it almost came across like a wall of family. He shook away the musing. Selene had said she had a thing for the wolf and that her father was a talented artist. Mitch wouldn't argue the talent, so why not show them, and him, off?

He'd visited the cabin once or twice before. That was when he'd been in Bend flying over the neighboring mountains fighting the forest fires. He remembered he'd been impressed by the paintings then when he'd dropped in to see his recuperating brother and Selene. On a cornering wall were the family pictures and photos, one of them being a large print of Bram and Selene from their wedding. It had been a beautiful day for a wedding: sunshine and cool Minnesota weather. Her family owned the most amazing house. It resembled an old castle in design, but it didn't feel like one. There'd been warmth, a home where love and laughter had been raised. He raised a hand in salute to the picture of the couple. They had a wonderful thing going for them.

Mitch didn't moon over his own state of bachelorhood, not after Janice. She'd almost made him reconsider his life. Almost. Until he'd realized what a mistake it would have been. Until he realized he'd be doing no less than chopping off an arm to satisfy her. No one was worth it. He couldn't change who he was, no sooner than he could change the fact that he lived for what he did—fight fires. But the danger element had frightened Janice to the point where she'd expected him to quit. Mitch couldn't, and thankfully he realized it before he'd made the biggest mistake of his life.

Bram was lucky. He and Selene were on the same page. Selene was nothing like Rebecca, Bram's ex-wife. Selene wasn't the center of her own universe, for one thing, and she adored Bram. It was in her gaze, apparent in each of the pictures on the wall.

"When I said go stare at a wall, I wasn't serious," Selene observed from behind him, her humor clear.

"I always get stuck admiring the paintings," he admitted with a sheepish glance over his shoulder. "Does anyone besides your father paint?"

"Brooke can, but she's the nature girl." Selene stepped forward, and he noticed a sincere gaze of adoration as she perused the paintings. "She's all into flowers and herbs. That's why she wasn't here for the wedding. She was in Belgium helping Aunt Jerry with a problem. They are two of a kind. Brooke helped keep her steady until she was stronger."

"I remember you mentioning her once before."

She chuckled at his side, her expression telling him she remembered exactly what he meant. "Don't worry, I'm not going to play cupid. I was teasing with Bram. He had awakened right before you came into the room and seeing him smiling, knowing he was recovering, was such a relief."

Mitch remembered those moments. His brother's injury was the only reason he'd been given a break from the fire lines. "That was some story, too. Rebecca swears it was a wolf, at least the last time I saw her she did. It's been a while, but she hasn't changed her story."

"No, no wolves. Just Bram and my brother. I was hiding." Selene shivered. Mitch knew from his brother exactly how close it had been for all of them. "I was the bait to draw Markson out of the shadows, where he'd been hiding. He'd given us an exchange location, but he wanted me first. Bram took advantage and located the camp, allowing Rebecca to escape. No one had any idea it was him until we managed to do at least that. He'd been successful for two years trapping small game and tanning the pelts, selling them on the black market. A lot of the wildlife he'd been trapping was protected. I hate to say it, but I don't look anything like what he'd been catching."

"No, you're prettier," Bram said from the doorway,

bringing Mitch's attention to the front of the cabin. "Hey, Mitch. Surprise visit?" Bram closed the door behind him, hanging his keys on the wood pegs by the door.

"My vacation, but with Brooke here, I'll crash in town." Mitch's brow furrowed. "But why would he want you if he was poaching?"

"Because we were getting close to finding him out. Morgan is an excellent tracker, and it came down to who would get caught first," Selene explained with utter unconcern. "His plan was to stop us either with blackmail or by threatening something once he had me. It didn't work out the way he'd planned. The police made the news, and not in a good way, because of their lackadaisical approach to our requests for searches to be done when we turned in proof of the traps. It turned out the reports were taken by Markson, the man we were after. No police department stays sparkly when they're harboring the enemy."

Mitch shook his head. "No, I imagine not."

"Why don't we go get your Jeep? I saw it on the road," Bram said. Mitch nodded and followed his brother out the door.

Chapter Three

Selene walked into the guest room carrying a cup of tea. She brushed hair from Brooke's cheek, and Brooke sighed into her touch.

"Are they gone?" Brooke asked.

"Yes, but not for long." Selene sank to the bed. "What happened?" She placed the tea on the table and waited.

Brooke's eyes blinked open, finding Selene's worried gray gaze. "I wish I knew. I remember turning on my blinker and then a tank disguised as a Ford shoved me off the road. I heard him ask how fast, probably forty, trying not to be the car under the tank." Brooke groaned as she sat up, pressing a shaky hand to her forehead. "This hurts like no one's business."

"It won't last. You've never really been hurt, have you?"

Brooke shook her head carefully, not wanting to test the ache's limits. "No, not that I can remember."

Selene patted her arm, reaching for the tea. "Here, drink this. You'll be back to normal in a few hours. You weren't hurt too badly."

Brooke sipped, feeling the warmth all the way to her toes, where she wiggled them. "I never meant to be a problem. I just wanted to see everyone before I left for Mom and Dad's."

"You're not being a problem," Selene replied, soothing her. "You scared me a little, that's all. You're as punctual as the seasons."

Brooke's gaze wandered over her younger sister. She had a healthy glow and an easy smile. "Married life is working for you too." She couldn't help the wistful sound in the statement.

"Bram is the best," Selene admitted with a rosy blush. "I had no idea how to make things work, but somehow they did."

"How? How do I do it?" Brooke asked. "I feel so old, and I want my own family."

"Oh, Brooke. It'll happen." Selene cupped a palm to her sister's cheek. "To be honest, I was scared spitless when Bram showed up. I had no clue how to make it work, but when you find him, you'll know."

"Yeah, but will he?" Brooke asked, her shoulders rounding inward.

Selene gave her a sharp, concerned look. "Aunt Jerry messed with your head, didn't she?"

"Yeah, I guess she did, but jeez, she's a hundred and forty-eight! And regardless of whether she looks our age, she hasn't found her mate!"

Selene smirked knowingly at her sister's show of temper. Brooke scowled back. She wasn't in the mood to be pacified.

"Aunt Jerry is a different egg from us."

"Only because we're different from the rest of the damn planet!" she argued. Brooke pulled up her legs to sit Indian style on the bed, propping her chin in her clasped hands. "I'm sorry, Selene. It was hard staying at Roman's too. I'd probably be more comfortable with Morgan," Brooke muttered.

"Yeah, if there ever was a loner, he'd be the mold for it," Selene agreed. "Why don't you come eat?" Selene's expression grew devilish, her eyes glinting with her mirth. "Want to shock Bram's brother? Be at the table when they get back. He almost had a cow when you twisted out of the car."

Brooke's shoulders shook with her laughter. "When did you get so devious?" she asked, standing from the bed. She felt all right, only a little headachy overall.

"When I discovered how easy it is to fool some people," she admitted. "And he didn't see anything either. I made him leave."

Brooke shrugged as Selene collected the cup. "I didn't think about it. I did what you said. I trust you."

Selene pecked a kiss to Brooke's cheek. "And I trust you, Babs," she trilled with a playful grin, then fled from the room.

"Ooh! Just you wait, Selene!" Brooke was laughing too as she dashed down the hallway, chasing after her sister with a pillow from the bed clutched in her hands. Only she smacked into the solid wall of a male chest. Her air left her in a rush as thickly muscled arms crushed her into a warm, incredibly hard body.

"Hey, shouldn't you be lying down or something?"

She inhaled and found the scent of the man who held her. This was who had carried her in after her accident. "Mitch?" She gasped sharply, trying to straighten out her thoughts and other things. Everything about him swarmed her senses, from the heated strength of his body where he held her in his embrace to the scent of skin-warmed cotton. She licked her lips looking up at him. He was even cuter than his pictures.

Her grip tightened on the pillow in her hands as her lungs fought to drag in air. Apparently, they'd forgotten how. Her mind didn't want to work either, and her fingers clutched tighter. "Sorry," she brokenly managed to say. "I was intent on harming my sister. I didn't see you there." She relaxed in increments as he gradually loosened the impressive cage of his arms, but he didn't let her go.

His gaze was chocolaty smooth as he stared at her. Mitch's face was a little more squared and sharper than Bram's angular length, but the hair was almost the same color, maybe a shade lighter than his brother's. He had it trimmed short, and for some reason Brooke wanted to touch it.

"We brought your bags in with us," he was saying, bringing her back with a jolt. His hands dropped completely, and he blinked, breaking whatever thoughts had been about to take shape for her.

"Thank you," she said, meaning it. "I am sorry for running into you."

"I'm surprised you're even running," he told her, unsure. "What are you doing out of bed?"

"Selene mentioned food," she answered with an embarrassed heat filling her cheeks.

He took a long, sweeping perusal over her. "You're not hurting anywhere? Nothing feels broken?"

"Just my head," she replied with a disturbed frown, her hand rising to the sore spot over and between her eyes. "Thank you for the rescue, but I'm fine."

"If you're sure," he said in an unconvinced tone.

"Mitch, leave the girl alone," Bram warned from the kitchen. "She says she's fine."

Mitch muttered something under his breath aimed at his brother, but he stepped back, letting her pass. She tossed the pillow to the couch. Ganging up on Selene wasn't as appealing now.

* * * *

Mitch kept a concerned eye on Brooke. He couldn't understand how she was up and moving after her accident. No muscle spasms or cramps, no flashbacks or aches. He thought she'd been hit harder with all the damage to the car, but if she wasn't feeling the aftereffects of the collision, he shouldn't wish them on her, either. Had someone purposely forced her off the road? If it had been an accident, why didn't someone call for help when it happened? Even out here in the quiet stretches of wilderness, someone should have called for emergency help, but instead she'd been left in the car. It made him more than a little angry that someone had left her without staying to make sure she was all right.

She was a nice enough woman, sweet and soft-spoken. Mitch knew the history of the brothers and sisters. Except for the blonde hair, which to him wasn't that similar, he couldn't see much family resemblance between the two women. The eyes were the most startling. He'd never met a blonde with such dark black-brown eyes before.

After dinner, the brothers were relaxing on the porch when Selene walked up with Brooke not too far behind. "Bram, we're going for a run."

"Okay, be careful," he said as she gave him a kiss.

"We will. Listen for me," she said.

"Always," Bram replied tenderly.

Selene tossed a glance over her shoulder to Brooke and without another word, they vanished around the corner of the house.

"Are there trails back there?" Mitch asked, surprised the two would want to go running at night in the thick woods behind the house.

"Sort of. She's lived here for years. She'll be back in about an hour," Bram said with absolute confidence. "Don't worry. With the poacher problem gone, no one is here but us and the squirrels."

Mitch examined his older brother, noticing how much more serene he seemed to be. "You've really grown into living out here, in the quiet. You seem so much more comfortable here than I think I ever saw you in St. Louis."

"You sound surprised," Bram said, sipping his tea. Mitch had noticed he didn't drink beer anymore. He'd had to run to the local store to grab some for himself.

"I guess when you dropped the bomb about moving out here, I expected you to come home bored out of your mind," Mitch said.

Beyond the clearing where the vehicles were parked, there was an endless stretch of sky loaded with bright stars. Mitch picked up the small block of wood resting on his thigh and opened his knife. This was a perfect time to relax and do a little carving.

"I had no idea what I was doing for the longest time. Rebecca had become controlling again. Stalking wouldn't even be too far off the mark. I needed a change. I was lucky. I found everything right here."

Mitch turned a little to see him better in the ambient porch and streaming lights from the large picture windows at the front of the cabin-styled house. "You don't miss the big city?"

Bram shook his head as he relaxed in the porch chair. "No, not at all. Maybe for a nice dinner and a bit of change, but essentially, not at all. What are you working on, by the way?" Bram flicked a motion toward the wood in Mitch's hands.

"I don't know. A bear, maybe. Depends on how I feel when I start chopping into it," he said, joking.

Bram nodded and settled deeper into his chair, his eyes closed once more. "You don't chop. You do great work. I have three of them, remember?"

Mitch declined to answer. Bram was his biggest fan. Mitch had become interested in carving as a kid, tromping around the woods with their father. It helped to pass time and as he'd grown older, Mitch found it settled him when he was at odds over something.

"Bram," Mitch began, picking his words

thoughtfully. "When you left, how restless were you?"

He barked a gruff sound. "Restless enough. I felt hunted and overworked. I felt beaten," his brother admitted in a faraway voice. "Coming out here was better than getting a breath of life." Bram cracked an eye open, catching Mitch's gaze. "I never told you this, but I thought I had a vision the year I came out here to hike."

"You're kidding?" Mitch said, disbelief dripping from his words, his hands freezing in their actions. "A vision? Of what?"

Bram swatted a hand, waving away the question. "Not important, but what I believed was important was that it gave me a very solid memory of this part of the country and that there was something more in store for me. I got lost for four whole days, lost my compass, my direction, and was sure my sanity wasn't too far behind."

"I remember. Not long after Dad died," Mitch remarked thoughtfully, remembering to that time and the changes he could recall in his brother. "You seemed quieter when you came back. If that was possible." His hands started moving again. Wood flakes flew to the ground. "So what happened?"

"My vision led me on the third night to a trailhead. I will never forget it." Bram's gaze had floated shut, but it was almost as if Mitch could see the peacefulness descend on his brother. "Maybe you need to find what you're seeking but don't know it's missing."

"Am I that obvious? Even Tory questioned my trip." Mitch reached for a drink of his beer and grimaced. It tasted sour for some reason. It wasn't hot, but it wasn't what he wanted either. He placed it beside him, not wanting more. "A vision, huh?" he asked, wondering, distracted. Mitch started rambling. "I don't know, I feel restless, but you're right, I don't know what for. I love what I do, and I don't know if I could give up the big city. I told Tory I wanted to explore, search for property out here, and I might find something. A little spot for me for later." Mitch stretched his shoulders, staring up into the night sky. A sky so large he could lose himself in the vastness. The moon was a slim crescent, a whimsical shape hovering magically in the darkness. "I know Mom doesn't need us as much as she did, not with Harold around."

"Yeah, she did good with him. I'm happy for her too," Bram said.

"So, what am I missing, Bram? What's out there that I don't know about?" Mitch asked with only half a mind. The cool Oregon air streamed around both men, sending him wisps of nature instead of the heated odors of the big city. That was something he could get used to if he had the chance, he admitted silently. At the moment, he had a nice block of cedar to play with, a full stomach of damn good, well-cooked steak, and his brother for company for the first time in months. What was he missing?

Mitch had a full life, a great career, and a full-time schedule. He didn't date much, but it was more by choice. So if he wasn't missing the company of a woman, why was he feeling restless? Now that he'd openly voiced it, the nagging urge sat next to his ear, whispering to him.

A lamenting howl rolled out of the darkness as he stared out into the night. He sat up with a jerk and tensed. "Hell, what was that?"

"Just the wolves," Bram intoned with ease.

"But the girls!" He jumped to his feet, but Bram's unconcerned form made him pause.

"They'll be fine. They won't be hurt."

Mitch stared at his brother, collapsing slack onto

his chair. "Wolves don't live out here! They must have traveled to hunt," Mitch said as his heart accelerated when another cry followed the first one.

"No, they don't hunt here. They live here." Bram hadn't moved an inch, his hands twined across his chest as if there was nothing out in the darkness at all.

"You mean you have wolves in your backyard and you let your wife take off into the woods! At night!" Mitch gaped at his brother, wondering if his sanity had been damaged.

"Depending on which one is around, up to three, and they won't hurt anyone. They avoid people like the plague."

"Are you insane? They should be in a protected park! Wolves can't survive with people around," Mitch argued, dumbfounded and angry that Bram wasn't moving. Selene and Brooke were out there!

"Technically, we're the only people around. Selene knows them by sight. She won't be harmed."

"Are they at least monitored? Good grief, what happens if they attack a person?" Mitch was sitting, but barely hanging on to the edge of his chair.

"They never have, and they never will," was Bram's easy answer.

"How do you know that?" Mitch asked sarcastically. He cringed when he heard the call again, sharper and longer than the other two. He stared in comprehension at his brother as he smiled with a sublime pleasure into the darkness. "My God, the poacher *was* after a wolf!" Mitch barked incredulously.

"Yes, he was, but I knew he wasn't going to get one. Not while I breathed."

Mitch fell into his chair, astonishment giving him chills. "You almost died saving Rebecca, all for a wolf?"

Bram shrugged in the darkness. "We make our choices."

Mitch vaulted to his feet, unable to sit quietly any longer. "How can you be so calm? Your wife is out there!"

Bram's eyes shot open at Mitch's scathing shout, spearing his brother with a gaze that was as direct as it was secretive. "Because there is nothing to fear. The women are safe. No one will ever be harmed by the wolves living in these woods and hills. I can give you that promise in blood," Bram said bluntly with a gaze of steely brown.

"Have you seen them?" Mitch asked, shocked at his brother's vehemence. His wife was out there somewhere, and he sat in his chair as if there was nothing wrong with it. Bram was silent for a long time. "Well, have you?" Mitch almost had to leap out of the way when Bram thrust himself from his chair. Mitch stared into his brother's cool gaze and for the first time saw the secret harbored there. "You have! You knew they were here."

Bram nodded once, purposefully. "They are protected by the people who know they live here. That means by me, Selene, and her brother, Morgan. We have seen them, and they are safe."

"Are you safe?" Mitch asked, completely unprepared for his brother's protective stance.

"Always," Bram' replied adamantly. Mitch stared at his brother. There was an evasiveness to him now that a year ago Mitch would have had an explanation for or Bram would have cleared between them. Mitch realized his brother had changed.

The brothers turned as one when laughter carried from the rear of the house. "God, I needed that," Brooke said as she cleared the corner. She stopped cold in her tracks, noticing the expressions of the brothers. "What did we miss?" Selene slowed also when she joined her, studying the two men.

Bram held out a hand to Selene. "Mitchell was worried because he heard the wolves. I've been trying to convince him you two were going to come back in one piece. I think he understands now. No harm done," Bram murmured, brushing a kiss to the top of Selene's blonde hair.

No, not quite. Not hardly. He didn't understand at all as he watched Selene curl into Bram's side.

Brooke stood off the porch with her fingers hidden in the rear pockets of her shorts. "Sorry, didn't mean to ruin the evening," Brooke said, her cheeks warming with a tinge of guilt.

Mitch's gaze swept between the women, wondering how nuts the two sisters could be to not be concerned that wild wolves were somewhere out in the woods, possibly stalking them, running with them. "You didn't hear them?"

Brooke twitched a shoulder. "Sure, we know they're out there."

Mitch knew his gaze widened. "It's your skin," he finally retorted, unable to fathom their complete ambivalence. "I'm gonna go get a room. See y'all tomorrow." It came out in a disgusted statement.

"Mitch, you can stay, you don't have to get a room," Selene offered.

"What about Brooke?" he immediately asked.

Brooke's face smoothed, now that the worrying crisis seemed to be over. "I can take the couch. Being small, I don't need much." She toppled his indecision with her next argument. "Besides, you're here for a while, right? I'm only here for a few days, then I'm going to pester Morgan and go home to Mom's. No sense in wasting the money," she told them all.

Mitch faced his brother and Selene. "If you're both sure? Four is gonna be a squeeze."

"Jesus, Mitch. Get your crap and move in already,"

Bram said with a fuller, chuckled laugh.

Mitch threw up his hands in defeat. "All right, all right. Come on, Brooke, I'll get yours first." He forced himself to calm down when Brooke smiled up at him. Maybe he'd overreacted. Neither of the women were hurt, no matter how unconcerned they were about the fact that wolves were out there, too. Maybe next time they'd go for their traipse through the trees before nightfall. It was a small hope.

He pocketed his knife and tossed the block of wood on the chair where he'd been sitting. He followed as she strolled out to the Jeep. She and Selene both acted fine for being out after dark, running around with wolves in their backyard. Maybe they did know enough to stay away from them. Maybe they hadn't gone too far. He didn't know how close the two had been, only guessing at how close the howls had sounded. He wasn't so chauvinistic to believe the two didn't know they needed to avoid something as dangerous as a wolf.

Brooke turned to him from the Jeep with a bag handle in her grip as he neared, and he froze in shock. "Hey," he exclaimed abruptly. The light from the house shined on her, and there was no denying it. "Your bruise is gone!"

A tentative hand rose to where it should have been. "Really? I never saw how bad it was." After stroking the spot, her arm fell to her side. "Was it bad?"

Mitch touched where her hand had been, where the bruise should have been. Her skin felt flawless under his fingers. "I guess it wasn't as bad as I had first thought," he muttered. He forced an unassuming smile to his mouth. Something just wasn't right in Kansas. First the wolves, then the ugly bruise that should've been there for several days had vanished. He shook his head, silencing the crazy, whirling disbelief. "Glad to know you're feeling better." Nothing was making sense, and no one was acting as he would have expected about anything.

He was captivated though to see her blush, her pale cream skin warming with a summer-rose hue. "Yeah, thanks for finding me," she told him with a shy smile. Her gaze dipped to a point beneath his chin, and he was struck again by her eyes. So dark against her fair skin and honey hair.

He made some room for her to get by. "No problem." He tilted a shoulder behind him. "I guess we better get this stuff inside."

She nodded a second later.

Chapter Four

Brooke watched as Mitch disappeared with his bags into what was now his room. Her heart rocked hard behind her ribs. His touch had been so gentle. Her eyes drifted closed for a heartbeat as she recalled the feeling on her skin.

The way he filled her senses, the way he made her heart race, left her feeling raw. His scent was unique. No cologne, nothing on his skin but warm flesh and pulsing blood. She wondered if this was how her mate would make her feel, if she ever found him.

He had a nice walk in his blue jeans. He was well carved, manly but sleek in a T-shirt printed with the firehouse number. She wrapped her arms around her middle, remembering those few seconds when he had held her tight after running into him in the hall.

She faced the window to stare unseeing outside, feeling the strong grip of melancholy move in on her. Just because Mitch made her feel flushed, made her feel hungry to have his touch or his arms around her, didn't make him her mate. It was because he was a guy, and he was here when she was at her lowest. He was also her brother-in-law. Her gaze became unfocused, letting her mind meander in its own way as she let the memory of him, his scent, become part of her. The unexpected impact when it hit her full force made her reel.

Her eyes snapped wide open, and she froze solid where she stood. Was it possible? Was Mitch *supposed* to be her mate? She'd thought he was cute, undeniably good-looking in the wedding photos in Delilah's album. In person, he was so much more.

She frowned on the next heartbeat. No. She refused to fall under some spell simply because he was there. It was a fluke. Mitch wasn't her mate. Selene and Bram had found something special between them. Brooke didn't know when or where she would find that special connection or with whom. She only knew she wanted it desperately, which was probably what made Mitch so appealing. A single, sexy guy around her age. She laughed once, without a trace of humor. *Desperation, thy name is Brooke,* she scolded herself.

She just needed to be patient. It would happen. She would find her mate. After all, thirty-one wasn't the end of the world.

* * * *

The next morning she woke before the sun was a threat on the horizon. The cabin was silent in the predawn stillness as she dressed and used the restroom. She'd always been an early riser, especially after spending so much time with Aunt Jerry. She loved her aunt, but if someone wanted a great example of a sporadic sleeper, she was it. So it only behooved Brooke to follow suit, not that she minded. Brooke was flexible, in a lot of ways.

She made herself a mug of tea, heading out to the porch to watch the sun rise. The air was a smidge cool, and there was a hint of summer in the breeze. Fall was probably her favorite season. She loved the nip in the air, warmed by a noonday sun, loved the bright colors of nature as it changed, preparing for a long sleep. Spring was breathtaking too, but there was a feeling of acceptance with fall. Expectation. Knowing the coming season was inevitable and that on the other side of winter, life would be reborn all around her.

She missed fall in the Northern Pacific Rim. She stayed with her family a lot in Minnesota, but when her brothers and sister could put up with her, she spent weeks or even months with any of them.

Brooke curled up on a chair as the first rays of dawn hit the trees, arcs of yellow light breaking the sky wide open. Life didn't get any better than this.

"You're up early," a sleepy male voice said from the doorway.

"I hope I didn't wake you," she offered with an apologetic grin over her shoulder at Mitch. His hair was tousled in an unruly kind of way, making him scrumptious in jeans and no shirt. The man had a chest; that was for sure. Her heart rate picked up while she admired him.

"No, I usually wake early too," he explained. "So, no effects from your up-close-and-personal introduction to the trees, huh?"

She twisted until her chin rested on her shoulder to talk with him. He propped himself against the door frame, equally unhurried. "No. I feel great."

There was mild disbelief on his face when he shook his head once. "I don't know how Selene got you out from under that dash," he remarked. "But you're all right, and that's what matters." His bemused grin was kind in the morning light.

"There's hot water if you want to make coffee or tea. Neither Selene nor I drink coffee."

"Sure, if you don't mind the company. I'll be right back." He slipped inside, closing the door quietly.

She settled more comfortably into her chair, trying to get her heart rate to calm before he returned. Why did he have so much of an effect on her? It was obvious to her he didn't see her as any more than a sister. She wrinkled her nose when she smelled the drip of the coffee maker. She could handle it—restaurants reeked of the stuff—but she personally could live without it.

He returned roughly ten minutes later, dressed sans shoes, with a hot cup of coffee.

"Why don't you drink coffee?" he asked as he joined her on the porch. He sat on the top step, leaning against the rails.

"Something about the oils in the beans, I think. It turns my stomach faster than ipecac."

He grimaced. "Well, now I'll know if I need it."

"Sorry, I'll try to keep my personal quirks under wraps," she said, teasing him with an apologetic stare. Strong, lean fingers wrapped around his mug. He was a virile male, and her heart rate was thundering like a racehorse, apparently worse now with him sitting so close to her. She took a breath, searching for the morning scents of life around her to help clear her mind and her head.

Instead, she was hit with the essence of Mitchell Benedetti right between the eyes. She gulped as her eyes clanged shut. She took a few shallower breaths, trying to understand what the heck was going on.

His hand cupped her chin in the next instant, and she quivered. She actually quivered.

"Hey, you okay?"

Her tongue snaked out. "Yeah, just a head rush, I think. I guess I'm not at a hundred percent after all," she replied, fibbing with a tremulous laugh. She met his concerned gaze, flicking away once or twice, unable to keep it, fearing what she'd see or what he would within her own eyes. "I'm fine, really."

Mitch's touch was concerned, gentle, and supportive, until he was satisfied she wasn't going to faint, most likely. "You sure? You were shaking there for a second."

Oh no, he felt that! Humiliation stole her voice for

a span of seconds. She nodded against his palm instead, his caressing tenderness sending shots of something strong and drugging down her spine.

"Yeah, I'll be fine."

He settled on the step, sipping at his coffee, as they took in the sunrise. Unerringly, his worried gaze returned to her, the weight of the sunlight-warmed brown eyes doing more to wake her up than her tea at the moment. Unable to look at him for more than a second or two, fearing he'd see more than he already had, she sipped at her tea, finishing the last of the cooling liquid before she tried to form words again.

"So what are you going to do while you're on vacation?" she asked him a moment later when she felt equipped to do so.

He stretched out his arms, rolling his shoulders to lean against a post. "I was going to look into some property. Try to ruin some wood carving. Maybe fly a little."

"You fly?" she asked, curious. She'd never known someone who flew planes.

"Yep, jump certified with a pilot's license. Watch out, world!" He chuckled. "What about you?"

Holding her mug, she ran a finger over the rim, being frugal in her glances. "I've only been home a couple of weeks. I was at Roman and Delilah's before I came here. I'll be going to Morgan's next and then to Minnesota to see Mom and Dad, I guess."

"Selene said you paint. I really like the paintings she has." He had tugged up a leg, resting his arm across his knee, his other hand resting with his cup by his side.

"Yeah, I can paint, but not like Dad. He's a real talent. It's more of a hobby quality for me. And I love your carvings. They're very exact." She'd seen the ones Bram kept over the fireplace. There was a bear, an eagle launching to fly, and a deer with a very respectable rack, all of them roughly four inches tall.

He shrugged away the compliment. "What do you do?" he asked. The sunlight reflected in his eyes, making them almost bottomless, like a full cup of her favorite tea. She had to fight to find her voice. Why was she feeling so off kilter around Bram's brother?

She shook herself, skirting away from the dazed sensations washing over her. She needed to stop being pathetic. "Sorry, I spaced out for a minute. I'm an herbalist," she answered eventually. "These teas, they're my recipe."

"Really? You make stuff like that?"

Was that admiration in his voice? She couldn't hold his stare long enough to be able to tell. "I know, it's boring to a lot of people, but I love it. If I settle down enough, I'm going to grow my own ingredients: flowers and herbs. Healthier for you, too."

They twisted to glance over their shoulders simultaneously when the door popped open. "You guys hungry?" Bram asked.

"If you're cooking," Mitch said.

"Lazy," Bram shot back with a grin.

"No, vacation," Mitch replied, saluting with his cup.

"All right, give me a few minutes. Selene's getting ready for the morning shift." Bram slipped inside, closing the door on them.

Brooke let her mind wander in the quiet again. She was going to have to cut her visit short. Selene and Bram were too happy, and Mitch, he was too appealing. Besides, she hated feeling like a third wheel. They didn't need her hanging around.

Morgan could put up with her no matter her mood. He wasn't home half the time anyway. He ran wild a lot more than either of the girls. Her brother knew his land like the back of his hand, too. If anyone sneezed, he knew about it.

Mitch broke into her rambled musings. "When you and Selene went for your run last night, didn't you worry at all about the wolves?"

"No."

His expression was rueful, a shake of his head saying as much as his tone. "I don't understand how you can be so unconcerned. Bram said there can be as many as three prowling together. That makes a lethal hunting pack." She studied him and saw his brow furrow.

"Were you really worried?" she asked, surprised to see and hear that he truly was.

He rubbed a stiff hand down his face. "Evidently more than my brother," he replied with an annoyed twist on his lips. "He didn't even blink. He was smiling when he heard the howls."

"He's accepted like we have. We all live together in harmony."

Mitch shook his head, and she could hear his adamant concern wanting for her to understand. She did, but she wasn't worried for reasons Mitch would never know. "But what if they get too close? What if someone gets hurt?"

"Doubtful," she said, offering him a tentative touch to his arm, wanting to add weight to her own argument. "We protect them, and they never come within any distance to people." She met his direct gaze with what she hoped was an equally dismissive look rather than exposing the growing confusion she'd been stumbling through because she was sitting next to him. "Don't worry about it. You will probably be here the whole time of your vacation and not hear them again."

"At least you guys are keeping track of them," he said.

"Yes, we do." She rose from her chair. "I'm getting some more tea. Do you want anything?" She waited until he refused the offer.

She closed the front door on him, wondering why he was worried for their welfare. People and wolves could live together if they respected one another. She grinned, avoiding the scene in the cabin's kitchen when she found her sister and Bram lip-locked. Yep, they can all live together really well given the chance.

She cleared her throat, and they were just shy of obnoxiously slow to separate. She rolled her eyes. "You don't have to rub it in, you know," she groused good-naturedly.

"We weren't," Selene said breathlessly. "We're celebrating."

Brooke's eyes widened. "Really? What?"

Bram's fingers formed to Selene's shoulders. "We're pregnant!" he announced.

The door opened behind her right then. "You are? That's fantastic!" She squealed, rushing for Selene to hug her first.

"I heard that! Congratulations," Mitch said. He hugged his brother and then picked up Selene and gave her a quick spin. "I get to be an uncle! I'll warn you, I'm an expert at underage spoilage," he informed them with a pleased, beaming grin for the couple.

"There goes Roman's throne," Brooke said jokingly. "So when?"

"Roughly seven months, possibly less," Selene told them with a happy gleam of anticipation in her eyes.

Brooke swallowed, determined to hold herself together. She felt ready to cry suddenly. Her sister was pregnant. Roman was married and deliriously happy as a father to Adrian. Brooke was on the verge of shattering. Her emotions were taking too hard of a battering this morning. She hugged Selene again, tighter. She was thrilled for her sister, but their news only seemed to exacerbate the hollowness Brooke had been fighting since she'd returned from Belgium. "Look, you guys eat. I'm going for a walk," she said in a thick voice, barely managing to get the words out. Tears were already daring to press against her eyes. She had to get out of there.

She avoided her sister's disquieted stare. Brooke couldn't explain it, and the truth would only spoil their happy moment. "I'll be back," she called, wearing the fakest smile she'd ever known. She almost made it off the porch before Selene caught up to her.

"Brooke, what's the matter?" Her halting grip was light, an attempt at comfort on Brooke's arm.

"Nothing. I don't want to ruin your announcement." She dug fingers into her pockets, looking anywhere but at Selene.

Selene turned her around, forcing her to meet her searching gaze, making it impossible to evade her. "Brooke? Come on, tell me."

"I'm going to Morgan's later today. You and Bram don't need me here."

"But we want you!" she cried, staring harder. "What's the matter?"

Brooke broke down and explained it like she had to Delilah. The melancholy. The lost chance. Feeling so old. "I'm sorry. This isn't your problem." Brooke waved a flippant hand toward the house. "And Mitch is too damned appealing. I feel like I'm so desperate for a family, I'm having reactions because he's here, alive and breathing." Frustration made her voice brittle.

"What reactions?" Selene asked, watching her too closely for Brooke's comfort.

"It doesn't matter. He's Bram's brother. I'm the other sister," she uttered flatly.

"Boy, you are having a pity party, aren't you?"

Selene murmured sympathetically. She let Brooke go. "Don't leave. We do want you to stay."

"I'll come by before I leave for Mom's, but you and Bram need your family time." Brooke reached for her sister's hands, clasping them firmly. "I'm happy you're pregnant. I am. I'm just feeling a little left out."

"You're not old, Babs. We're all the same age."

Brooke hugged her sister. "I know. I just feel ancient. I guess it's because I left and came back and so much changed. Except with me. Go eat," Brooke told her, letting her go with a tender shove toward the cabin. "I'll wait until you get home this afternoon before I leave. I need to do something to replace the car anyway."

Selene brushed her sister's hair back. "If you're sure?" Brooke nodded again. "All right, then. Take one of the guys when you get the car. Small town mentality when it comes to women. They'll make sure you don't pay a fortune."

"Will do," she said.

Brooke spun from Selene before she had the chance to see the tears weighing heavily on her lashes as she all but stalked away from the house. She swiped at them angrily. She should be ecstatic for her sister. She was, at least a part of her was, but she felt like the odd man, or woman, out.

She kicked at a stone on the ground as she ambled a sluggish, meandering path toward the creek bridge on the south side of the property. She crossed the bridge and kept going. Not surprisingly, the glow of the morning had dimmed exponentially.

* * * *

The rest of her morning was spent car shopping. The old sedan had been towed and the insurance filed. She didn't get just one, but both of the Benedetti men to help her. They piled into Bram's Explorer and drove into town.

She tried to ignore how Mitch made her pulse react, how every breath was redolent with his scent, how every other word was a rich sound from his lips. She needed to get away, to escape if she had to. She needed to find her mate. All she really needed to do was get far away from him. Brooke fought to ignore his presence in the vehicle, counting down to when she'd be able to leave for Morgan's.

Mitch seemed barely aware of her, talking with his brother in the front seat as Bram drove them all into town. She kept her attention focused on the outside world. It lasted until they reached the downtown area where businesses lined the streets.

"Hey," she said with a sharp, stunned cry, sitting up and pointing out her window. "That looks like the tank that ran me off the road."

"That black Ford?" Bram asked as he automatically turned in its direction and then slowed to let her study the vehicle.

"Yeah, that sure does look like it," she said. She turned in her seat, studying it closely as they crawled past. "But I could be wrong. I didn't get a real clear look at it except in my mirror. I imagine there are a lot of those up here."

Bram shook his head. "No, I don't think so. I've never seen one in the months I've been here."

Mitch held up a piece of paper between his fingers. "I've got the plates. I'll see if I can get a rundown in case there's something there after all."

"You can do that?" Brooke asked him.

"A friend of mine can," he replied, tucking the paper into a pocket. "If it's a visitor, no harm, no foul. If it's something more, you can make a complaint with the description and the plates."

"Oh, I don't have to do that," she quickly said. "I was just surprised to see it. Besides, I didn't make the police report after the accident. Who would believe me?"

"I'd back you up," Bram said.

"I would too," Mitch agreed. "I did find you, after all."

"Oh. Okay. Thanks," she said, then sat in troubled silence.

Chapter Five

Mitch waited with Bram while Brooke finished the documents to purchase her Sequoia. "I swear, that woman needs a keeper," he drawled in a joking grumble. "Not make a complaint? If I got run off the road, I'd complain to everyone I know."

"Yes, and we would all be hearing about it in detail, too," Bram said. He ducked when Mitch aimed a hit at his arm. "She's a very quiet kind of person. She's the last of the quads to make waves."

Mitch regarded him with curiosity. "I can't believe those four are quadruplets. They look nothing like one another."

Bram shrugged, leaning against his Explorer, his long sleeves rolled up at the cuffs. "What about that set of, what was it, seven or something born in the '90's? They had mostly dark hair, but I think there were some strong differences between them too. Besides, it's not her fault Roman stole her height."

"He stole everyone's height!" Mitch straightened when he spotted her coming toward them from the sales offices. "Here she comes. She should smile more," he said, drawn to the lightness in her expression.

"I think so too," Bram responded in agreement. "But she's making some adjustments after being gone so long with an older relative."

She glanced at both, saying, "I'm ready. I'm going to the cabin, unless you guys have a plan."

"No, I guess we're done. So how bad did they get

you?" Mitch asked as her new silver SUV came from the prep shop.

"Not bad at all. They dropped fifteen for me," she said with a note of pride.

"Fifteen hundred! Was that all?" Mitch was about to go in and beat up a salesman when her bubbling laughter captured him.

"No, fifteen thousand."

He kept himself from tripping by spinning on a heel. "How'd you do that?" he cried with a raised eyebrow.

"I paid in cash," she explained.

"Hell, you didn't need us," Bram muttered.

"It wasn't worth arguing over with Selene this morning, not after your happy news."

Mitch noticed that the brightness of her effervescence vanished with saying that, like a candle blown out in a stiff breeze. He lost her unique gaze as the salesman came from the offices and personally offered her the new keys.

"Thank you again, Miss Aiza," he said in a purr.

"Sure thing, Charlie."

"Hey, I'm going to go say hi to my wife," Bram said, getting their attention.

Mitch turned and faced Brooke, speaking with a drawl. "Can I ride with you? I can't take any more of those two."

She shrugged, her expression giving him nothing of her thoughts. "Yeah, I don't see why not."

"'Bye," Bram called as he slid into his Explorer and drove away.

"Thanks, they were a bit much over breakfast," he confessed.

"I'm glad they're happy," she said as they started out of town.

"Then why do you sound so sad?" he asked.

He saw her shoulder roll. "Just personal stuff," she said indirectly. "Nothing you'd be interested in hearing, I'm sure. Besides, you're on vacation. I'm not going to be blamed for ruining any of it."

He sat beside her in silence, wondering what that meant the entire trip out of town.

That afternoon, amid hugs and well-wishes, Brooke left for Morgan's. Mitch didn't understand why she felt she couldn't stay, but as Bram had said, maybe she was adjusting to being in the States with her own family. She was a sweet woman, he thought, but he wasn't in the market for a woman, especially one with issues.

* * * *

Three days later, Mitch rented the two-prop plane he'd reserved to do aerial excursions and scope out the possibility of finding a square to call his own. He was antsy to get outside and feel the sun on his face for a while. Bram was behind the idea of him settling in the area, and when he was ready, Mitch was thinking he probably would.

The day couldn't have started out better as far as he was concerned. Sharp, pristine blue sky, the kind where clouds feared to show themselves. A light layer breeze right above the treetops, but nothing he couldn't fly through.

He flew east toward the Rocky Mountains, soaring over the area where the fire damage had been over half a year before. He settled in around nine thousand feet and simply enjoyed the view. The controls curved with familiarity under his palms while he watched his airspeed and fuel, confident at the wheel. His gaze took in the scorched earth and gaping holes where trees had burned down, noting that the wilderness was beginning to grow into the damaged spaces.

He banked to the left, aiming west, watching the emerald treetops whisk underneath in a thick blanket of color. The humming roar of the propellers vibrated in his ears, but he could tune it out for his own thoughts.

For some reason, Brooke was still in them.

Brooke had been at Morgan's since she'd left Selene's. Mitch knew because she'd called the night before to talk to Selene. He'd never felt the need to comfort a woman, but the day they'd driven together with her new SUV, he had wanted to. There had been something troubling her deeply. He'd forwarded the plate information on the Ford to his pal, John Davis, in the St. Louis PD. He hadn't received a return e-mail yet, but he'd explained it wasn't a rush, merely a favor for a friend, describing the reason for the search and Brooke's accident in brief detail.

He didn't understand why she was hesitant to report being knocked off the road, either. Her car had been totaled, and regardless of how minor it had seemed then, he knew she had been hurt in the impact. Maybe he had made the bruise on her head larger in his own mind for it to have been gone within a few hours, but she had been hurt.

Without warning, the crystal-clear image of her golden-blonde hair and coffee-brown eyes rose up in his mind. She was pretty in a petite way, standing barely an inch or two shorter than Selene. Both girls were trim but Brooke was a lightweight, delicate like the flowers he knew she loved, and he couldn't argue that she had nice legs. She loved to wear shorts. With unspoken male interest, he appreciated the view of those shorts.

He blinked when he realized he was smiling. Over a woman. He rumbled a disgusted sound, rubbing annoyed eyes beneath his sunglasses with stiff fingers. She was his sister-in-law. Not necessarily off-limits, but not a prime choice, either. He knew better than that. You didn't date family. It complicated matters when things inevitably failed, when things fell apart and you both had no choice but to make small talk at family gatherings, like weddings and reunions, when both would have to pretend that neither had been hurt or even involved. He shook his head sharply. Some things were just better left alone.

He stretched and grabbed one of his snack bars, tearing it open with his teeth. He munched in contented silence as he continued to soar, gliding over the earth. It felt almost Godlike when he could fly without restraint, without a reason other than for the enjoyment of it. Some people may feel that way about a boat or rock climbing, but for Mitch it was flying. Man and machine. Ability. It gave him peace.

The morning had started out cool so he'd worn a light jacket. As he made his journey, picking out details of the land beneath him, sunshine poured through the glass surrounding him and a contentment stole over him. He finished his snack, tucking the wrapper into a jacket pocket. He took a long drink of water from the bottle stuffed between the seats. He grinned when he belched.

"Take that," he said, laughing, feeling at peace to just be himself.

His focus fell without concern to the dials and meters in front of him: gauges for pressure and altitude, fuel, and temperatures. The little Cessna was humming along smoothly. The rental hangar said it had been running well since its last tune-up. Mitch would have to agree. Maybe someday, he'd get one. They weren't just for the rich anymore. Not exactly economical to get you to work—it was a plane, after all—but not a bad investment.

His laugh was deeper, feeling the freedom,

enjoying the moment to the fullest. Maybe Tory had been right, maybe he was hungry for a change. Bram seemed to think he was missing something. He was only twenty-nine. How much could he be missing?

He noted a flock of ducks ahead in the distance and started to rise above them to avoid any turbulence in their flight path, but he wasn't fast enough. Two of the trailers thought he was the mother ship coming home and shot up, straight for him.

He cursed, then glided higher once more. *Crazy birds. I must have startled them somehow.* A moment later, his body relaxed, his grip loosening on the split wheel. They had passed like ships in the night, close but no damage. Odd they would do that, he mused, instead of fleeing like he was the *USS Roosevelt* on maneuvers for target practice. He glanced at the dash, checking his fuel again. He didn't want to go too far and run out of gas. Rookie mistake.

He snapped around barely seconds later when a sharp whine, then an explosive *pop* overrode the hum of the engines. His gaze widened in shock as a plume of blue-black smoke trailed out of his right propeller. It ground to a halt. "Shit!" He hadn't hit one of the birds, but something had locked up in the engine casing.

He tried to restart the engine, punching on the engage button for the dual motors with a persistent thumb. Nothing. He gripped the receiver for his radio as he banked toward the hangar. He threw the communicator away as the wheel jerked savagely in his hand, fighting him all the way. "What the hell?" The rudder refused to cooperate, no matter how hard he turned or twisted the control wheel. It wasn't budging.

"He said it was working fine!" he shouted, cursing the man at the hangar.

Mitch snatched up the radio, shouting, praying. "Mayday, mayday, Cessna C7359 going down! Mayday!"

He kept his unblinking gaze on the horizon, desperate for a clearing. Relief. There was one ahead, surrounded by trees. Dangerous in such close confines, but it was his only chance. He wrenched at the rudder to point north. "Come on, you stubborn ass! Move!" He ground out words between clenched teeth. The wheel bucked and pitched against his strength, not giving an inch. He swept his gaze down, catching his altimeter. Five thousand and falling fast. He swore between stiff lips. He gripped his radio and gave the mayday call again. Still nothing.

Mitch swore violently as the rudder kicked in his hands. Something was jamming the movement. His knuckles whitened as he fought with the little plane. There wasn't a chance in hell he was going to make the clearing. He couldn't get enough movement out of the rudder. He couldn't get enough of a northern bank.

Thirty seconds later, no amount of fighting for control mattered. His second engine overheated and froze worse than a block of ice. "Aw, hell!" His hands clenched the wheel while he desolately watched his altitude drop like the steep side of a black diamond ski slope. He worked the tail pedals, fighting to keep the plane stable to glide. He was going to crash in the trees, and there was very little he could do about it. Mitch cursed colorfully as the tree line began to brush the underbelly of the plane. His jaw tensed as he fought to keep it straight, fought to keep the plane from going nose first into the ground.

He sent a silent prayer for his mom and Bram as the trees began to claw at the wings. The wrenching, screeching sound of metal tearing roared through the amplified pounding in his ears as the wings collapsed, stripped like feathers from their welds. When the Cessna hit the ground, the sound echoed for miles around. The silence that followed was long and deafening, but no one heard it.

* * * *

"Selene, have you heard from Mitch?" Bram stood next to her at the kitchen counter as they worked together on dinner.

She offered a light frown over her shoulder but shook her head. "No, he left at about eight thirty to go fly."

"I wonder when he was planning on returning," Bram remarked. He glanced for at least the fifth time at his wristwatch. It was well after five. "It'll be dark soon. Surely he's still not out there," he said, more to comfort himself than as a logical statement. Bram knew if Mitch could have, he'd be home. It wasn't like him to disappear for the day when there was nowhere to go. Bend was nothing like St. Louis. A knot in his stomach told him he wasn't worrying for nothing.

"Why don't you call the rental place? Maybe he's back, just not here." Selene heated the pan for dinner. Well, for his dinner anyway. There wasn't any way he could eat steaks as rare as she did.

He nodded in agreement, turning to search for the number in the phone book. Bram waited for someone to answer, tapping his fingers on his elbow as he stared out the window to the front clearing.

His brother's Jeep wasn't out there.

"Yeah, hi," he said when they picked up at the rental offices. "I'm looking for Mitch Benedetti. He had a Cessna reserved for today."

Bram's worry sharpened as the other man began speaking in a belligerent tone. "Benedetti. Yeah, he was supposed to be in by one. I need to close up."

"At one," Bram echoed, feeling something cold slam into his stomach. "Has he called in or anything?"

Bram heard the man shuffle on the other end, losing the gruff undertone, if not the impatience.

"The plane was in working order. I had a mechanic on it yesterday, but the radio was acting up." There was an embarrassed apology for the lapse, not that it helped Bram at the moment.

"I see. Did he give you a flight path?" Bram asked, willing a calm. It didn't last.

"North. Said he wanted to check out the scorches from the fires he was here for a few months back."

"But those are nearly forty-five miles away!" Bram shouted.

"Hey, he's the one who's late! Don't get pissed at me. It's my plane," the other man said, reminding him.

"And he's my brother!" Bram enunciated. He hung up before he growled something foul. He usually didn't feel the need for it. This time he did.

He turned with a rock in his stomach the size of a dinner plate and locked on to Selene's worried gaze. "He's missing." Bram was positive of it. The feeling was far too real to ignore. Mitch did not just disappear.

"Call Morgan. He's the best."

Bram didn't hesitate as he dialed his brother-in-law.

* * * *

Mitch groaned, the rough sound hoarse and loud. He was breathing. He was alive! The thrill was short-lived. He hurt all over the damned place! His pounding head was pressed lopsided to the control panel where the landing had thrown him. At least he wasn't upside down. Bleary eyes cracked, unable to miss the harsh pull of dried blood on his forehead as he shifted, trying to focus. He groaned again, wiggling his toes. Felt like he had all of those. He counted his fingers. Good to go. He closed his eyes and breathed for a few minutes, hearing the tick of his pulse and dry bellow of his lungs. He was alive. Mitch allowed himself a grateful prayer to whomever was responsible, even if he did hurt like hell.

Mitch's left shoulder was killing him. With a groping hand, the one not attached to the arm that was killing him, he tried to find all of his injuries. It dropped before he accomplished much of anything but more pain. He hurt in so many places. Hurt wasn't even a strong enough word for all the pain coursing and stabbing at his nerves. He forced his eyes open once more and started for a split second when he realized why he couldn't focus. It was dark outside. Pitch black, and not because he was buried. Night had come. He swore vividly through a swollen, busted lip.

He lifted a shaky hand and planted it on the console. Rolling his head, gathering his strength, he shoved his body from the twisted position he was in. He swore like a heathen when he twisted his hips and a lightning-hot pain blistered his right leg. He was panting heavily by the time he was sitting upright in the captain's seat. With a palm running over his injured shoulder, he discovered the dip in the joint.

To count, one broken leg, one dislocated shoulder, and a head injury, and that was provided he hadn't done anything major on the inside. He drew several deep, slow breaths and was only punished with a few twinging discomforts. Bruised but not broken sounded damn good to him at that point.

He closed his eyes and rested, propped nearly slack in the cockpit. He was protected there, and he didn't smell gas. Two pluses in his book.

Mitch blinked in a flurry of awareness as light clobbered his eyelids. He had passed out again, but he was breathing, and somehow alive. He built up steam to move something else. He searched to his side, but his water bottle had disappeared. He'd try to find it later if it was somewhere close by.

Regarding his situation, trying to get some bearing on where he'd crashed, all he found were trees.

The plane had knocked down quite a few, creating spaces and gaps. If he wiggled, there was a little room to open his door. With his one good hand reaching across his body, he yanked on the door handle. It burst open with a caterwauling shriek of protest after a short-lived struggle. He freed himself from the belt buckle to pivot in the seat and see what else was outside his cubicle of safety. If he was lucky, there wouldn't be much, and if there was something, it wouldn't be hungry.

His howling curses startled birds to take to the air when he moved his busted leg. By the time he accomplished a turn and faced outward, he was panting again and starting to sweat. Christ, he needed to pee! Why does the body do that at the worst possible times?

He focused in the brightening morning light, examining his legs. The right one was definitely broken. Feet don't twist to that angle naturally. Flexing his left leg, nothing happened. He didn't know if he'd earned any internal damage but he imagined by now, he would be dead if he had. That thought didn't really cheer him any. With a steadying effort, he shifted his weight to his left leg, grimacing and clenching his jaw against the pain in his right until he was standing in front of the plane door. His left arm was useless, dangling painfully at his side.

He managed to relieve himself, then sagged once more against the pilot's chair. He was going to have to sit or lie down. With his one strong leg beginning to shake, he didn't have long before the decision would be made for him.

Mitch clung to the door, using it for support as he stiffly completed a falling slide to the ground. He fought the urge to black out as he maneuvered his broken leg until it was stretched out in front of him. By the time he slumped on solid ground, the world tilted precariously. The blackness of nothing swooped in and took over before he could garner strength to halt it.

He was dreaming, or at least he thought he was. Dry eyes slit open to mere cracks, taking in the long shadows of the late evening sun to find not one, but two wolves standing at the edge of his crash site. They faced each other for a surreal moment, then the dark one disappeared, loping into the trees.

Mitch tiredly closed his eyes, knowing he was about to become lunch, or dinner.

The dark one was off to get the pack and tell them he was ready for dining. He would have laughed if he hadn't hurt so much. It was impossible to do anything more than breathe.

The next time he opened his eyes, it was pitch-black night once more. Mitch sensed it to be early evening, though. The air didn't have the cool stillness of late night. His right hand jerked with a spasm and brushed against something that wasn't forest ground remnants. He rolled his gaze and found his water bottle.

How did that get there? He didn't remember grabbing it. He thought he'd lost it. When the thirst hit, he quit questioning the divine gift. Propping up the bottle between his thighs, he unscrewed the top, gulping several deep swallows, ceasing before he gorged on the entire thing. He had no idea how long it would take for someone to find him.

His gaze snapped wide, searching the tree line. The

wolves! Where were they? Had they left? Were there more of them? His aching head found the pilot's door behind him. What did he care if wolves found him? He couldn't fight off a gnat with the way he felt. Drifting in and out of consciousness, he lost track of time as the night chilled around him. Where was he? How far had he flown before the problems started? How long had he been down? Had anyone noticed he was missing?

It was very late when his discordant musings were broken. One of the wolves was slinking through the trees, except it wasn't focused on him. Its teeth were bared, and he could almost hear the low warning snarl. The animal's dark eyes glittered in the moonlight. An answering hiss echoed from beyond his view. He ducked his head and shuddered. He dimly recognized a paw on the other side of the body of the destroyed plane. A very large paw.

A loud feline howl of anger split the silence between the two combatants, and a tremor shot down his spine. He watched in silent fear as the cat leaped into the air, a tawny arc of claws and teeth wanting to impale the wolf. The blended yellow pelt of the wolf flashed as it avoided the attack, snapping at a hind leg of the feline as it raced past.

The wolf positioned itself between him and the cat, refusing to give ground with strong jaws and determined growls. Mitch winced as the cat's claws raked viciously into the wolf's shoulder, but that seemed to only make it madder as it advanced on the cat again.

Mitch held his breath as the wolf lunged, aiming for a furry throat. The cat's panicked roar was sharp when the wolf found tender flesh. The large mountain lion reared up on its hind legs and then swept a clawed paw solidly into the body of the wolf, yanking itself free. The cat didn't earn freedom without paying a price, though. The wolf held a huge chunk of feline skin clamped between its pearly teeth as it rose from where it rolled from the momentum of the strike. It spit out the chunk, shaking its head and squaring its body, growling menacingly at the cat.

The cat called defeat, whirling and running for the woods, convinced it would find easier pickings somewhere else. Mitch watched in stunned silence as the wolf took two steps and collapsed, breathing heavily. Shaking, it rose and limped into the trees a few minutes later, but he had seen the blood on its shoulder. It had been hurt. Protecting him.

He searched the tree line again for the body of his guardian angel. He eased his breathing and could nearly make out the sound of heavy panting. It was there, probably too tired to go far.

"Why are you here?" Mitch said into the darkness. "Are you my protector, like Bram's vision?" His voice cracked, his lips unbearably sore as he spoke.

Mitch listened to the growing quiet and he thought he heard a rustle in the inky shadows of the trees. Cautiously, the shape of a nose came into view. He could make out eyes and then ears, its body covered in undiscerning shadows. It lay down again, regarding him.

"I'm dreaming. I know that," he whispered, his voice reedy as pain racked his body. His head tipped with exhaustion, and his eyes closed, but he was able to think mostly coherently. A few moments later, he gathered his strength, and his attention landed on the animal once more. It hadn't moved. "Wolves don't like people."

Eyes almost as black as the night sky stared at him, then blinked, gripping him in their power. "You're one of Brooke's wolves, aren't you?" He tried to smile, but it probably came across as a grimace. He watched as the beautiful beast rose on its haunches to lick its wounds.

"My God!" he exclaimed. The wolf snapped up at his hoarse shout. "That cat shredded your shoulder!"

The wolf made a sighing sound and began to lick at the deep scratches again. "So, are you a vision? My guardian angel?" The animal paused and then resumed its care, as if it were getting what Mitch was saying. "Would you let me look?" he asked soothingly.

The wolf whipped up, its eyes huge in its pale head. "Yeah, I know. I'm sitting here hallucinating over a wolf. Imagining you can understand what I'm saying, like you're my protector," he said, guardedly keeping an eye on the animal. His head sagged to the door, fighting the growing strain to stay awake, but he refused to succumb. "I must have hit my head harder than I thought."

The animal hefted itself to all fours. It almost appeared to be grinning at him! But that wasn't possible. Was it? Wolves didn't understand people. They didn't even like people, and wolves couldn't laugh. Could they? The whirling questions made his head ache beyond the throbbing pain.

The wolf limped as it moved around. Mitch reached a hand toward the animal. "Come here," he said coaxingly. He couldn't stand to see an animal in pain. Dream or not, he wanted to help.

The wolf hesitated but inched closer with its head lowered, approaching with tentative, lengthened steps until it was near enough for its warm tongue to flick out and lick his fingers. "I don't taste good," he joked, silently thrilled the animal was trusting him to come so close. He was taken by complete surprise when it flopped next to his leg. "You're pretty tame for a wolf," he said, thinking out loud to try to stay awake. He carefully rested a hand on its muscled shoulder, brushing the coat out of the way to examine the deep gouges from the cat's claws. They didn't look good. "Poor beauty. You're not going to the ball looking like that."

The animal actually stretched under his touch, long legs flexing in relaxation. He smiled, ignoring the pain-filled tightness around his lips. "You like that, huh?" It sighed a contented sound. His hand roamed leisurely. Its pelt was a rich, honeyed yellow, thick and wild under his fingers. It had to be a hybrid of some sort. "You probably belong to someone," he said, not wanting to fall asleep again. He was sleeping a lot, passing out. He'd suffered a concussion on some level. "You're too tame, too gentle."

Two dark eyes closed as he caressed fur. "I don't even know where I am. I'm sure I'm at least twenty miles out of the way I had intended. I wonder how long it will take for them to find us." He chuckled, feeling considerably better when the wolf's tail slapped the ground. "Not long, huh? Glad you're an optimist. I've only been gone a day and a half. That's not too bad. I wonder if they've started searching. I'm sure Bram's figured something happened by now."

He tilted up, but all he could see for what seemed like miles were the crowns of the large firs overhead. "Can't see me unless you look straight down," he muttered, feeling utterly lost. The wolf pressed against his leg more, a snug warmth against the chill of the air. He closed his eyes and let himself relax, making it a conscious decision this time, the beating of the heart under his palm telling him he was as alive as he could be.

When he fell asleep this time, he knew he wasn't alone.

Chapter Six

The whirling, lopping sound of a chopper jerked him awake with a start. Mitch blinked and groaned as he moved stiff muscles. Body parts blazed with renewed pain for the effort. A basket lowered along with a body in a harness from overhead.

"Hey, man," Morgan shouted, kneeling next to Mitch. "Next time, let us know when you want to break a plane. We'll buy you a model kit," he shouted with a grin over the high whining sound of the chopper.

Mitch managed a dry, chuckled laugh. "Glad to see you, too." Morgan did a quick once-over, then splinted his leg.

"Do you want to do the shoulder now?"

"No, I'm getting used to the pain. Drug me first," Mitch shouted, and Morgan gave him a thumb's-up sign. Mitch knew when he'd maxed out on endurance.

"All right, I'm going to lay you out and roll you onto the body board." Mitch nodded. Gritting his teeth, he waited for the pain. Sharp and hot, it sliced straight up the middle of his body as Morgan did his job. Mitch didn't breathe an easy breath until he was strapped into the chopper. Morgan joined him. He passed out at some point on the way to the hospital.

* * * *

"He'll be fine, Bram. He received a mild concussion and suffered shock." Mitch heard the voice but didn't recognize it.

"Good. He gave us a scare," Bram said in answer. Mitch felt as cool fingers lifted his hand and squeezed his wrist.

"The leg should heal without a problem, and the shoulder sling will be needed for a few weeks, but I guess you already know that," the humoring voice said.

Mitch's eyes opened, and he found someone he didn't know taking his pulse. When the doctor finished, he laid his arm on the sheet of the bed. "Hello, Mitch. I'm Dr. Lin."

"Hello," he said weakly. "I feel like shit."

"Aftereffects of your ordeal, nothing else," he reassured Mitch.

Mitch turned the other way and found his brother's worried but relieved gaze. "Hey, welcome back," Bram offered.

"How long have I been here?"

"Only since this morning. They found you at the crack of dawn." Bram looked across the bed to the other doctor. "Thanks, Dr. Lin. Selene and I can take over."

"Sure, I know it's hard to work on family," he said in sympathy. "I was worse than my son-in-law when my daughter went into labor." Dr. Lin read over the paperwork, signed off on the chart then left the brothers alone.

Bram closed the door when they were alone. "I know you may not remember much, but you may need to," he warned cautiously. "A small device was found on your rudder. A low-grade plastics bomb."

Mitch gaped at his brother, shocked. "You're kidding! Someone tried to kill me?"

"I think so." Bram sank onto the bedside chair, his hands clasped between his knees, seeming to want to avoid Mitch's stares. "Tory called us last night, wanting to talk to you."

That was not a good thing. "Why?" Tory wouldn't have bugged him for anything on his vacation. Unless it was bad.

"He wanted to know if you could be in town for a funeral at the end of the week." Bram's gaze darkened, becoming apologetic and pained.

"Shit," Mitch whispered. "Give me my button; I have to sit up." Bram handed it to him and let Mitch get comfortable. When he wasn't flat on his back, he said apprehensively, "Tell me what happened."

Bram hesitated. "John Davis was shot outside his house two days ago."

Mitch lay in stunned silence. Not possible. He couldn't believe it. Davis was dead? Mitch and Bram had known him their entire lives. "But how? Why?"

"If it weren't for your plane going down, I'd say there wasn't any connection," Bram said, his eyes flitting between Mitch's gaze and his own hands. "Nothing has been released yet by the police department. Right now it's being called a random homicide. He had made a few enemies over the years," Bram muttered ruefully.

Mitch's eyes closed, feeling queasy all of a sudden. "But you don't think so," he said. "And it doesn't feel like it."

"Why would someone intentionally bomb your plane? You're miles away from St. Louis," Bram said with drawn anger.

"It wasn't just that. I lost a propeller too. It might have been as intentional." Mitch explained what happened during the flight, Bram growing more serious with each passing minute. Tension rolled off his shoulders in waves. Mitch's uneasiness was growing under the circumstances.

"And now you're laid up here for another day at least, until you can come home. I don't like this, Mitch.

Did you send something to Davis?"

"I asked him to run the plates on that Ford Excursion Brooke thought had run her off the road." Bram rubbed stiff palms down his face, groaning into the sterile quiet of the hospital room. "You don't think someone is after her, do you?" Mitch asked his brother uncomfortably.

Bram gave Mitch a wry smile. "The Aiza women draw trouble like nothing I've ever seen."

"But that's pretty thin," Mitch argued. "Run plates and Davis gets shot down, then someone supposedly tries to kill me." He shook his head. It was the craziest scenario Mitch had ever tried to piece together.

"No, someone did try with you, Mitch. That's why I'm worried. Small plastics don't get camouflaged and hidden on their own."

"How did you find all of that out?" Mitch asked, bewildered Bram would have so much worked out already. Someone had really planted an explosive device on his plane? It explained a lot, but... His brain wasn't wrapping around it quite yet.

"Roman. He's an expert with explosives, and Lord only knows what else. Del is as good, but she has a different kind of talent."

"What kind of a family did you marry into?" Mitch asked, only half joking.

Bram's grin tightened. "A very unique one." He rose from the chair, placing a flat hand on Mitch's unwrapped shoulder. "Rest; we'll see you for a few this evening and get you home tomorrow morning."

Bram was reaching for the door when Mitch stopped him. "Hey, about those wolves. Is one a golden-yellow one?"

"Why?" Mitch was taken aback at the shadow of evasion in his brother's posture.

"Nothing, I guess. I probably imagined it. I did hit

my head hard. It just seemed too tame to be a wild wolf. It was probably a dog and belonged to someone."

"Probably; they really don't like being near people," Bram said. "See you later." Then Bram left him to rest.

Mitch let his weary eyes close, but rest was the last thing on his mind. Someone killed Davis. Someone had tried to kill him and had very nearly succeeded. Were the incidents connected? Were they tied to the black Ford? Was it all connected to Brooke somehow? Had someone intentionally run her off the road? Why? Brooke was harmless. And what had Bram meant when he said that the Aiza women could draw trouble? Selene? Mitch knew the story about the poacher, but it had been a case of an overzealous man thinking he could get something from her. *What* had always been the question. His motive had never been released. Of course, the poacher hiding as a deputy had died the night of the rescue, so nothing else could be investigated.

Mitch could admit his sister-in-law was a lovely woman. It had been rationalized that the poaching man had a loose screw somewhere after Rebecca's report, anyway. With no known motive, what else could they do?

Was Brooke involved in this somehow? Did all of this mean Brooke was in danger? He frowned at the thought, not sure why it bothered him, yet knowing it did. Why would she be in danger? And why on earth would someone want to hurt her? She'd been out of the country for over a year and back maybe a month, if he remembered correctly.

His eyes popped open when there was a light tapping on his door. He smiled at the petite blonde who stood visible outside his room, waiting patiently by the door. "Hey, didn't think I'd see you here," he said.

Brooke peeked through the door. "Wanted to see you how you were doing. Can I come in?"

He sat up straighter, glad he wasn't lying flat on his back. "Yeah, sure." Of course she would ask; Brooke was like that. With his one good arm, he pushed himself up, doing what he could to at least look like he was okay. She aimed for the chair Bram had used and sat down. He managed a long glimpse of her legs. She still had great legs.

"How are you feeling?"

"Like hell," he told her truthfully. "But I'll bounce back." He reached up unconsciously and brushed away a length of hair which had fallen to her cheek. She blushed a petal pink, and it made him smile. No, he couldn't see how this tender, sweet woman could be the cause of their problems.

He watched her tongue sweep her bottom lip and felt an answering reaction under his sheet, sudden and heated. He dropped his hand and plucked at the sheet to try to hide it, but her gaze stayed on his face. Thankfully.

"So, how long until you get to go home?" Brooke asked.

"Bram said tomorrow morning. I'm a mess. My leg and my shoulder." Mitch sighed, disgusted. "Tory's gonna kill me," he told her, pushing irritably into the practically regulation flat pillow behind him.

She laughed at his woeful expression. "No, he won't. I talked to him this morning. He's a nice guy once you get past his bulldog mentality."

Mitch studied her from beneath his lashes. "Did he mention, you know, stuff?"

She reached for his hand. "Your friend?" Where she threaded her fingers through his, comfort spread out and up his arm. "Not this morning, but I did find out. Today he wanted to make sure you'd been found," she said in that quiet way of hers. "I assured him you had been and warned him that he could only kick your butt after you'd healed. Not before."

He couldn't hide the chuckle that rose from his chest at the mischievous light in her gaze. "I bet you were your daddy's favorite," he said, teasing her.

She flipped her hair, adding a cheeky smile. "I had my moments."

His eyes closed, soaking up her company when her touch flitted over his forehead. She swept a delicate finger across the gashes there. "Poor baby," she said in a breathy voice. "I guess you don't get to go to the ball, either."

At her words, his eyes snapped open, but her gaze was only concerned, her fingers following the rough scratches he had on his brow and over his face. He felt the heat coming off her skin, flowing over him everywhere she touched. Tugging her with his hand, she tipped closer. Mitch slipped his hand from hers and wound it into her hair. The thick waves felt like heaven beneath his seeking fingers. "Come here," he murmured against her lips.

Burning heat like a shot of bourbon going down his throat enveloped him when he covered her mouth with his. Her softness was better than a gentle wave, a cool breeze of sun-drenched air. If a lightning bolt had ever been described as gentle, then he'd found the cause.

Her lips were sweet as he brought her close. He didn't know why he did it. He only knew he needed to discover her taste. When her small hands lifted to cradle his face, his thoughts stopped, frozen like he'd been blindsided by a red light. She was gentleness and tenderness, a spark of passion and ripe need right under his touch.

She whimpered once when he deepened the kiss, tipping to revel in the feeling of her in his hold. He had never enjoyed a kiss like hers. Blood pulsed through his body. Nerves tingled as the sweet heat of her kiss infused him.

Brooke tore away from his lips, his eyes popping open to find her staring at him with a startled, wide-eyed shock. "You," she exclaimed. "Oh, God! It is you!" She ripped her hands away as though she had been burned. His fingers pulled free of his hold within the silk of her golden strands as she continued to move away. "I'm sorry, Mitch. I didn't... Oh, I'm sorry!"

"Wait!" he called out, his heart racing as though he'd climbed ladders all day. He clenched at the sheet, damning his inability. She was gone.

* * * *

Brooke raced down the hall, ignoring the gawking stares as she barely avoided a food cart. She slammed open the entrance doors and kept going. She swore she'd been imagining it, but as she snared gulping breaths of fresh air, he was there. In her mind, on her tongue, on her skin. And she wanted to cry.

Her head bowed while she fought burning tears of frustration and confusion. She collapsed under a tree on the grass of the manicured lawn of the parking lot. Curling up into a shapeless pile, she crossed her arms over her knees.

How could this have happened? Bram's brother! She thought it was because she'd been using him as a fantasy filler. She prayed it was only because she'd been so lonely. Last night when she'd slept under his hand, his touch comforting with his nearness while she kept an eye over him, his scent had filled her, flowed over her, and she'd silently thrilled at his closeness.

Except...she was not wolf. Not today. And it had

been a thousand times stronger, a million times more potent. Her blood had boiled and her body ached from his kiss. The intensity of it terrified her. The sheer want to be possessed overwhelmed her. She couldn't believe it.

Mitch *was* her mate. Brooke was afraid she might be sick from the discovery.

She sobbed miserably against her arms. How could this have happened? She would have to hide it. That was the answer. She couldn't let him know. He wouldn't understand. He'd convinced himself he'd imagined last night anyway. That was better, for the both of them.

Mitch wasn't the kind to understand. He wouldn't believe her. He would hate her. She didn't want his hate.

Brooke staggered, rising to her feet, steadying herself with the closest tree to stand. She swiped a shaking hand across shocked eyes. She would go to Morgan's and then go home. There wasn't any reason to stay, not while Mitch was here, because sooner or later she would slip up. She would make the mistake and then she'd have to run the same way Aunt Jerry had for most of her life. She'd have to live a life of seclusion, alone and lonely, living in deeper misery than she already was. If she was going to spend eternity alone, Brooke didn't want to have to do it on the run.

She stalked to her Toyota, unlocking it on the way. Why did life have to be so cruel? She actually liked Mitch. He was strong and compassionate. He was damned good looking and well made. He would physically be a great mate. Her lips thinned. No, she couldn't think like that.

He was Bram's younger brother!

She slammed the door and felt no better as she twisted the key in the ignition. Maybe Morgan had a suggestion on how to forget, how to purge this heat coursing through her blood. Even with her knowledge of herbs, there was nothing she could think of powerful enough to drive him from her system. From her point of view, it was worse than hopeless. That fact only made her more depressed.

She drove north of Bend, wanting nothing more than to reach Morgan's. Absently her hand rose and massaged the bandaged healing gashes on her shoulder. She should have known last night, when instincts had taken over and she'd fought the cougar. She'd never fought in either form in her life, but she'd halted the cat in its tracks and would have fought until she had no breath left to protect Mitch. There was no doubt with the way he'd slouched against the plane that he had been severely injured, and it bothered her that she couldn't do anything to help him.

How do you explain appearing out of thin air? Naked? She snorted a disgusted sound. She couldn't, so when she and Morgan had tracked the plane, finding the debris after hours of searching, he'd returned home and brought Mitch help. She'd stayed behind to keep watch, hidden in the trees.

Keeping others from intruding on him was a precaution until he was picked up. Brooke hadn't expected for anything to happen overnight, but that stupid cat had to test the easy-meal theory. If it was wounded and bleeding, it had to be easy, right?

Brooke refused to regret being there, even if he thought he had imagined the fact that she was a wolf, if he'd convinced himself into believing she was someone's dog. Weirder things have happened in nature when people have been hurt.

He'd said she was too tame, too gentle. That should have been her first clue. She wanted to smack herself for ignoring the obvious. By instinct, she would be gentle with her mate. In her wolf form, she wouldn't have wanted to be anywhere near him, but she'd gone right to him. She'd accounted it to his being a friend, not her mate. Her grip clenched around the steering wheel as she drove, seething inside.

It was the kiss. If only she had stopped him. If only she hadn't allowed him to do it. Her heart had raced while she'd cupped his hand, and warmth had suffused her when he'd brushed her hair back. She'd been ignoring those signals for almost a week. Whenever she was near him, her body, her pulse, her mind, reacted. There was no mistaking it. No denying it. Not now. The heat of his kiss had melted her to the core.

She held her legs together, pushing away the heated ache his kiss and touch had unknowingly created.

Brooke ground to a sliding stop on the driveway and shoved the door open, leaping from her seat and marching into Morgan's. He hardly blinked at her as he reclined on his couch, his job done for the day with Mitch now safe at the hospital. He was the epitome of an animal at rest: relaxed but alert. She didn't pay him an ounce of attention as she paced across the living room floor.

Out of the corner of her eye, she followed him as he uncurled and sat up. His heavy stare crashed like an anvil into her senses. He crossed his arms, his face darkening as she continued to pace.

"Christ, not you too," he muttered.

She gave him a cold stare. "Me too what?" She kept pacing.

"I can smell it. You're in heat. Who is he?"

She slammed on the brakes, jarring herself so brutally her jaw swung open as if it were attached to a well-oiled hinge. "What are you talking about?"

"First Selene was a walking pheromone factory,

now you," he said as his gaze crawled all over her. His storm-gray eyes narrowed. "You weren't when you left. Who did you meet?"

"I don't know what you're talking about!" she snapped, her fists clenching at her sides in fury. "I didn't see anyone! I haven't met anyone!"

He rose from the couch, closing in on her, then around her. She shut her eyes as he made his judgment. "You found your mate," he said starkly. "Who is it?"

"You don't need to know. I'm not staying!" She gave him a stony glare. "God, did you give Selene this much hell?"

"Actually, yes, I did," he informed her, unrepentant. His stance relaxed as she locked him in a battle of wills with his gaze. "Brooke, you don't have to leave. I can put up with it." He shoved a palm through his hair. "Hell, that just leaves me."

"I guess it does, because I'm not staying," she repeated. "He doesn't know. He doesn't even like me!"

"Who is it, then?" Morgan asked again. "It takes time, Brooke. Selene and Bram took months to find the connection. Even Roman and Delilah took months, and that doesn't account for feelings. That's just to form a bond."

She shook her head evasively, wanting to step back, to run. "It doesn't matter, Morgan. I can't do this."

She ducked away from his searching when Morgan's hands formed to her shoulders. "Why not? You have to give it a chance. It doesn't happen overnight."

"He's younger, for one. No one likes an older woman. He doesn't understand." Her voice trailed away, losing the worst heat of her anger. She felt beaten. How could this happen to her? All she wanted seemed to be right in front of her but so far out of reach.

"Aunt Jerry. She did this to you, didn't she?" He snarled once, his gray eyes churning in his irritation. "She didn't have the right to scare you. You were there to help her!"

Defensive, her annoyance matched his. "She didn't scare me! She just made sure I saw the truth from every angle, and I'm not helping matters. I want my family. I want what Selene and Roman have!" The gnawing need was a desperation she didn't know how to silence. Realizing who Mitch was to her was sending somersaulting attacks careening against her insides.

"And she made sure you'd think you'd never be able to get it, didn't she? We are not that different, Brooke! We bleed, we hurt, we die," he said firmly with a brother's concern.

"We are very different," she whispered. "I'm going to Mom's in the morning."

"No, stay. You need to work this out. You'll be miserable now that you've hit this point."

Sad and worn, she sagged dejectedly into his hands. "I'm already miserable. I have been since I came home. Now I know why. I can't have what I want." She didn't fight him when he pulled her into a hug and rocked her soothingly.

Morgan had always been the girls' champion, but in this case, he couldn't do one thing to save her.

Chapter Seven

Brooke's departure was completely thrown out the window by seven the following morning. She pressed the phone to her ear and couldn't think of one excuse to not do what Selene was asking.

"So, could you please? I know you've been feeling out of sorts. Maybe keeping Mitch company would be a nice break for you," Selene suggested helpfully.

"It's really not a good idea," Brooke hedged, desperate to find a deeper reason, knowing she was undeniably the only one available to help Mitch during his forced recovery.

"Sure it is. You get to nurse him with your wonderful healing. He'll be bored out of his mind before he can count to ten," her sister prompted. "I know he'd like the company. He's used to cable and takeout."

"And you think I won't drive him crazy?" she asked weakly. "Little quiet, no-fuss me?" Her ploy didn't work. It was a colossal backfire.

"No, in fact that's exactly what he needs for at least a few days. No quick movements, nothing to strain himself over."

Crap! "Oh, all right. When is he going to be at your place?" She cradled her middle with her loose arm, glowering at the floor.

"Thank you, Brooke! I owe you big. So does Bram. He'll be dropped off a little after nine. Can you meet him there?"

"Sure, I'll bring a deck of cards," she retorted snidely. "Sorry." She muttered the word, immediately contrite.

"I know, you're still adjusting," Selene said in an understanding way.

If you only knew. "I'll live," she replied. *Somehow.* Morgan stood at the hallway entrance when she hung up the phone, and she wanted to rip the grin from his mouth.

"I'm still sleeping here!" she informed him coolly.

"If you say so," Morgan replied innocently. "So, the younger man? Would his name be Mitch by chance?"

She grabbed a pillow from the couch and threw it at him as hard as she could instead. He laughed long and loud when he caught it, watching as she stomped into the spare room she'd taken over.

She waited on Selene's porch a few minutes after nine, listening for Bram's Explorer coming over the bridge. She clutched her elbows in her cold hands, fighting her instincts and her own racing heart. What he didn't know couldn't hurt her. That's what she kept telling herself. Steeling herself, she had no more time to gather her defenses as the vehicle stopped in front of her, both doors swinging open.

Watching him struggle to get out of the vehicle, her feet moved on their own accord as she raced to his side. "Here, lean on me."

"I'll topple us both," he said through a gritted jaw, white with pain and strain.

"I'm strong enough," she assured him. "You can't even use a crutch!" Brooke wound an arm around his waist, refusing to let him try to walk without her help.

"No, not until the sling comes off," he said with notable disgust.

"Don't worry about it," Bram said, coming up on

his other side. "Tory gave you medical leave. You can't do anything until the cast comes off anyway."

"Yeah, but it doesn't mean I have to like it," Mitch snapped with a glowered snarl. "Some vacation."

Brooke listened as Mitch grouched and cursed under his breath. He was not going to be an easy patient. He did not take well to being incapacitated.

She had already set up the couch with a clear view of the TV, a step for his broken leg, and pillows to make him as comfortable as she could. She noted he tried to take the situation with a grain of salt, but evidently he didn't have one big enough. He glared at the wall over her head until he was finally sitting.

"All right. Call the hospital for me or Selene if either of you need anything," Bram said, backing for the door. Brooke thought escaping was more appropriate.

"A time machine to get through the next six weeks," Mitch said with an aggrieved air.

Bram gave Brooke a sympathetic glance along with a sincere and silent thank you, then he vanished out the door.

"Now let's get this straight," Mitch ranted the second the door closed behind his brother. "I'm not a good patient. I don't like the fact that I can't move for another two days and if I get mad, I'm apologizing now, up front."

She crossed her arms and halted in front of him. Even beat up, scratched and bruised, he looked delicious. She was in a world of trouble.

"I'm sorry this happened to you," she answered him, her voice calm on the outside even if her heart rate wasn't. His body next to hers had sent her pulse into overdrive on the short walk from the car. "My rules are simple. Whatever the doctor said, that's the bottom line. I don't care if you get mad, scream, or cuss. If you throw something, have the decency to yell duck." His grim expression flickered, as though he were forcing the harsh exterior and falling short. "And if you need anything, I can help. If you do, my name is not slave, maid, or hey you."

"Fine!" He glared at her, and her lip twitched. "Can you move then, please? I'd like to see what I can find on the tube."

She lowered her head in acquiescence and stepped out of his line of sight. She all but ran for the kitchen to escape the room where his scent filled every corner. Brooke braced herself on the counter.

There was no one to blame but herself. She'd agreed to be tortured.

Brooke made a hot cup of tea and strolled to the porch, leaving the door open in case Mitch needed her. Listening to the wind sighing through the trees, Brooke prayed for deliverance, or maybe just a distraction from the solid form in the living room currently sending signals careening through her body, building waves of electricity she not only had to ignore, but had to hide. Folding a leg up, she planted her chin to her knee. How long would he need help? At least as long as his arm was immobile in a sling, she guessed. He couldn't use the crutches until then.

"Hey, Brooke. I'm sorry. I should have asked before you sat down, but could you find my laptop? I need to check my messages." She arched, peering through the door, and found him staring over the top of the couch in her direction.

"Sure," she said, unfolding from her spot. "Your room?" She placed her cup on the phone table. He nodded, and she went to find it.

* * * *

Mitch stared as those legs attached to the best rear

on the planet walked away from him. He blinked, yanking himself away from the view, the direction she had taken. What was going on with him? She was pretty and everything, and she did have some awesome legs, but the way she moved was phenomenal, and she was wearing shorts again. A creamy, buttery color. How does she wear shorts and make them so alluring?

He smiled for her as she came out and handed him the laptop. "Anything else? Power cord? Medication?" He shook his head. His tongue had deserted him. "All right. I'm making some fresh tea. Would you like to try it?"

"Sure," he managed to say, then blew out a breath. Tea? He'd never had hot tea in his life.

It wasn't her fault she'd been given Mitch detail. He didn't have to lay it on so thick, but if she got too close, he might be tempted to kiss her again. He still couldn't find the reason, *any* reason, for the first one.

He reached for the phone and plugged in his computer. There were noises behind him in the kitchen, running water and stuff moving around as he waited for the screen to pop up. He wasn't used to using only one hand, either, so it took time to get through all the passwords and locks.

He inhaled, his eyes drifting shut in appreciation. "That smells wonderful," he told her. "What else are you doing?"

"Just tea," she answered. "Are you hungry?"

"No, not yet." He started reading his messages, scrolling specifically for one from Davis. He found it, opened it, and read it quickly. His mouth became a pinched line by the time he'd read it and gone through it once more.

The Excursion had been stolen, for starters. If that was the case, who could have connected him, Davis, and Brooke all together? Brooke had been driven off the road his first day there. The plane was four days later, with Davis going down before he had been found. So who had stolen the Ford? And why would they want to hurt Brooke?

"Here you go," Brooke said in a lilting voice. He pushed the top of the computer down when she approached.

He curled the cup into his working hand. "Thanks."

"Try it first. If you don't like it, I can get you something else. Tea is an acquired taste for a lot of people."

He took a sip and felt the tingling-with-flavor warmth in his mouth. "Orange? What's the spice in it?"

"Ginger. It's a basic black leaf with my own flavors." She waited at his side with her fingers tucked into one of her rear pockets. He tried to keep his attention from straying to her legs. Not easy with her standing so close.

"Promise not to tell, but I like it," he told her with a smile he meant. He found it was incredibly easy to smile around Brooke.

"Good. Let me know if you need anything," she offered, disappearing to sit outside. He placed the cup on the table and raised the computer screen again, needing to dissect the connection of the murder and his crash. What if her accident had just been a fluke? What if Davis was a random homicide? But none of it explained one single thing about how a bomb found its way onto his plane either.

"Hey, Brooke, does Roman have an e-mail address?" He had to shout to be heard outside.

"Yeah." She rattled it off to him, saying, "It will take him a day or two to answer you, probably. He doesn't keep up with it as much since Adrian's arrival."

"I have a lot of time right now," Mitch muttered.

He typed out his message and sent it. Hopefully, Roman had a few answers to the endless questions Bram had stirred up regarding the wreck and everything that had happened since.

* * * *

Two days later, he was resting on the couch as Brooke sat outside. Again. 'The television wasn't on, and she was reading a book. So why was she outside?

He peeked over the couch and caught the glow of sunshine in her hair. She was curled up with her chin on her knee, tucked into a pretzel shape on one of the chairs. She could sit for hours in that position, and he had no idea how. It didn't seem remotely comfortable to him. Her hand rose and stroked loose hair behind an ear, moving the sun-soaked length. It was impossible to look away.

Her feet were bare, and the shorts of choice for today were red. She tilted her head and noticed his staring gaze, her lips curving.

"Yes?" she asked in a sweet voice that was only hers.

"I was wondering if I stink."

She laughed, a quizzical, light sound. "I don't think so. Why?"

"Because you spend so much time outside."

She blushed a telltale pink, and he smiled more. She was lovelier than anyone he could name when color warmed her skin. "I didn't want to smother you. You're more than capable. I'm just here for the hard stuff."

Hard stuff, huh? Yeah, lately he'd had more than his share of that, too. "Well, how about you come keep me company? I can't take any more soaps."

Her dark eyes sparkled at his humor. She rose with an easy grace that made his mouth go dry. She placed her book on the phone table and sat on the floor, tucking her legs up underneath her.

"Can't take your own company any longer, huh?" she teased him with a smile.

"I guess not." He rolled his shoulder, his head rocking in not-so-feigned misery. "This hasn't been so bad. Except for sitting all day."

"When can you remove the sling?"

"In a few more days. Then I can walk with crutches." He would if it killed him. No way was he waiting two whole weeks to move on his own again.

She observed him with a musing gaze. "Are you going home, then?"

"Why? So I can rattle around my apartment all alone? I'd rather stay here and pester Bram and Selene. They're good sports for putting up with me."

"You're family. Family is everything to the Aiza clan," she stated.

"Is that why you agreed to stay here with me?"

Her gaze flickered away, cooling to two dark pools. Those coffee brown orbs were enigmatic, bewitching. Mitch knew of no one else with eyes like them.

"Mostly. The rest of it is personal and very boring."

"So far, your family is not boring. I doubt you are," he told her honestly. "I know you are not boring." Mitch wanted to lean forward when she raised her chin, to be closer, touching her. He felt a surge of wanting when she licked her lips, felt it in his groin as heat pooled. The need to feel her lips against his own was so strong, a fire in his blood. Forcing his body to relax, he managed to stay right where he was. Why did he feel so drawn to her?

Her attention returned fully to him. "Have you heard from Roman?" She glanced at his laptop under the phone table.

Regaining his composure, he replied, "No, I

haven't checked."

"I'll be right back, if you want some privacy," she offered, gliding down the hall to the restroom. What was the saying, she looked beautiful walking up and even better walking away? It may not happen today, but he was going to get another kiss. He had to. The fact that he couldn't explain the first one just didn't seem to be deterrent enough.

He reached for his computer, plugged it in, and signed on, checking his messages. He found a get-well card from the gang at the firehouse, which made him smile. The firetruck on the card winked playfully at him. He'd show that to Brooke when she returned.

He scrolled through the messages and found Roman's response, reading it quickly.

You're right to be worried. The plastics were professional. I don't know who, but if you have a suspicion about the Ford and Brooke, don't dismiss it. Morgan and I went over the site carefully. The engine had been tampered with also. Someone didn't want you to walk away. If you need me, I can be there in a few hours.

Well, he couldn't move, but did he want to include more of the family in this than he believed safe? Roman had a child and a wife. Bram had Selene. Mitch was on his own.

He heard her steps nearing from the hallway. Typing a quick reply, he sent the e-mail to Roman. He'd ask for help if it was the last choice, but for now he'd do his own legwork, or as much as he could from his planted spot on the couch, he thought with a rueful grimace.

He reopened the card on his screen and sought her gaze as Brooke came into the room. How does a blonde get such fathomless, compelling eyes? She neared to peer over his shoulder and laughed at the playful firetruck.

"Cute," she said. "From friends?"

"The guys back home." He shut off the computer and set it to the side. Somber, he questioned her about the accident. "Brooke, when you were knocked off the road, do you remember anything specific about it?"

"Like what?"

He tapped his fingers against his elbow encased in the sling. "Were you followed for a long time? Or did they just show up? Did you notice the Ford anywhere else? And how did they knock you off the road? You'd said you were trying to turn, but they did something to keep you from doing it."

"Well," she said thoughtfully. "I guess they were behind me for a while. I don't remember if it was all the way from town or not. I came from Roman's, so I did go through town." She straightened and sauntered around the couch to sit on the floor again in front of him. "I remember turning on my blinker and then..." Her eyes drifted shut as she tried to remember for him. "I think they hit me!" she said, her eyes snapping open again. "Yes, now that I think about it, there was a jolt of some sort. I blinked and then I remember opening my eyes and seeing you!"

"Have you seen your car?"

She shook her head. "No, I never did. Bram said he emptied it. I didn't have anything in it but my luggage. I never keep anything in the glovebox."

"No records or maintenance manuals?" he asked her.

"No, I kept all of that at Mom's. It's probably a huge square by now," she said with a bitter turn of her mouth.

"I don't know what's going on, but that Ford was reported stolen from the northern side of the state a few days before I arrived." He made himself comfortable on the stack of pillows, staring upward and wiggling his toes. Man, he hated the cast.

"Stolen!" Her chin dropped to her raised knees. "So it was on purpose," she whispered. She paled as things became more clear, sort of. Mitch wasn't any more sure of anything than she was.

He felt torn. He couldn't walk, couldn't ask questions, and he didn't want to put Brooke in any danger, provided it hadn't found her to begin with.

"Maybe," he told her, "I'm not a hundred percent sure of anything right now." He searched her pensive expression. "Has Bram said anything to you about the plane accident?"

"No, not to me, but Morgan seemed confused that you crashed right after the plane had been worked on the day before," she replied.

He jerked up from where he'd been slouching. He tugged on the sling, wanting it gone and now. "The day before?"

"Apparently the guy at the hangar told Bram a mechanic had been on it right before you took it out. Oh, and he knew the radio was on the blink."

"You're kidding! That ass knew the radio was out?" He couldn't believe it! He'd walked right into it!

"That was what I understood," she replied self-consciously. "Why?"

"Damn it!" He swore under his breath. "Where is the connection?"

"What connection?"

"I wish I knew," he said, more frustrated than he'd been just a few minutes before. Mitch thrust a hand through his short hair. "Don't go anywhere alone anymore, Brooke."

She startled at the gravity of his warning, her spine stiffening. "Why? What's going on?"

Mitch moved forward, putting a seriousness in his

tone that he prayed was just overkill, fearing the danger was all too real and getting too close. "Something. You were run off the road. When I sent the plates to Davis, he was shot the same day a mechanic worked on my plane." He knew when she began to make her own connections as the wariness and worry paled her cheeks further. "Look, I'm not doing this to scare you," he told her, meaning it, getting as close as he could to hold her gaze better. "But whoever that mechanic was, I think he set my plane to crash."

"Crash? How?" Her eyes flew wide open, filled with her growing fears as her fingers dug into her knees.

"Roman found a small plastics device on the rudder of the plane. I can remember feeling the controller jump in my hand. I thought I'd hit a duck, but the snap of the control happened after one of my engines blew." He sighed, rubbing his eyes, feeling more tired than he had an hour ago. "After that, it was just a matter of landing. I wasn't going anywhere."

"Someone sabotaged your plane?" she gasped in a disbelieving tone.

"I think so. So please, no more driving back and forth. I know it's not far, but I don't want you getting forced off the road again. SUV's are known for rolling if they aren't handled well." And the thought of that happening to her made his stomach cringe with unwelcome spasms.

She nodded, her eyes darting around for a moment or two. "I'll have Morgan bring my stuff tonight. Does anyone else know?"

"Bram knows some, so does Roman." Mitch sat back, feeling helpless in his current condition. "I wish I wasn't stuck here."

She peeked at him out of the corner of her eye. "Would it be better if I went home? Let you go home, too?"

He grimaced. "I doubt it. Killers hate it when their targets don't do the polite thing and die," he said. "I don't know if you were supposed to die, though. The hit you took wasn't all that bad. Your bruises weren't substantial; they only lasted a few hours. But when you purposely do what was done to my plane, and what they did to my friend in St. Louis..." He trailed off, then shook his head with a heavy, sad motion. "I think you're safer here."

Mitch waited until she agreed and then let his head plop to the cushions. His eyes felt like dead weights when they shut.

"I can help," she said earnestly. "I can go and ask around town—"

"See right there," he replied, breaking in with a chuckle. "I wasn't kidding when I told Bram you needed a keeper." His gaze was kind as he sought hers. "If you go and stick your nose around town, then they will know you didn't die, for one, and two, will know that you're on to whoever this is. You might as well paste a bullseye on your cute rear." He closed his mouth with a snap. Okay, he hadn't meant to say that, even if it was God's honest truth.

She blushed but didn't avoid his concerns. "But what if I could get a name of the mechanic? Surely the guy who owns the rental place would know who his mechanics are."

"Brooke, I don't want you getting hurt," he stated firmly. "No." He smiled, softening the blow when her dark eyes flashed at him. "We'll figure this out. I really only told you so you'd be aware. Yours might have really been an accident, and I stirred the hornet's nest with my snooping into the plates." Her face was tight, but she finally relented.

"All right, but if you want help, call Roman."

"I don't want to include anyone I don't have to," he explained, reiterating his own thoughts.

She rose from her spot, effectively silencing him with her honeyed hair sweeping across her shoulders in a thick wave. "And I told you, family is everything to us," she said, equally direct. "Don't ignore it to save your pride, Mitchell."

He watched her walk out the door. Only his mother ever called him Mitchell, and only when she was pissed.

Chapter Eight

Mitch didn't blink an eye a few nights later when Selene said she and Brooke were going for a walk in the dark. After spending days to think, he wasn't getting any answers to the problems and questions revolving around his crash and Brooke's wreck. So, with Bram next to him on the porch enjoying the evening, Mitch called Roman.

"Hey, Mitch." Mitch shot a look at his brother to find him listening, but it was just as well. The more Bram knew, the safer he could be.

"I got your e-mail, and I have a few questions." Mitch shifted and rolled his unbound shoulder. His sore one was feeling better, and he was thinking he might try it without the sling the next day.

"Sure. How can I help?"

"I was wondering, do you know if the Ford's been picked up yet?"

"No, but I can find out. Do you still have the plate info?" Mitch gave it to Roman.

"What can you tell me about what you found on the plane?" Mitch asked.

"Well, the setup on the rudder had been painted, for one. We found paint chips in the enamel. It was likely something small, maybe the size of a silver dollar to make it easier to camouflage, but large enough to jam your tail rudder."

"So, if I did a quick once-over, I could miss it. Which I did," Mitch said with a note of disgust. "Most people don't need to inspect their planes for small bombs either."

"Yes, but it seemed to be working by remote. I didn't find a timer mechanism on it or any wires leading to an ignition box."

"Good grief! Who the hell did I piss off?" Mitch asked the world at large.

"If you want, I can go be scary and question the owner," Roman offered with a rumbled timbre, a sinister smile heard attached underneath.

Mitch could appreciate his ability to be scary. Very few could look directly at Roman and not feel a twinge of fear. "I do, and I don't. I don't know who the target was. I mean, myself, I got that. But why John Davis all the way in St. Louis? And did Brooke really have anything to do with it? She does remember getting hit before she blacked out." Mitch tapped his trapped fingers against his side, silently cursing the sling one more time.

"Really? Hmm. Well, that does change things a little," Roman said thoughtfully. "That makes her wreck intentional rather than accidental."

"But who and why?" Mitch asked. Staring out into the clearing, he sifted through what he knew about those days and drew a blank no matter how hard he tried to wrap his mind around it all.

"Thanks," Roman said off the phone. "Let's see, the Ford was found fifty-five miles from Bend, deserted, two days ago."

"Wow, how'd you get that? And so fast?" Mitch asked with admiration.

He replied with a touch of pride, "I'm married to the best. Del can find a black grain on a white beach." His tone went serious on his next words. "Well, let's look at it as if she had been the target. The accident wasn't enough to hurt her. So what did she do to make someone want to scare her?"

"I don't have an answer to that one. She's only been back a month."

"From Aunt Jerry's," Roman stated suspiciously. "I bet she had something to do with this."

"You're kidding, right?" Mitch almost barked his laughter, except something in Roman's tone made him swallow it instead.

Mitch heard a sigh of resignation. "No, I'm not. Aunt Jerry is a bit...different. If she did something, and Brooke knows about it... I'm guessing you need to ask her."

"I don't get it," Mitch said. "Even if she were supposed to get the life scared out of her, how did my sending the plates on the Ford get Davis murdered? Not to mention my landing." The frown he couldn't fight grew with his confusion.

"Hold on a sec," Roman said from the other end. Mitch could hear him talking to Delilah in the background. Then he said, "Well, that was something different."

"What?" Mitch didn't like the burn lodging in his gut.

"The owner of the Ford was found dead the day he reported it stolen."

Mitch closed his eyes. "Hell," he muttered. "People are dropping like flies because Brooke got ran off the road," he said with a very worried growl.

"No, people are dying because she knows something," Roman retorted decisively. "And whoever is out there is eliminating the trail as they track her."

"But that means the whole family is in danger!" Mitch sat up straight. Bram stiffened in his own chair, closely paying attention now.

"I'm going to take Del and Adrian to a safe place, then I'll be there in a few hours. When you find that sister of mine, sit on her if you have to, but we're going to get to the bottom of this."

"All right. I'll be here." Mitch hung up the phone, setting it on his lap. Tapping the heel of his cast on the porch, he had never felt more trapped, or less capable of solving this crisis. Apparently, he was in as much danger as Brooke was if what Roman hinted at was possible because, like Mitch had told her, killers tended to get bent out of shape when their targets didn't die.

Bram spoke up calmly, immediately. "I'm staying."

Mitch released an irate breath, but not aimed at his brother. "Bram, I don't know if it's safe to stay, for you or Selene."

"Well, I can tell you, there is power in numbers, and no one messes with this family," Bram said. "Believe me. I know."

"How do I qualify as family? I'm extended."

Bram shot Mitch a no-arguments glare. "You are my brother. You are family, and you are accountable."

"Jeez, all right," Mitch said. He closed his eyes, trying to think. Unfortunately, all he could manage were circles with no answers.

He didn't understand Bram's attitude. Mitch didn't understand much of anything at the moment. A few minutes later, his eyes widened as wolf song traveled on the breeze from the darkness. "They're back," Mitch whispered.

"Yes, they are.'"

* * * *

The next morning, Selene left for her shift at the hospital while Bram and Mitch tested his shoulder in the living room of the cabin.

"How's that feel?" Bram asked, studying Mitch's motions.

"A little weak and twitchy, but not too bad," Mitch said as Bram rotated the shoulder. He couldn't take the sling anymore. Mitch could get used to the soreness and pain.

"If you get tired, go ahead and use the sling for a few hours, but I think you can stop using it all day now." Bram let Mitch's arm go, and he managed to hold it steady for a solid count. "Great."

Mitch glanced at the cast. "Any hope for that?"

Bram smiled. "Nope. Gotta stick that one out."

"Damn," Mitch replied, dejected. He adjusted the crutches that had been waiting for him in the closet and tried to use them. He clenched his jaw as the pressure on his shoulder caused a burning ache.

"Not too much too soon," Bram warned.

"Yes, doctor," he replied. They both turned toward the front of the house as a motorcycle neared the clearing.

"Roman's here," Bram said.

"Good. Is she even awake?" Mitch asked. He hadn't seen Brooke all morning.

"She went for a run before dawn. She'll come in now with Roman here."

"She just took off?" Mitch asked, bewildered. "With all of this over her head?"

Bram shrugged. "Sometimes a run is all they need."

"I will never understand this family," Mitch muttered.

Bram's gaze turned evasive. "No, probably not. But it's better for you that way."

Mitch gaped at Bram when he turned away from Mitch's stunned stare to open the door. Was Bram holding back? Did he know something he wasn't telling Mitch? Why would he keep secrets from his own brother? And what was it about the Aizas, especially Brooke, that made no sense?

Bram and Roman began talking while they all waited for Brooke to reappear. And as Bram had said, within five minutes, she walked through the door. She closed it and went right to Roman to be enveloped within his large arms for a brother's hug.

Her hair was slightly tousled from being outdoors, her face flushed. Mitch still wanted that kiss, but she'd been keeping an arm's length between them. The more no-man's land she kept between them, the more he discovered he didn't like it.

"All right, Babs," Roman said as Bram heated water for tea. "What did Aunt Jerry do?"

"Do?" she asked.

Roman rested against the counter and stared at her. He seemed to make the kitchen shrink with his height and broad shoulders. Roman was a block of a man. Maybe Mitch should let him go and torment the plane's owner after all.

Mitch stood nearby, leaning on his crutches, but gave in to the pain and found a chair when it became too unbearable. He couldn't help that he was injured.

Roman rubbed his eyes, then crossed his arms over his chest. He gave her the information he'd shared with Mitch the night before, including the now known death of the Ford's owner, along with one little tidbit he'd found out after hanging up with Mitch.

"Del found out the owner was a Mr. Kavanaugh, who recently traveled to Belgium. His stay put him within hours of where Aunt Jerry lives," he explained with a cautious note. "Did he go see Aunt Jerry? And why would someone want to kill or try to hurt you?"

Brooke pulled out a chair to sit with stilted moves, her face pale. Her expression grew distressed. "I don't know. I didn't meet anyone while I was there."

"Did Aunt Jerry do any business while you were there?" Roman asked her.

"Why?"

Mitch followed the conversation between the two, hoping for a clue to his own wreck.

Roman's gaze turned thoughtful. "Because Mr. Kavanaugh was a collector of rare..." Mitch watched him try to find a word. "...antiquities is the best way to put it."

Brooke's fingers twisted together on her lap. "Whenever someone came to see her, I stayed out of the way."

Roman cursed a sigh. "I imagine that's what she would've wanted."

"Um, sorry for asking, but who is Aunt Jerry?" Mitch asked. Brooke's worry continued to deepen, and Roman was definitely furious at the situation.

Roman and Brooke exchanged a look, and he gave her a nod of allowance. Her voice was quiet, unable to physically meet his confused and disbelieving stares. "She's a witch. Among other things."

Mitch barked a laugh. "You're kidding, right?"

"No, we're not," Roman said. "Brooke, do you remember seeing anyone at all while you were in Belgium?"

"I'm sorry, no."

She closed her eyes, and Mitch wanted to hold her to tell her it would be all right. Her voice was a shadow of her usual self when she spoke again.

"She did give me a small box. She told me to keep it until I needed it, or until she asked for it back."

"Until you needed it? That's odd," Mitch said, rolling his shoulder to ease the growing suffering in the joint.

"Not if you knew our aunt. Where is it?" Roman demanded.

"In my bags. I'll get it." She jumped from her chair and returned a few minutes later holding a simple metal box, nothing extravagant or special from what Mitch could see of it. She held it out for Roman to take it, but he didn't want to touch it.

"Don't give it to me!" he said in a growl.

"What is it?" she asked, her face paling.

"Hold it out," he ordered her. Mitch watched as Roman gave it an unblinking once-over. Mitch was surprised when he heard a deep hiss come from the bigger man. "Hell," he said, the word sounding strangled. "Open it, slowly."

Mitch waited in bewildered silence while she flicked a small clasp and cracked the cover to what looked to be nothing more than a very plain tin or aluminum box. Roman swore again.

"I thought Dad said that had been destroyed!" he practically yelped, gripping on to the counter, bending his body backward away from the box in Brooke's hands. "Close it!"

"What is it?" she asked, carefully holding it between her hands, snapping the clasp into place.

Roman spun and gripped the counter with bloodless fingers. "The blood amulet. Christ, how the hell did Mitch get into this? He's not one of us," he demanded, perplexed.

"That's what I told Bram. I'm extended. I don't understand the connection," Mitch agreed, puzzled. What could he possibly have to do with any of this? His gaze flicked from Roman to Bram to Brooke. All of their expressions were different.

"Roman, can I talk to you? In private?" Brooke asked, clutching the box close in her trembling hands.

Her request was so forlorn, Mitch almost didn't hear her.

Roman stalked away, and Brooke followed with a dejected pace. They were gone a short minute before he returned, following her. Her dark eyes glistened with pools of tears, ready to cry.

"All right. I need to call Morgan and tell him the amulet is back in the family. Bram, you and your brother don't need to worry since you can't be affected by what's in the box. Selene and Brooke can control it, but neither Morgan nor I can touch it." Roman faced them all again from his place at the counter, his arms crossed with a brooding glare pinned on the box.

"Would someone explain what is going on?" Mitch asked, getting angry that he felt like the only person who didn't know what everyone else was talking about, staring in from the outside. "Who are you people, and what the hell is in that box?" he snapped, pointing at it in Brooke's shaking hands.

Roman fell silent for several minutes. "Mitch, I wish I could tell you what you want to know, but I can't. I don't know why you were targeted unless someone spotted you helping Brooke the day of her accident and assumed you and she..." Roman clamped his jaw shut. "But regardless, they traced your e-mail to Davis, which tracked the Ford, and will lead them right back to here." He ran a hand over his face. "Damn, I wish Del were here."

"You want to risk your wife?" Mitch asked. Was the man insane?

Roman made a rude sound, pinning Mitch with a stare that sent a shot of wariness across his nerves. "No, of course not, but out of all of us, she could probably use the amulet and split the world in two."

"Amulet? What amulet? Use it how?" Mitch scowled, wondering when he'd entered a Dungeons & Dragons game.

"It's an amulet that, if the wearer knows how, can control certain bodies," Brooke answered when no one else seemed willing to offer even a token explanation. Her smooth cheeks were still chalky pale. "It makes the user very powerful over ones like my family." She bowed her head and the tears began to fall, glistening like dewdrops on her lashes. "I had no idea it was *that* amulet," she whispered thickly. Her head snapped up. "Can't we destroy it? You said Dad thought it had been," she pleaded with a brash light of hopefulness.

Roman shook his head. "No, whoever wants it followed you from Belgium, tracking it. They won't know either way, and you could still be hurt before they know we have destroyed it." He dropped his chin to his chest, a bleak sense surrounding him. "Besides, if memory serves me right, only the one who made it can destroy it."

Brooke's despairing groan filled the room. "Well, that's not going to happen."

Roman crouched in front of her chair. "Brooke, you trained with Aunt Jerry when you were younger. She said you could harness the ability. Have you kept up on it?"

She nodded once, a stiff motion expressing her worry clearly. "Of course. How else could someone like me find so much trouble?" Brooke searched Roman with a beseeching gaze. "I never meant for this to happen, Roman."

Roman tucked her hair behind an ear as her head fell forward to land on the broad strength of her brother's shoulder, the weight of her problem obvious in her slumped frame in her chair. Mitch felt useless.

"I know you didn't, Babs. Do you think you're strong enough to control it?"

Brooke nodded. "But if those hunting for it aren't like us, it won't affect them. It'll be powerless."

Mitch blinked. *Hunting? Ability?* He knew less now than when Roman had first arrived. He was only convinced he was more confused than ever.

"I think they might be, now that I know what

they're after." Roman's voice was deadpan serious.

Her head whipped up as though it had been yanked with a string. "What do you mean?"

Roman glanced over his shoulder at Bram. "Does he know?" Bram shook his head.

"Hey, I'm right here," Mitch pointed out, exasperated. Roman delivered a menacing glare, and Mitch forced himself to not flinch. No doubt, Roman was intimidating as hell. Mitch was there only as an unavoidable witness. Roman obviously would have preferred he wasn't there at all.

"Sorry, Mitch," Bram said, giving him a slanted glance. "I know this is weird."

"And this happens regularly, is that it?" His hand clenched where it rested on the table, feeling his brow tighten, helpless to help Brooke, helpless in his condition.

"No, actually. It's been three hundred years since someone tried to capture one of us, not counting Selene." Roman stood again. "But this is a different situation completely if I'm right. Having the blood amulet changes everything."

Mitch's gaze jumped between the three other people in the kitchen. "Capture? What are you talking about? People don't capture one another."

Brooke's tears were flowing freely now. "They do when you're us," she said in a choked whisper, leaping from her chair and running for the spare room. Mitch waited for the other two in the kitchen to do something, anything, when the door slapped closed.

Bram let out a sigh, pinching the bridge of his nose. "You should probably go home to St. Louis. This really isn't your fight, Mitch."

"But they tried to kill me!" he shouted. His head was spinning. Nothing made sense. "And what about John Davis? He was murdered!"

"Because they thought you and Brooke... Well, that doesn't matter right now," Roman said heavily. "It's really a guess at this point."

"What is a guess?" He bit out the words, grinding his jaw in some shallow attempt at restraint. Roman didn't pay him any attention, already dismissing him. He wanted to snarl, demand, that they explain all of this. "What is it about Brooke? She's pretty, but come on. She couldn't hurt a fly," Mitch retorted scathingly.

Mitch could only gape in bewildered and hurt shock as his brother—*his* brother—and Roman shared a telling look.

What was that about? What weren't they telling him? How could Brooke be in enough danger to make someone want him out of the way to get to her?

He rose from his chair, leaning heavily on his crutches, and without another word went to find Brooke.

Chapter Nine

How stupid could she have been? Brooke should have known Aunt Jerry was up to something. Sweet, kind, and trusting, Brooke's largest faults were now glaring at her from inside the little tin box. The damn blood amulet! Why did Aunt Jerry give it to her?

Now, because of it and her, Mitch was in trouble. They all were if what Roman hinted at was possible. Who knew what they were? What had Aunt Jerry been thinking? Why hadn't she told her what she was giving Brooke to begin with? And who would have known enough to be able to track her to Oregon?

She flinched when she heard Mitch's shout at the other end of the cabin. He didn't deserve this. He was innocent in all of this. Brooke knew having him as a mate would prove to be impossible. She'd kept a constant space between them, but the last week had been a tortured hell while fighting against throwing herself at him at the same time. His heat, his warmth, his kind laugh when he wasn't mad at being stuck on the couch, had been agony without relief.

She'd been going out every night to run herself numb, trying to wipe him from her mind, out of her senses. If anything, his presence was becoming harder and harder to ignore, and she couldn't just get up and walk out. Especially now.

Sitting on the same bed with his scent permeating the air like an elixir was driving her slowly insane. She'd had to tell Roman what she knew. If he said something assuming Mitch and she had…it was only an assumption at this point, but if she knew it then they probably knew it too. If the hunters thought she and Mitch had connected, he was in grave danger. Brooke's stomach heaved. She didn't want anyone to be in danger. She shook her head, tossing her hair around her. They hadn't bonded, and they never would. It was too much to hope for. Morgan had more faith in her than she did believing it would all work out.

She drew a breath and knew before the door opened that he was outside. His troubled gaze became visible as the door opened. "Hey, you all right?"

"Sure," she said sarcastically. "I always doom my family this time of year."

He slipped in and shut the door enclosing them together into the room, haltingly hopping his way to sit next to her on the bed. She moved over and gave him more room. He turned on a hip to face her.

She swallowed. *It's hard to talk when you're salivating for your company*, she thought

For the first time in days he was close. Very, *very* close. Her eyes drifted shut as he pushed her hair back. Using a gentle thumb, he wiped away tears of frustration and worry.

"I'm sorry. I had no idea when she gave this to me how much it would affect everyone." She sniffed, clearing her throat, and fought the urge to hold him, to feel him. It was taking a Herculean effort to suppress.

"Well, I have to admit, I don't remember asking the travel agent if there were witch hunts on this tour, but I'm game," he replied with a tender smile. "Can you tell me what's going on? I'm not going to leave you to face this alone. Bram's ready to pack me up and send me home, and I don't feel like I can."

She raised her chin, seeking his gaze, and found

how caramel rich his eyes became when he was serious. "There's a lot you don't know about me, about my family." She searched deep for the strength to continue. "Aunt Jerry is just the tip of the iceberg, and very few outside of the family have even met her. I was born with a little more aptitude than the other three and when I was in my teens, I went to her and studied the art of witchcraft."

"Is that why you're so good with the flowers and stuff?" He tipped in, narrowing more of the gap between them, his expression completely earnest and curious.

A small sigh escaped before she could stop it. "I was good with herbs and flowers before. I excelled in school when it came to natural science and biology."

He nodded thoughtfully. "But that doesn't explain why Roman the Terrible is terrified of what's in that box," he said, prompting her.

She bit her lips, fighting the smile he'd coaxed out of her, and he joined her.

"You're prettier when you smile," he said. "I think so, anyway."

Her blood hummed when his voice deepened to a rumble. She clenched her fists. She would not touch him.

Brooke made her mind kick in to talk to keep from doing exactly that. "The amulet is dangerous to the men of my family. It was created centuries ago and like Roman said, we all thought it had been destroyed." She lowered her stare to the bed. If she didn't look right at him... Frustration tightened her body, urges and hungers pounding at her. She wanted to cry! It didn't help, not in the least.

"And when you left, your aunt gave it to you to protect? To use? To bury?" he asked.

"I don't know!" she cried, tortured by the truth of

her answer. "I don't know if Aunt Jerry was trying to get it out of someone's reach or if she thought it would be fun to have us hunted instead of her for a change," she said on a spiteful breath.

"Hunt you? I still don't understand that."

She looked up and caught his gaze. Utter confusion. "Mitch! I want to trust you. I really do!" She gave in and reached for his hand, feeling his body's heat down to her toes. His smooth brown eyes widened as they zeroed in on where she covered his hand. "But ever since you and I crossed paths, it's been nothing but trouble. I've been nothing but trouble."

"That's not entirely true," he said, his voice acquiring a hoarse quality she'd never really heard before. "You've helped me when you didn't want to. You've avoided me unless I asked for something. I know you don't exactly like me, but I thought we were almost friends."

"No, I do like you," she exclaimed, her wide gaze rising hurriedly to meet his, wanting to remove that assumption. "There's just so much involved." She was dying to say what was on her mind, in her heart, but the fear of utter rejection kept the truth frozen in her chest.

"I agree," he whispered, then he reached and touched her lips with his. Her eyes fluttered closed as he shifted, cupping a hand to her face, holding her. Her entire body reacted. Not her senses, not her mind, and not only her heart.

Everything ignited into a hot liquid flame at once. He was warmth and heat, desire and need, and she drank from his well as he kissed her. She shuddered as he moved, pressing closer, and her hand rose from her lap to curl longingly around his neck.

His kiss deepened, and she begged for more. Brooke whimpered against his lips when he cradled her with both hands and sought her with his tongue. It felt like she was falling, flying as he did things she'd never experienced, touched her in ways she'd never dreamed, with the merest brush of his lips.

He angled upward from her mouth while he traveled over her skin with a gaze as gentle as a caress. "Brooke," he said, tender and hungry at the same time. She fell backward, his lips guiding her as he floated to the bed with her. "God, I've wanted this for so long," he said breathily against her mouth. "To touch you."

She held on as his lips worshipped her, dropping little explosions across her cheek to meet the warmth of her throat, and she groaned, an aching need bombarding her. She tipped her head and let him roam. He wound one hand into her hair, and she shivered as he licked and kissed her, nibbling in delicious discoveries of sensation that stole her sanity.

"Like that?" Mitch asked, his voice roughened with pure desire. "You taste so sweet." He went to where he had started. "You're like candy. I don't want to stop," he said, flicking his tongue against her ear.

She stiffened in his hold and tried to push against him. "No! We can't!"

"Shh. We won't," he said with aching tenderness, resuming his attack. "I don't want to stop tasting you." He hummed against her throat, right beneath her ear, and a shot of electricity sparked the nerves of her spine. "I would never hurt you." She shuddered and cried out when he raked his teeth over the exact same spot. "You're incredible," he murmured.

She sucked in a hot moan when he found the beating of her heart at the top of her shoulder. He sighed his approval.

"I want," she said, gasping.

"What?" His response was a purr, nuzzling beneath her ear.

"I want to taste," she managed to say in the next breath. He'd gone no lower than her collarbone, and she was a quivering mass of screaming nerves.

He cradled her in his arms and rolled onto his back, his brown eyes heavy with desire. "Please do," he said in invitation, his strong fingers winding through her hair again.

His gaze slid closed when she discovered the heated sensation of his skin and felt the rush of him on her tongue. She traveled from his jaw to anywhere she could reach. He moaned shakily through parted lips when she nibbled the skin beneath his ear and gave it a tender treatment, mimicking his previous attacks on her nerves. "Yes." He sighed, encouraging her, and it fanned her flame of desire higher.

"You taste like hot honey," she whispered. "I've never..." She shook with an untested wanting as she gave up trying to talk and instead kissed and suckled on his skin. "Oh God, Mitch."

"We need to stop," he said on a rolling groan, sadly mere moments later.

She did in a heartbeat. "Oh, God! I'm sorry!" He captured her before she could retreat and tugged her to his side.

"Don't be." He kept her close, running a hand up and down her spine as she gradually cooled to a simmering pool of awakened desire. "That was the most erotic kiss I've ever enjoyed," he told her with a mused sense of wonderment. "You taste so good." She heard him lick his lips and quivered in reaction, knowing exactly how hot those lips were on her skin.

Her palm rested over his heart, and its hard rhythm rocked beneath her. He tilted his head and inhaled. "Even your hair smells like a summer garden," he murmured, as absorbed as she was in the discoveries between them. He released a breath. "No,

I am definitely not leaving. Not now."

"Do you trust me?" she asked with an apprehensive feeling settling in her stomach. She had a chance now, a bare one, but it was better than anything up to then.

"Yes, I do," he said without hesitation. "Why?"

"You asked about the amulet." He nodded and she told him, "I have something to ask you first." Desperately, she wanted him to believe, she wanted to know he could believe.

"All right." He lay relaxed under her touch, enjoying the moment, she hoped, as much as she was.

She prayed she wasn't about to make the largest mistake of her life. There wasn't exactly a beginner's course for telling your family's largest, deepest secret to a person.

"Please understand I need to do this," she told him. "But when your plane went down, do you remember anything about a golden-yellow wolf?"

She felt his gaze on her when he twisted next her. His hand stopped in its gentle meandering. "How do you know? I never told anyone but Bram. Unless he said something."

"No, he didn't tell me anything." She made herself sit up on a hip to watch his face. Being that close to him, under his touch, made speaking difficult, and she had to tell him the truth to let him decide. Her heart beat with a thudding, sluggish tune as she tried to keep the fear of rejection at bay. "Explain your water bottle to me," she said warily. His gaze narrowed, and he sat up with her.

"It fell out when I opened the door," he replied.

She shook her head. "You and I both know it didn't. I know how it got there, by your hand." Her voice became tentative as his expression drew blank, already fighting to dismiss what she had to share.

Brooke knew he wouldn't trust this, her, not yet, but she had to take the chance. She knew that now. His entire body tightened though, like a board had been shoved flush against him, his spine rigid. His gaze never left her but she could feel his reaction regardless.

"I want to trust you." His gaze didn't deviate, challenging her.

"Then just tell me, trust me." His tone was even but she heard the charged caution, felt the apprehension swirling in the very air around them. She knew he was already rejecting the possibility before she'd even had a chance to put it into words. Brooke couldn't blame him.

Her gaze fell when she found her courage lacking. She groaned at herself. "I can't. I would rather have you at least as a friend than watch you leave in hate and disgust," she told him, feeling the weight of her decision in her soul. At least this was indeed her choice.

"What do you know about the wolf?" he asked her with quiet sincerity. "Tell me I didn't imagine it."

His prodding destroyed her hesitation. If he wanted to know he hadn't dreamed that much, maybe it would create the opening to go the final step.

"I know she helped you when you needed it, that she kept watch over you when you were lost," she said.

"I thought it was a tame dog," he told her, accepting, for the moment, with quiet awe. "It was really one of the wolves you've told me about, wasn't it?"

"More than that." Brooke caged the butterflies before they escaped. "I'm trusting you with a lot of me." A single finger supported her chin, bringing her up to meet his stare, and she dived into the truth. "I know about the cougar."

His hand jerked away as if she'd burned him. She could tell he'd have jumped up if he hadn't been injured. "But how?" His lips parted and his pulse was erratic, beating sharply beneath the skin of his neck.

"Do you still want to know? Do you still trust me?"

She watched as he moved his attention to the floor. "This has to do with the whole family and why Bram won't discuss anything with me anymore, doesn't it?"

"Yes, but this is between you and me." She stood from the edge of the bed and offered him his crutches. "I need to show you something."

She opened the bedroom door and led the way to the living room. With a single, studied observation, both Bram and Roman exited for the outdoors without a word spoken. *Some things don't have to be explained at that point,* she thought pensively as she stood in front of the wall of paintings, too grateful for their understanding to get the hell out of the house. The last thing she wanted was an audience.

Brooke crossed her arms and began pacing. How was she supposed to do this? Would he hate her after all? After what she'd just experienced, she knew better than to think he wasn't the one meant for her. Nothing, no one, had ever reached her so deeply, made her raging and desperate for more. Mitch was definitely the man she'd been waiting for. She was sorry he had been hurt. She was sorry he'd ever been placed in danger because of whatever was tangled around the amulet, around her.

"I don't know how to do this," she finally admitted when he stood near her. "So I guess I'll just tell you." She took a deep breath and squared her shoulders. Facing him, she said, "I know you won't believe me, but I do hope you'll understand I'm doing it to help keep you safe."

"What?" He propped himself on his good foot, landing on her with a confused gaze.

"You were the only one who saw the yellow wolf?"

she asked, purposefully examining the wall again.

"Yes."

She cleared the few paces until she stood next to the painting of the pack and pointed to herself. "Is this the one?"

"That's not hard to guess. There are only two up there," he stated as he hobbled closer.

"Why do you think Selene has paintings of so many if only a few live here?" Her finger traced the yellow form, then fell. She longingly wished she could be that creature now, to escape the next few minutes.

"She said she liked the wolf, and your dad could paint them well." The weight of his confusion filled the silence of the room. She wasn't being clear enough.

"How do I know what happened that night, what you saw?" she asked him, unable to meet his gawking stare, fixated as she was on the wall of paintings, her family. There was a tremor in her voice she couldn't, and didn't, try to hide. "And how do I know she wasn't alone when she found you?" She motioned to a dark animal with light gray tips, her hand pale against his thick coat. "He was with me," she whispered.

She heard his air leave him with a violent whoosh.

"This is our family secret. This is what Bram protects to his grave. This is why someone wants that amulet. Because whoever wears it, if they know how, can control us in this form. Roman and Morgan can't touch it. The effects are irreversible."

She heard him gulp.

"What are you?" he asked in a wavering voice. She sensed more than saw the way his body moved away, tipping on the crutches.

"Shape-shifters. The only ones of our line any of us know of." She turned and faced him, baring it all. "You have a right to know."

"Why? Why me?" His gaze was huge, stuck on the

paintings, yet unseeing, looking right through them.

"Because I was so convinced I would never find what I wanted, I was willing to absolutely ignore everything under my own nose. Because..." She paused, took a deep breath, and continued. "...you are my mate."

He stumbled on his feet. "What?" he shouted. "Are you insane?" He fought with his crutches, getting his feet underneath him.

"No, I'm not, but I don't blame you for doubting, either. I'm telling you because someone thinks you and I are already together. I don't know how that came to happen. It's the only connection Roman or I can come up with for you being sabotaged and for someone going after your friend. You are connected to me by association." She sounded calm. She felt fairly calm. She could tell by every atom of his body that he wasn't.

"You're all looney," he cried sharply, tilting his head in disbelieving emphasis. "Did you brainwash Bram? Drugs?" He all but snarled the thrown accusations. "I can't believe you would tell me this." He shook his head hard, his gaze empty. "An amulet? Do I look like an idiot? It was a rock! It wasn't even a crystal. Magic and witches and," he threw a hand toward the wall, "wolves! I can't believe I came out here thinking I'd have a good vacation either. How long has all of this been going on, anyway?"

"I didn't expect you to believe so much," she replied evenly, hiding her broken dreams. "And I can take your anger. Just please, stay close until we find out who this is."

"Fuck you! I'm going home." He spun on a heel and clumped down the hall.

She clasped her shaking hands and let him go. Roman became a furious wall behind her, and she stopped him from following Mitch. "No, let him go. I knew what my chances were."

"He didn't have to say that." Roman's palms rested on her shoulders, gentle and caring. His voice vibrated unmistakably with his fury at Mitch's behavior.

"He's scared. So was I. I took the leap. I lost." She hid the quiver in her voice, knowing tears weren't far behind. "Don't try to force it. I know Del didn't jump for joy, and neither did Bram. I can only hope he's careful enough to not get himself killed before we have this figured out."

"Do you think he might accept it later?" her brother asked quietly. She faced the wall of paintings as she listened to Mitch move in staccato thumps in his room. A room where she had experienced a whole new world in his kiss, a few moments out of time where she had felt maybe, for the first time, that she had a chance for more.

"No, I don't. I've known since I came home I wasn't meant to have what I want. I just proved it." She allowed him to cradle her into his chest for a few minutes. By the time Mitch came out demanding to go to the airport, Brooke had fled the house.

* * * *

Bram was silent on the drive. Mitch couldn't blame him. He'd cussed, insulted, and hurt Brooke, all within minutes of promising he wouldn't. But she was crazy! Wolves! He snorted derisively. "So how long have they been drugging you?" he asked sarcastically.

"They don't," Bram replied evenly. Mitch noted the way his hands whitened on the wheel and felt a pang of remorse for his tone, but Christ, it wasn't possible.

"You can't tell me you believe all that crap?" he said in disbelieving exasperation.

"Just forget what you heard. You can think she's

crazy if you want, but try to keep yourself out of trouble." Bram made a right turn into town. Two blocks farther, and he made another right.

Mitch glared out the window, watching scenery. "I can't believe you fell for all of their lies. Hey, didn't we just pass this block? I thought we were going to the airport?"

"We're being followed."

Mitch rolled his eyes. "God, you need help. You need to come home to Missouri. They're messing with your mind." He was convinced of it now.

Bram tossed his chin at his brother, urging his cooperation. "Look in your mirror. See the blue Crown Vic? Watch it." Bram turned again. The blue car turned two cars later, remaining the same distance behind them.

"Yeah, so? They drive like you do. Aimlessly," he said, mocking his brother. Mitch crossed his arms, but his gaze stayed on his mirror, and three blocks and two turns later, the car remained in their shadow, one lane over and two cars back.

"Believe me now?" came Bram's caustic question.

"So now what?" Mitch asked, a little less perturbed, maybe a little more worried.

Bram grabbed his cell phone. "Roman, we need a diversion. We're being followed. Yeah, I know the road. All right, see you there." He dropped the phone into the console catch-all. "Hang on!"

Mitch reached for the hold bar over the window as Bram careened wildly into an alley.

Chapter Ten

Mitch shoved his stomach into place as they sped out of town with the Crown Victoria barely lengths behind them. High-speed chases didn't have the same adrenaline rush appeal when you were actually a part of it. Mitch didn't want to look at the speedometer. It was a fact that Explorers and ninety didn't mix well. "So the amulet crap was real?" he panted, trying to keep his heart in his chest.

"Yes, Mitch."

"So what the hell is going on?" He closed his eyes when Bram swept into a curve, tires squealing in protest as they bit at asphalt for purchase, then let out his breath when he could see the horizon on the other side. Bram juiced the vehicle for more speed.

"I don't know, not really." Bram's jaw tightened as a turnoff came into view.

Mitch sat up straight. "Hey! That's Brooke's SUV!"

"I know."

Mitch felt his stomach shrivel when she stepped out in plain sight and flagged the other car, as if she were expecting them. "Christ! They're stopping. We have to go back!" he shouted as they barreled right past Brooke. Black smoke billowed as the other car hit their brakes, skidding to a stop a short distance beyond the Toyota. Whatever she had planned had worked to get their attention. Mitch's stomach did another flip. He gripped the dash in front of him, wishing he could tear the damn thing out.

"Don't worry. She'll be fine."

"What are you? Mental? That car just chased us for ten miles!" Mitch tried to turn in his seat, but he couldn't see anything now. Bram picked up his cell when it rang.

He gave a terse response and hung up again.

"You have lost it," Mitch muttered. "How you ever got tied up with this family, I'll never know, but you need to come home. You have got to get yourself away from these lunatics. Car chases and crazy stories about witches and wolves."

Mitch was still fuming, finding two men bound and gagged behind Brooke's car, hidden from the highway. Not that it mattered. There hadn't been another car outside of town at all. "Great. Now they're taking hostages," he grumbled. Bram aimed a warning glare right at him. That was when Roman stepped into view holding an automatic rifle, and Mitch snapped his jaw shut. He with the gun, rules.

"We need to get them off the main road to question them," Roman was saying. Bram didn't hesitate, simply grabbed one of the two and dragged the dead weight, who wasn't even struggling against his bonds, into the trees. Mitch hobbled out of the vehicle on his crutches.

"What is with you people?" he yelled at Roman, gesturing emphatically. "They're not terrorists!"

He pointed to the one left next to the car. In fact, they were nothing but two young guys in jeans and T-shirts.

"No, they're not. They're hunters," he said with absolute chilled confidence.

"It isn't against the law to hunt," Mitch exasperatedly reminded him. Bram reappeared and brushing his hands off, shackled the remaining young man and forced him into the trees with the first. He didn't go as willingly, kicking and struggling against the ropes wrapped around his wrists and Bram.

"Mitch," Roman snapped with icy meaning, stabbing him with a stone-hard, black glare. "Stay here, and stay out of the way."

"Wait! Where's Brooke?" Mitch was worried because he hadn't seen her since he and his brother had pulled up. She had been there, standing right next to the road. Where was she?

Roman didn't bother to answer him, turning to follow the path the men's dragged feet had cut through the forest debris. Impenetrable trees immediately created a heavy private wall. After a few feet, at most, there was nothing to see from the roadside except for green and tree trunks.

Mitch cursed inside. What the hell was this? Commando central? How had Bram become so mixed up in this? Mitch muttered profanely, then hobbled his way into the tree line until he could hear and see. Once close enough, he almost fell into the underbrush with shock.

One of the bound men's eyes were glowing yellow! *Oh shit.* He froze, unable to move further but not sure he wanted to, either.

"I know you're after the amulet," Roman growled. "Who sent you?" Neither man seemed inclined to answer. Then he heard her voice, a musical chanting cadence that rose from everywhere, stirring the fallen leaves on the ground. Mitch watched as both men tried to escape, jerking and fighting against their ties, desperation making them twitch violently. By the time Brooke quit chanting, both slumped against the trees that supported them, heaving with their exertions.

"Ask them again," she said. Mitch had no idea where she was. He couldn't find her anywhere, searching through the trees as far as he was able without moving. He didn't really want Roman's glare locked on him again, or the gun. He could only hope she was hiding somewhere, safe.

Roman kicked the shoes of the closest one. Bram reached to unwrap the gag, with a caution from Roman. He released the man and leaped quickly out of reach.

"One more time, who sent you?" Roman raised the gun until there was no way he could miss his target.

The one with the glowing eyes began to talk, his jaw popping with a brash cracking sound as he fought against the question. "The demon lord."

"Why? He has no use for us." Roman snarled lowly.

"He did not tell his purpose. We are only hunters." The voice was gravelly, rough, and dry. It hurt Mitch's ears.

"Why are you hunting nonshifters? He cannot serve," Roman demanded.

"The master wants the one who holds the heart. She will follow if he is taken." Mitch's breath hitched at the answer. The man's eyes glowed menacingly at Roman with a cruel light. Retribution glittered in those yellow orbs.

"Roman, they're going to implode! I can't hold them much longer." Brooke's cry echoed from the depths of the woods.

He nodded and stepped back. "Then let them. Let him know we are not going quietly." Roman's thunderous gaze watched the duo. Mitch was unable to tear away for a second. The one with the cruel eyes started to disintegrate and then the second followed. Mitch clenched his jaw to keep from losing it as he witnessed it all with his own eyes. Skin peeled from their skulls, and what lay beneath was not human in form. The skeleton was elongated with a putrid smell of death and something he couldn't name, but it rivaled the worst odors he'd found in the city until eventually even the bones turned to a powdered dust. It fell deathly silent for a long moment once the only sign the two had been there were the bindings and the lone gag lying on the leaves.

"Aunt Jerry set you up!" Roman roared with a violent curse, breaking the silence wide open. "She knew this was coming! That woman doesn't do a damn thing without a reason." He spun, glaring into the tree line.

"Roman, that's not fair!" she argued.

"She knew she couldn't fight off a damn demon! But you could!" Roman slammed his fist against a tree. Mitch flinched when he heard it crack like a walnut shell. "You send her back that damn amulet now!"

"And how am I supposed to do that?" she shot back.

"Brooke, just do it," Roman snapped. "You're not the one to fight this one!"

Mitch's mouth dried in disbelief as she emerged, literally, out of thin air. She held the amulet above her head, drawing it off her neck, then lowering her arms. "Look, Roman. I can handle this. I'm not going to let this follow us. If I can do it, then I will!"

She gave her older brother an equally determined glaring stare, and Mitch swore he felt the hair on his arms rise.

She sought Bram beyond the piles of dust. "You can take Mitch to the airport now," she told him with a hollow, saddened voice. She rubbed a weary hand across her brow. "You won't be bothered, and I'm sure he won't be now that it knows I have, without a doubt, the blood stone."

"Wait just a damn minute!" Mitch shouted, whipping three heads in his direction.

"I told you to stay at the road," Roman said with a

menacing curl to his lip.

Mitch tried to think. His brain had gone numb. "I need to talk to Brooke," he said cautiously. A few things clinked together in his mind, and possibly, he understood. Maybe.

Roman glanced at him as he passed, going toward the road and the vehicles. His gaze was flat and lethal. "You swear at her again, and I'll break your other leg," he warned with a menacing snarl.

Mitch nodded, keeping his trap shut. He understood without needing pictures drawn. Bram didn't say a word as he strode past. Mitch avoided him, ashamed at his earlier outbursts against his brother.

"Just go home," she told him in a low, tired voice, approaching him. "I'm sorry you were connected to me, but now that it knows I have the amulet, it'll focus on me."

He didn't argue with the impulse. With a tender hand, he sifted through her hair. "I'm sorry," he said in a bare, shocked whisper, trying to understand what he'd seen, what she'd been trying to tell him. "I shouldn't have yelled at you." What he wanted to say was that he was sorry he hadn't believed her.

"It doesn't matter. I'm the one who should apologize for dragging you into this mess. You almost died," she told him. He caught her anguished expression and felt a stab of emotion he couldn't have named if he'd had to.

"But I didn't, and I have you to thank for that. I wouldn't have tasted good as kitty food." He smiled as a hopeful light flickered in her swirling gaze when he mentioned the cougar. If the wolf...if she had told the truth... Mitch knew he owed her, to give himself the chance to try to believe. He hurt inside when her hope faded. He couldn't let it end like this. "If I beg right now, can I have a second chance? To understand what you are?" He massaged her scalp, unprepared for the deeper need to feel her beneath his fingers. He needed to understand, but waited for her to accept him. He knew he'd blown it at the cabin. Mitch had no idea what he was doing, but he couldn't leave. Not now. Not after what he'd seen.

"Mitch." She sighed forlornly. "There really isn't a reason to. I understand you don't want to believe. I can't force anything on you. I can't force you to be my mate, and I won't." Her eyes closed her away from him, and he knew she was putting up walls. He'd screwed this up bad by the hurt he found in those pools before they'd disappeared. "I'm older than you, too."

"You look twenty-six, maybe. How old can you be?" He tipped her to search her features, teasing her lightly as he stroked her with a thumb.

"Thirty-one, same as the others. Give or take a few minutes," she said. Then he saw the twist of her mouth and knew he was winning. "I forgive you. I was asking a lot of you to believe when all you had done was kiss me." Her gaze opened and turned brokenhearted again. "I shouldn't have..." He shut her up by kissing her and felt the slam of hungry heat invade him, course over him, and he trembled. He would help protect her. He would protect what she was, her secrets.

"I'm staying," he managed to say a minute later, still hovering over her lips. "Just try to get rid of me now." He held her carefully in his arms, and she curved into him. "You forgive me? I'll do anything to take back what I said."

She smiled. "Yes, you're forgiven, but if we don't walk out soon, Roman is going to come get me, and he doesn't make idle threats."

He let out a deep breath. "Yeah, I need to get back on everyone's good side."

No one spoke on the drive to the cabin. Roman

rode with Brooke, and Mitch returned with his disapprovingly silent brother. He had no idea where to start with the apologies.

Once inside, Mitch owned up and apologized. He apologized to Brooke again, in front of her brother and his. He apologized for accusing his brother of being a gullible idiot. Then he ate crow a third time and apologized for intruding when Roman had made it abundantly clear he hadn't been invited to the interrogation party, but he didn't regret it.

"So who is this demon that wants the rock?" Mitch asked a while later when everyone had settled and said their piece. The amulet was in its little box, tucked away.

"We don't say its name," Brooke said. "Draws its attention, but it's very real." Watching Mitch over the rim of her cup, she saw a new understanding in his gaze, a willingness that hadn't been there before he'd left. She was glad something had finally made it through. She'd been miserable from the second he had turned away from her. The demons hadn't hurt her argument any. Now maybe all they needed was time and a way to keep everyone alive and unharmed.

"Any ideas on getting rid of him?" Mitch asked.

Brooke knew no one was going to like her answer. "I'll have to challenge it."

Roman glared, Bram frowned, and Mitch hit the table with a reverberating palm. A unanimous no. "I don't think so!" Mitch said sharply. "I agree with Roman. Give back the amulet."

She sipped her tea, patiently, avoiding what she was going to tell them. "I wish I could, really." None of them were going to like what she had to say.

Roman's ominous voice filled the corners of the cabin. He hunched over the kitchen table, pinning her with a cold stare across the bared width. "Care to tell me why you can't?"

She traced a moisture ring, evading gazes. "She, um, spelled it to me."

Roman cursed, his almost black eyes snapping with his growing ire at her and at Aunt Jerry.

"What does that mean?" Bram asked.

"It means," Roman said, looking not in the least bit pleased by the scowl on his features, "Aunt Jerry knew what she was doing. Brooke would have to spell it back, in person. Basically, she put a protection spell on it. No one else can take it from her with that spell on it unless it is given willingly. It attacks the thief to protect itself." Brooke noted as Mitch's face continued to slacken with degrees of incredulity as Roman explained it.

"Could she pass it on?" Mitch asked, looking at those around the table.

"To who? Anyone less skilled or trained would be toast in five minutes, and the amulet would be gone. I don't know of anyone stronger." Brooke hated the fact that she had been given this, but she wasn't going to pass the buck either.

"Del could." There was pride in his voice when Roman mentioned her name.

Brooke shook her head adamantly. "No, there's Adrian to think of. I won't let you or her do anything." That would be too much guilt if something went wrong.

She heard Mitch clear his throat. "That guy, whatever, said something about why they were after me. What did he mean?"

She buried her face in her palms and silently cursed every man she could name.

"Well," Roman began, trying to be gentle while Brooke could have smacked him with something large and iron, "it's basic chemistry. When a female shifter finds her mate, their body goes into heat."

"Like dogs?" Mitch blurted, gaping at Brooke.

"Worse," she groaned, wondering how many more shocks he could take before he ran screaming from the house again. "You are not as blessed as we are, so you and Bram don't notice it. We, and those hunters, can follow it like the yellow brick road. It's very distinct. They could track you by my scent." She hung her head and admitted quietly, "And yes, I would have followed to try to find you."

"But why did they try to kill me?"

"Probably to remove whoever had started the search for the leader, eliminating the trail of the amulet. The fewer people between them and the stone, the easier the take would have been," Roman told him. "But now that they assume the two of you are bonded, you became a bargaining chip to force her hand."

Brooke set her knotted fingers on her lap. When she found Mitch's gaze, she blushed from the roots of her hair at his assessing stare. He sat cornered to her side and moved close enough to whisper just for her, "In heat, huh?"

"Shut. Up," she warned with a stiff frown. Why did men have such infuriating grins?

"So what do we do from here?" Bram asked. He glanced up at the clock on the wall. "Selene will be home soon. How safe are we?"

"Safe enough," Brooke replied. "The demon won't trespass, and it won't send anyone to do the deed for it."

"An honorable demon?" Bram laughed caustically. "I don't believe it."

"No, it has nothing to do with honor. Our family is a very old line. Our dens are protected," Brooke told them. "The safeguard comes from way back in our history and being what we are. So long as we are true to ourselves and our mates, never force ourselves on the outside world and never abuse a mate or offspring, our secret remains sacred and untouchable. We remain safe." Roman nodded in agreement when she finished.

"Wow. It sounds so, I don't know, archaic," Mitch said, stretching out his cast-covered leg.

"That's what Selene meant then when we had the poacher problem. She knew if she was captured, she would be powerless," Bram said thoughtfully. "She would be limited on how to defend herself."

"Yes. What happened between you and the poacher was protection of our secret. It's frowned on, but gray hairs are gray hairs when it comes to our world. We may only have to answer to ourselves, but we still have to respect the laws, or it can trickle down to every following generation." She glanced toward Roman. "How are Del and Adrian holding up?"

"I called her earlier. Adrian was cranky from traveling, but she's doing all right." He asked Brooke, "Do you think they'd be safer here?"

"Did she feel safe? She'd know better than us if she thought she was being threatened." When he offered a positive gesture, she continued. "But then again, she's not directly involved with this or the amulet. I don't want to include her and the baby if she can stay out of it," Brooke told him honestly. She turned to Bram. "The same for Selene. She's your mate and pregnant. I know you would die for us, Bram, but this one isn't your fight."

"What happened to power in numbers?" Mitch asked in a concerned rush. "I don't like the idea of you trying to do this alone. I mean, I'll be here, but..." He looked at his cast. "I'm not going to be much good for anything."

Stiff fingers pressed into her eyes, wanting to obliterate the truth. Brooke wanted everyone gone, actually. She didn't want anyone else threatened, chased, hunted, or hurt.

All three of the men started talking at once, and she tuned them out. What was she going to do? How could she keep everyone safe? Was it a good idea to keep anyone there? Was it better to send everyone away?

She reviewed the facts. She had the blood amulet. That nasty what's-its-name wanted it and so far had done a good job of trying to find out who possessed it. Now, she was positive it knew she had the amulet. You can't go around stomping on lesser demons and expect to not be noticed. Might as well have rented a billboard; it would have had the same effect.

What else had Aunt Jerry been teaching her to prepare for this anyway? She wasn't a witch like her aunt. She was a shape-shifter with an affinity for nature and all things natural, and if things went well, she had found her mate.

What was going to happen there was anyone's guess. Roman and Selene had both fallen in love. She liked Mitch and cared for him. She wasn't betting on the love just yet. There was a demon in the way.

So, point one—get rid of pissy demon problem. Point two—enjoy Mitch for hours. Sounded like a great start, at least to her.

"What are you smiling about?" Mitch asked.

She startled out of her thoughts and realized it was only her and Mitch at the table. "Where did they go?"

"You've been daydreaming for a while. They're outside with Selene, bringing her up to date. We've had a busy day."

"Yeah, I guess we have." A tender fingertip caressed her bottom lip, creating a liquid reaction deep inside. Her mouth curved naturally, living in those sensations, craving them and more.

"See, there's that smile again. What's it for?" he asked. He drifted his finger over the side of her face, sending a slow sparking river through her body.

"Just some hopeful thoughts. Unfortunately, I'm still at a loss of how to get rid of the amulet and the demon."

"How about we work on the hopeful part of that statement," he murmured as he kissed her, a drugging kiss of discovery and enjoyment. Tilting into her, he nibbled and seduced with teasing lips. The light flick of his tongue to her bottom lip sent a shiver unlike any she'd known into her belly. Releasing her, he scooted his chair closer until he was flushed to hers. "You know, I want to taste you again. It's the weirdest thing." His breath flowed over her skin as she pressed into him, spellbound by the seductive timbre in his voice.

"I know. Me too," she told him, a rush of volcanic heat making her breathless. "I wonder if it has anything to do with that scent thing."

She heard him take a long leisurely inhalation along her neck. "You smell divine to me." She shivered in her shoes.

"Can you tell?" she asked him on a shaky note.

"You mean the heat? I can taste it on your skin, smell it in your hair." He groaned thickly, his lips a scant distance from her neck, each word sending a butterfly-light brush of his mouth to sensitive skin. "You've been driving me nuts for days, ever since I woke up in the hospital and got that first kiss." He nuzzled hungrily against her, and her heart rate tripled in needy answer.

"That's when Morgan said I became obvious." She sighed as he sipped and tugged at bared skin. "You have this clean scent. No colognes or..." She breathed deeply, gasping when he found her pulse point. "Or anything but hot flesh."

"God, I love it when you talk like that!" Her arms looped over him as he buried himself into her neck. She felt hot all over as he tasted her, roaming at will with teeth, lips, and tongue.

"Get a room, you two," Roman complained. She jerked away from Mitch, her cheeks burning, but he only let her go as far as his stretched reach.

"We will," he replied. "All in good time." She melted because of the tender heat in his gaze. "Something tells me Tory is going to be pissed but not surprised when I talk to him again."

Chapter Eleven

Mitch was there and staying. So why did that scare Brooke now? Why did it bother her more now when he had accepted her secrets? Why Aunt Jerry did this to her was another great question for the books. She didn't have the training Aunt Jerry had or the years of experience. Suddenly thirty-one didn't look old enough.

Brooke settled on the porch, surveying the stars as they coasted through the night sky. There wasn't a cloud to be seen. She pulled her legs up onto the chair seat, wrapping her arms around them.

She tried to remember what she knew about the amulet. Only a woman of shifter ability could ever use it. If a male touched it, he would be unable to shift for the rest of his life, but it could be used against them. All of them. Why would someone make such a thing? It had more warnings than the surgeon general's date book. If the demon got hold of the amulet, she knew without a doubt it would use the amulet against her family. No one had a single clue as to why, suddenly, they had become a curiosity to a demon lord.

She replayed the last year and a half. Aunt Jerry had suffered a severe case of depression, and when Brooke's dad had learned of her ordeals, he'd asked for Brooke to go to Belgium to stay with her. Brooke had a calming influence on most people, the same way Selene did. Selene could calm a person or an animal from anger or fear.

Brooke could heal, but Selene excelled in medicine and science. Brooke's knowledge circled natural agents and remedies, like using chamomile tea to relax or basil oil to clear sinuses. She was an herbalist, not a witch!

Her head thudded forward to her bent knees. It was late, but she wasn't tired enough to sleep, though today had been long and beyond weird. Figuring out the two lesser demons only created more questions for her. They had been too easy in hindsight. Roman hadn't believed her that they were demons at first but when they had all but ignored him for her, she'd clasped the amulet and used it to control them. Brooke hoped she hadn't broken a rule with that one! The guy with the glowing eyes hadn't hurt in the convincing department, either. Mindless souls in bodies, that's what they had been.

So why chase Mitch and Bram? If they wanted to get to Mitch, they could have nabbed him when he was injured and stuck in the woods.

She admitted she had been fighting what she now knew to be the truth. Her scent wasn't a part of him, then. He had only been an obstacle to them because he'd known enough to track the Ford. So take him and his friend out of the picture. Now she was emitting signals louder than a bell tower, and he was answering in kind.

What had Aunt Jerry told her? She sighed, trying to remember. Something about the power of her heart. Brooke rocked over her knee on her chin. She couldn't remember, and she really couldn't remember what she had been explaining when she'd been talking about it, either.

Aunt Jerry hadn't made any grand gesture regarding the amulet, simply passing it on, like Brooke had said, until she needed it or Aunt Jerry asked for it.

Her head lifted with dawning reality. "That witch!" she swore under her breath. "She did know!"

Her head bobbled loosely on her bent knees, resuming her musing pose. Aunt Jerry had known Brooke was going to need the blood amulet, but only because she'd given her the amulet to begin with! So if that were the case, why give it to her at all? Why not keep it hidden, like Aunt Jerry obviously had for over a century? Her father and at least Roman had believed that the amulet had been destroyed. So why bring it out in the open now? Why let the world know it still existed? Why make Brooke the keeper of the blood amulet? And why did Bel—oops! She stopped herself midthought. No names, she warned herself, smacking herself mentally. She steadied herself, then continued. Why did *it* want it? No one had bothered their family for centuries. No one bothered the demons in their world. Who would *want* to, she wondered sarcastically.

"Aunt Jerry! What did you do?" Her hands clenched in front of her legs in frustration. "Why me?" she demanded as strongly into the night.

She whipped her head up a few minutes later when a blanket covered her shoulders. Mitch smiled at her. "Hi. It's late, and you weren't in bed," he said, meaning that the couch was empty.

"No, I'm sorry. I know I should be," Brooke agreed. If she thought she could sleep. "How late is it, anyway?"

He clumped carefully to grab a chair and sit beside her. "After one. Aren't you tired?" He breathed deeply, rubbing his injured arm with an absent motion once he was comfortable.

She shook her head. "No, right now I'm extremely upset with Aunt Jerry." She tugged on a corner of the blanket to wrap herself tighter, then raised the edge. "Two would be warmer," she offered with a beckoning enticement.

She didn't have to ask twice as he folded up against her and cradled her into his good shoulder. When he had tucked the blanket around them he asked her, "All right, so what did she do now? Seems she's behind everything today."

"Almost, but I think she owes me a few answers," Brooke commented. Her hand fell to Mitch's thigh while her cheek rested against his chest. Her skin warmed immediately where they touched. "I always thought she was depressed. That's what I was led to believe, anyway. Now? Now I'm not so sure. I am convinced she did give me the amulet for a reason. I just don't know why."

"Maybe Roman's right. Maybe she wanted you to fight her battle. You did fight the demons and win," he said, nuzzling the top of her head with his chin. Her eyes closed as his voice washed over her.

"I wouldn't be surprised," she answered back. "She's older, but I don't get it. I'm not a witch. She is. I'm like the other three. Nothing more." If anyone was a witch—without it being an insult—in their family, that would be Aunt Jerry.

Unmoving and silent for a long time at her back, she listened to his heartbeat. She didn't think he had fallen asleep holding her.

"I'm not so sure about that," he finally told her, dropping his chin to her shoulder to brush light kisses to her temple. "I saw you appear out of nothing, something I've only seen done with special effects in movies or read about. As in fiction, and that's not going into detail over the two who didn't stay for the fireworks between you and your brother or the wolf thing." He shifted his position, bringing her snug into his embrace. "So, how much older is she? Seventy? Eighty?"

She told him in an unwavering voice, "She's a hundred and forty-eight."

His entire frame flinched. "I'd ask if you were kidding, but somehow I don't think you are," he answered with a murmured, tense tone.

"No, I'm not, but that isn't what is bothering me about all of this."

"I know I'm going to regret this, but all right. What is bothering you?"

"When I thought she was depressed and changing things on me, I think she had a purpose even then. As though she needed to prepare me, but couldn't put into words why." She shook her head, trying to make the thoughts line up and give her an answer to this problem. Unfortunately, it was late, and her brain seemed to have given up on cooperating.

He rocked her within his strong arms. "That's enough for tonight. You are tired. I'm tired." He let out a shuddered breath. "And I just hit my limit for really weird in one day."

Rising, she kissed the side of his neck. His hold tightened. "I know. We're a handful." When she tried to sit up, he kept her right where she was.

"Wait. Do that again," he said, panting against her hair.

"What? This?" Brooke kissed him again, and he purred richly, rumbling beneath her lips. "Or this?" She nibbled on the muscles under his skin, and he arched, offering himself to her, seeking exploration. She stopped talking, rather stealing the moment to enjoy him shamelessly on her tongue.

* * * *

Three days later, Brooke stood alone in the clearing, listening to the coming morning with her eyes closed. Bram and Selene were gone, riding with Roman to collect Delilah and Adrian since it appeared that nothing else was going to happen. They would be gone for a few short hours before returning, which didn't leave her much time to get to the bottom of this. Brooke didn't like the idea of having everyone here at once. She hadn't felt threatened, and no one had been followed or chased since the last attempt. It was with a dreaded certainty that she knew the quiet was only a lull. She didn't know how she was supposed to fix anything. At least Mitch had still been asleep when she'd come outside. The guy had suffered through shock after shock, and she was responsible.

She felt relaxed, almost serene in the morning gray. She'd been dreaming about her aunt right before she'd awakened. Somehow, that alone made her decision easier to take. She didn't like having to ask for help, but this time there was no choice. Too much was at stake, and too many were at risk. It was time to get those answers.

"Aunt Jerry, you better tell me what's going on," she intoned into the surrounding emptiness. The sun was barely cresting the horizon, soaking the world in its predawn glow of gold and red. There was an eerie, cool feeling on her skin. It skittered over her, skipping like a learning touch. "I am not like you. I am as my brothers are," she informed the world firmly. "I was there when you decided to give this to me. The least you could have done was tell me why. How I'm supposed to fix it would be nice too," she muttered without rancor.

She lifted her arms, and a breeze wound over her, a mere brush to her skin as it flowed around her. The warmth of the first rays hit her fingers and spread over her arms. "Come to me, Jeralynna Aiza. Welcome my voice and hear my summons."

"Do I get tea?" a whispery sound responded.

Brooke's lips twitched. "Of course. I am a hospitable woman," she replied in a clear, calm tone.

"Very well."

Brooke dropped her arms to her sides while the breeze picked up, blowing strands of hair around her face. When her arms had completely drifted down, she opened her eyes and found her aunt standing in front of her. She was a graceful woman with knee-length black hair and shimmery, silver-gray eyes. Aunt Jerry wore a silken shift of muted crimson with a flowing gauze tunic over it and silver bangles on her wrist. Her feet were bare except for a single wire of silver around one ankle. It bore one charm of a crescent moon, the mark of her heritage.

"Thank you for coming," Brooke told her.

"I knew you would call. I sent you the dream," her aunt informed her in a no-nonsense tone. "Let's start with tea, shall we?" she said, smoothly reaching for one of Brooke's hands and clasping it to her arm, cupping her own over it. "Has it gotten bad?"

"I don't know. How bad is bad?" she retorted back. "And why did you do this to me?"

Aunt Jerry patted her gently. "All in time, love. I do promise you that." Aunt Jerry waved toward the door, and it swung inward as they approached. It closed without a sound after they entered the cabin.

"Good morning, young man," Aunt Jerry said as Mitch appeared on his crutches.

"Uh, hello." He shot Brooke a questioning glance.

"Aunt Jerry," she said without preamble, rolling her shoulder at him.

"But I didn't hear a vehicle," he said with a confused frown. He whipped up a hand as soon as he'd finished speaking the thought. "No, never mind. I don't want to know."

Aunt Jerry smiled in warm welcome. "Come. Join

us for tea." She waved toward the counter, and the water began to run with three cups moving through the air to be filled. "Your favorite?" she asked Brooke. The mugs floated one by one under the water. Brooke watched as steam began to rise and the tea sank into the water. "Nothing better than hot, steeped tea," Aunt Jerry murmured appreciatively.

She pulled out a chair and, pointing at another on the other side, motioned for Mitch to join them.

It slid away from the table as he hobbled near, and Brooke saw him flinch. Seeing how hard all of this was on him, she told her aunt, "Aunt Jerry, stop showing off. He's just a regular guy."

"But he's your mate!" she said with an arched eyebrow. "Surely he understands?" Aunt Jerry offered in a remorseful voice, "Oh dear. I'm sorry! I thought he knew."

Brooke rested her forehead into a hand. "Aunt Jerry! He does know. But jeez, lay off already." Mitch all but plopped himself onto the waiting chair, following them warily. She couldn't blame him. She offered him a weak smile, but his gaze was shuttered.

When all three were sitting and Aunt Jerry had approved the tea with a sip, she began. "In answer to your question, Brooke, I gave you the amulet because I can't fix the problem."

"But why not?" Brooke cried, sloshing her tea by accident when her entire body jerked. "You gave me the amulet! You knew what it was when you gave it to me!"

Brooke clutched a napkin to dab at the mess while Aunt Jerry reclined in her chair. Too bad a napkin couldn't fix their current problem as easily. "I did," Aunt Jerry replied without regret. "I also know why Bel—" Brooke raised a swift hand, a sharp glare silencing her.

"No names!" Brooke reminded her.

"Yes, sorry. William, then. That was what he wanted to be called." Aunt Jerry looked momentarily contrite. "I know why he wants it," she said, followed by a sip of steaming tea. "You always could make the best tea," she offered as a compliment.

"So, why?" Mitch asked, his own fingers wrapped in a death grip around his cup. He bent forward, watching the women through pensive brown eyes.

"I'm glad to know you are involved. You are a strong force," Aunt Jerry said directly to Mitch.

"Answer the question, Aunt Jerry," Brooke said, rubbing her forehead, knowing her aunt could evade for hours.

For the first time, Brooke became aware of a cloud in her aunt's gaze. Aunt Jerry's thoughts focused inward. "When you came to see me in the beginning, I was very sad. Very upset. I guess a depression would have been appropriate."

Brooke listened, holding her cup. It never cooled in her hand. That was one thing she had liked about her stay with her aunt. The tea never cooled.

"I had found someone I believed was my mate, my love. I was fooled by him." Her aunt's gaze grew distracted, thoughtful. "I know you may not understand, but when you have lived as long as I have without the heart of a love, well..." She sighed. Her smile was limp when she met Brooke's gaze again. Gray orbs shimmered with a watery sheen as she continued with her story. "Anyway, I made a mistake. And two things happened because of it. He learned I had the blood stone amulet. I learned you cannot use it on a being you care for."

"You care for a demon?" Brooke shrieked, leaping from her chair. "Aunt Jerry! How could you have feelings for..." She waved her arms in agitation. "And you never bothered to tell me this while I was there?"

Her aunt regained her polite composure, sitting straight and relaxed as she said, "I couldn't. You needed training for one. It wasn't until that poor Mr. Kavanaugh arrived that I feared I had run out of time." She held her cup in her slim hands, bracelets jingling delicately over pale skin, her voice repentant in the early morning stillness of the kitchen. "I knew if Mr. Kavanaugh had bought it, then the demon lord could get it, like taking candy from a baby, and the whole family, the world, would have paid. When you left, I had no idea he believed I had sold the amulet to Mr. Kavanaugh." Aunt Jerry took a sip of her tea before she continued. "I will not hang my head in shame. I made my choice, and I fought him. But I paid the price in doing so. I cannot use the amulet again, for any purpose. He knows this. I could not keep it."

"So, now Brooke is a sitting duck." Mitch snarled, glaring at the woman at Brooke's elbow.

"Quite the opposite. She has your strength to hold her. She has her own ability, which she doesn't know about. She has already used the amulet once without knowing anything about it, with hardly a thought to how she did it," Aunt Jerry replied with an airy wave. "She is this generation's me." Her lips lifted into a very satisfied smile. She sipped at her tea again, apparently pleased with that announcement.

"And I'm supposed to be happy about that?" Brooke muttered, taking her chair again.

"Child, do not be snappish," she admonished Brooke. "Every one of you has a special ability. Your father is an artist without compare. Selene is a goddess of healing. Roman is the protector. He reminds me of the stories of Zeus. Morgan..." She trailed off. "He is the heart of the family. Morgan holds each of you close and breathes for you. He is the oldest and would die to protect this family." Aunt Jerry looked at Mitch with purpose. "Even your mates have an ability."

"Oh no. Don't even go there," Mitch argued back. He shrugged his shoulders in disbelief. "You people are the odd family, not me."

Aunt Jerry gave him a sympathetic moue. "I see. I thought you understood," she said with a disappointed air. "When a shifter, guardian, diviner, or anyone finds their heart's match, that person is unique in their own way. An everyday person doesn't have the capacity to embrace the differences. Your brother is equal in every way to Selene. His knowledge of life, balance, and the world surrounding him is his gift. Delilah, well," she said with gentle respect. "She truly is gifted in this world." Brooke noticed when Aunt Jerry pinned Mitch with her silvery stare. "You have a knowledge, an understanding of fire. You know how to follow the waves, read the paths." She gave him a smug look. "Some have even said that with you it is instinctual."

Mitch's entire face fell ashen at her words. "How do you know that? Crystal ball somewhere?" Mitch ducked his head, as if searching beneath the table for the offending tell-all ball.

She waved a hand, laughing glibly at him. "Crystal balls are for charlatans. Imagery is not everything," she replied as her thin-boned hand flitted between them.

Brooke raised her own hands, breaking up their conversation. "Okay, fine. I'm supposed to do something now with the amulet, is that it? Is the demon coming after the amulet?"

"You will have to summon him and defeat him," Aunt Jerry said without remorse. "But I know you can. You had already come to the same conclusion before you called for me."

"What if she doesn't summon him? Won't he leave us alone?" Mitch asked. Brooke noticed that he hadn't drunk any of the tea, as though he would be able to deny this moment in time if didn't.

"I cannot guarantee anything," Aunt Jerry replied. "But right now he is more in this world than out of it because of my attempt and my failure. And also, there is no way of knowing when another of Brooke's ability will be born. The fact that four mark this generation..." Aunt Jerry's gaze met with Brooke's, and she felt a chill when her aunt's gaze became intense and didn't waver. "It was rumored in the ancient texts that their birth marked the days of the four apocalyptic horsemen."

"You mean the end of the world?" Mitch barked a rude sound. He slouched into his chair and started laughing in utter disbelief. "Look, Brooke, honey, I like you and everything, but if this is your family, I don't think I want any part of it."

The weight of the decision she had to make was sobering. There weren't a lot of options out there for her to choose from. "There have never been multiple births like ours, Mitch. Never," she repeated with emphasis. "None of us even know why it happened." There was speculation their mother had done something, but none of the kids wanted to be the one to mention it, either. The chill deepened and spread within her soul. "I really don't have a choice, do I?" she asked, facing her aunt once more.

Aunt Jerry cupped her hand on the table. "I have faith in you, love. I always have. I tried, and I failed because I had feelings, regardless of how misplaced they were. But if he succeeds and reenters completely..." She didn't finish the statement. There wasn't a need for it.

"Just promise me something?" Brooke asked, staring at her own tea a moment later.

"Anything, love."

"Next time, before you fall for a guy, make sure he's a *guy*, all right?"

Brooke caught the sparkle of her aunt's gaze, made brighter by the light teasing. "Of course, love."

"So how do I get rid of him?" Brooke asked, serious once more.

"I trained you. It is in the power of your heart," Aunt Jerry replied. She rose from her chair, giving Brooke a brushed kiss on the forehead, and without another word, disappeared.

"All of that just happened, didn't it?" Mitch asked several seconds later, sounding less than sure of himself.

"Yes, Mitch. All of it. Your tea should still be hot if you want proof," she pointed out. "One of her specialties. She hates cold tea worse than I do."

Steam wafted from the top of his mug, and he sighed. "It is." Confused, he searched for her, every bit of his disbelief and worries visible in those brown eyes of his. "So now what?"

"Now I have to plan. I have a demon lord to trounce," she explained, planting her chin on a fist.

"She wasn't kidding? She really wants you to fix her problem?" His eyes widened at her across the table.

"I can't refuse, whether she meant it to happen or not. Family is family," she told him without regret. "But first I need to know, are you staying?"

"I said I would," he mumbled. His chin fell into his chest to stare at nothing, least of all at her.

"But you think you've fallen into the rabbit's magic hole now, don't you?" she asked him.

"That's one way of looking at it. God, how did Bram get around all of this?" Across the table she found his indecision, his doubts. "He's crazy about Selene."

"I guess I've become a little more complicated in the last week. But it doesn't change who I am. Or who you are." She wanted to reach for him. She craved to touch him. She needed to know he hadn't changed his mind about staying.

Scrubbing his palm over his face, he told her, "I said I would stay. Every day I'm finding out something about you that should make me run away as fast as possible. But I'm finding I can't." She didn't doubt him. The urge to run had been there since Aunt Jerry pulled the chair out for him.

Unable to resist any longer, she rose to stand next to him. "Let me do something to help you," she said as evenly as possible to not startle him, crouching in front of him. "At least you will be able to run if you need to." She curled her hands around his cast-covered leg.

He inhaled sharply as the unexpected warmth spread from her fingers. Her hands glided over the cast, and it cracked under her concentration. She followed her hands' floating path, watching as the cast broke apart in chunks and fell to the floor. Her heart thundered against her ears as she felt the bone heal, knitting beneath his skin. The rush of blood, the heat of his skin against her, echoed deep inside her.

She exhaled a long, slow breath when she was done. "What a mess." The cast lay beneath his chair in a pile of chunks of plaster and dust.

"How did you do that?" he asked, his voice shaky. He wiggled his toes. "There isn't even an ache. It feels fine," he whispered, staring at his bare foot.

"Aunt Jerry. When she kissed me, it was a gift from her. I don't have that much ability. At least I don't think I do," she clarified. "Maybe I do." Brooke's brow tightened as she examined that statement. Unfortunately, now wasn't the best time to test her theory on her ability.

"My shoulder. Try my shoulder."

"It still hurts?" She glanced up from watching his merrily dancing toes.

He turned away in avoidance. "I, uh, should have used the sling longer, but I didn't like being dependent on anyone. It hurts in the mornings," he admitted with a guilty tint to his cheeks.

She bit her lip to keep from grinning at him, but did as he asked. She rested her hands on his left shoulder and let the warmth spread outward again. He relaxed under her touch. "You still had a strained ligament or two," she said as she released him. "How does it feel now?"

He stretched his arm outward and rolled his shoulder. "That feels fantastic!" he told her with a note of excited awe. She squealed when he swept his arm around her waist and tugged her gently to his lap. "Now I get to pay for it," he murmured as he neared her lips with only one thing burning in his eyes. He paused barely more than a breath from touching her. "Brooke, I don't know what's happening. I don't know what I'm supposed to do about it, either. But I will stay. Somehow the thought of leaving you now isn't an option." He nuzzled against her ear. "And that still scares me. I wasn't looking for a relationship. Hell, Janice was the worst mistake I've almost ever made," he told her, holding her snug within his arms. "I haven't dated in over a year, and I haven't missed it."

"Do I still scare you?" she asked.

"No, you never really did. What you told me, what I faced, scared me more." He ran his mouth up her throat, and she shivered. "How do you taste so good?" There was an edge of wonder in his words. "I could do this all day."

She couldn't find it in her to tell him to stop, craving the rush of his touch, the caress of his lips.

There wasn't a part of her that wasn't hot and needy while he held her on his lap. Her hands clutched at him, sliding over muscled arms and shoulders.

"We need to stop. I can't take much more," she warned him, gasping for air, reaching the point of no return. He settled his forehead to rest against her, shuddering as he fought for control.

"I don't know what happened. I'm sorry," he managed to say on harsh pants of breath. "I can't get enough. I want to make love to you. I never thought I could lose control, but with you, I have none at all."

She wrapped him into her arms, letting the fire of his desire stretch against her length, from shoulder to hip to calf. "I know, but there's something you should know."

He sighed, then chuckled lightly. "Lay it on me, babe. I think I'm getting used to your surprises."

She licked her lips, tasting him on her skin. "We mate for life." The curve of his smile where he pressed into her shoulder eased her worry for her latest shock.

"That's the kind of surprise I can handle," he told her. Her lips rose in answer. Maybe she would get what she wanted after all.

Chapter Twelve

The first thing Brooke noticed was that Selene's little house was crowded. There were almost ten people in the quaint two-bedroom cabin including the silently sleeping baby, Adrian, oblivious to the goings-on of the people who filled the house in quiet conversation. They were all family. Mitch stood nearby, giving her his support. It was crowded, but it was a balm to her nerves to have everyone there.

The second thing she noticed was that it had become completely silent because of a single statement to her sister and sister-in-law, a statement which gave all of them the reason for being at Selene's.

There were only four days to the next full moon, when Brooke would be at her strongest. It was going to be a harvest moon. It was in the air, and the pressure was right. The elements were right. It would rise large and blood red. It was almost an omen, and she knew this, but didn't dare point it out. Brooke wasn't crazy enough to say she might die, that she might fail, out loud.

Their combined silence already made it abundantly clear that they knew. Their gazes, one by one, traveled until they rested on her. She wore a white linen shift and a gauze tunic rather than her usual shorts. There was no makeup, not that she usually used it, and her jewelry was nonexistent. She had begun to prepare earlier in the day after Aunt Jerry's visit. Four days wasn't nearly long enough, but somehow it would have to be. Once the cat—pardon,— *the demon*—was out of the bag, she had no choice but to make sure it went into its hole without any of them in tow.

The demon was furious with Aunt Jerry for being rejected. It was also angry it would not have them to control, that it had lost its chance to obtain the amulet from her once it discovered that the blood amulet still existed. Brooke was there to make sure it didn't get the amulet at all. She just wasn't entirely sure how she would accomplish that.

Brooke cleared her throat and repeated her answer to Selene's stunned question. "I said, I am going to summon a demon."

The silence was gone in the blink of an eye. "Are you insane?"

"Why?"

"You can't be serious!"

"Brooke, you can't!"

She raised a hand, silencing them. She searched each face and found the love underneath their concerns and fears. "I can, and I will. I must."

Roman spoke up. "Aunt Jerry, right? She put you up to this. Get her to solve her own damn problems." He snarled with a gleaming anger in his gaze, a gaze which nearly matched her own. "I knew it." He spat when she didn't argue.

"I have a choice in this, Roman. I made it. She is family, as each and every one of you are. If the amulet goes to it, all of us will suffer. If the demon remains in our world in limbo, it will search for the amulet until it has it. That is too large of a risk to ignore or chance."

Their expressions ranged from shock and bewilderment to lethal anger. She could deny no one their feelings.

"I have made my decision. All I ask is for your blessing. I will face him alone. I cannot risk another single soul," she said firmly with direct meaning. There was no choice but to see this through.

"What are you going to do?" Morgan asked. Turbulence swirled in his gaze, mocking the storm gray of nature.

"Honestly, I don't know," she conceded.

"How do you know you can beat him?" Bram asked. "You said yourself you aren't a witch."

"No, she's more," Mitch quietly interrupted as he stepped out from behind her, emerging from the depths of the shadows where he had been quasi-hiding in the kitchen. He set his crutches to the side and walked forward, unhindered and without pain.

Brooke knew he'd been keeping out of everyone's way to not alarm anyone. A cast doesn't fall off after less than two weeks. Thankfully, everyone had been rather absorbed since they'd arrived and no one had given him more than a quick greeting to have noticed his lack of injuries with him still camouflaged by the crutches. He hadn't planned on exposing himself tonight. Mitch had wanted to talk to Bram first, but apparently, his plans had changed.

"Where's your cast?" Bram asked suspiciously, noting its absence immediately.

"I don't need it anymore," he replied. Mitch reached for one of her hands, standing at her side. "Because of her. Brooke is what is good in this world. I'm not happy with this. I know what may happen, but I can't let everyone live in fear, either. She's right. If the demon stays, no one is safe. I met Jeralynna today, and I believe her." He gave Brooke a caring glance, not quite fully accepting everything that had happened in the last several days, but willing to try and willing to support her fully. Brooke knew how much that statement cost him. His pronouncement brought a round of shocked gasps.

"Are you serious?" Selene blurted, her gaze widening as she whipped her attention between the two of them. "You *met* her? And she didn't turn you into a rock or a toad?"

His lips twitched at her exclamation. "Yes, I met her."

"She was hurt, deceived, and has paid the price," Brooke tried to explain. "She is powerless now to defeat the demon. That leaves me. Now, I ask you as a sister, do I have your blessing?"

Brooke waited and watched as anger and fear warred over each person's features. She couldn't blame them. If she didn't destroy it, she would die, leaving everyone in that room vulnerable. Roman's gaze remained cold when she found him across the room. Aunt Jerry had been right. Morgan may be the strength between the siblings, but Roman was the protector, and he felt powerless to help her or to stop her.

Selene was the first to step forward, offering her hands to Brooke. "*Eadig beon geboren,*" she whispered. Brooke accepted her blessing and pressed a kiss of gratitude to her sister's pale cheek.

"Thank you," Brooke whispered, blinking away grateful tears.

Morgan came forward and gave her a penetrating, searching stare. "Is there any other way?"

She shook her head. Brooke wished there were. His hands tightened on hers, the battle difficult for him.

Finally he offered the blessing and brushed a kiss across her cheek.

Roman glared icily once more, then stiffly stalked through the door. Morgan acted as though to follow him, but Brooke's quiet entreaty stopped him.

"No, let him go. It is his right to deny me. He knows what I'm doing," she said. She rested a hand on his arm. "I know why he doesn't want to, and there is nothing he or I can do about it."

Morgan hesitated, giving her one quick appraisal over his shoulder and a nod before turning to talk to Selene.

"What were they whispering?" Mitch asked her privately a moment later.

"It's an old tongue. It means 'blessed be sibling'," Brooke explained.

"I wish I could do something," Delilah said, drawing near. She gave Brooke a quick hug. The want to help was apparent in her expression.

"I know you want to, but you have Adrian. And Roman will need you. I have faith, and so does Aunt Jerry," she said calmly.

Bram joined them. "I know there is more going on than I want to even try to understand. If we can, we will help. You do know that?" he asked her sincerely.

She nodded, feeling more at peace. "I do, Bram. With each heart I carry, I become stronger. I love you all. But I'm not going out there to die." She squeezed his hands within hers decisively where he had clasped them tightly with his misgivings. "I'm going to make sure you and my sister can raise your child without a threat following you, so Adrian can be happy. And so Aunt Jerry can finally forgive herself for falling in love."

"The sun has set," Mitch pointed out. "We need to go find the clearing."

She couldn't avoid it any longer, letting Mitch lead her from the house, his palm clasped firmly with hers. She needed to find a place to confront the demon, where she could summon it by name and not endanger anyone else. She needed to prepare the spot, purify it. Mitch was taking a lot more in stride since that morning. Maybe he had found a level of acceptance. Maybe he'd been shocked numb too many times for anything else to seem extraordinary. Whatever had made him change his mind, she was never more thankful for his quiet strength and wall of support, and for the next three nights she was going to stay close to him.

This was because on the fourth, she was going to have to walk away from him.

* * * *

Mitch followed her lead in absolute silence, his hand twined with hers as they strolled into the night. Once outside, she paused and closed her eyes, drawing a deep breath, listening to the night enveloping them. When she found her direction, she turned and began at an unhurried pace into the trees, and he trailed after her willingly. Her skin burned against his palm, like a small current racing across her flesh.

He'd sat through the morning with Aunt Jerry only half believing in what was real and what was not. So much had happened to him since he'd arrived in Oregon. So much he couldn't explain, more that he had experienced himself from the demons by the roadside to his now healed body, and it all circled around the woman within his clasp. But something inexplicable had happened when she'd placed a weightless hand on him. He had felt the surge of her power like a current, but it didn't burn. His cast had practically shattered with barely a flick of her finger, and he had felt her heart as clearly as his own as his leg healed underneath her palms. He had felt the bone warm, felt the blood surge, felt his strength return, and at that moment knew he could no longer deny what she was. Witch, wolf, woman. It had ceased to matter at all.

Because he was falling in love with her.

How it had come to this point he couldn't say because a woman wasn't on his list of priorities at all.

He had a life and responsibilities in St. Louis, a fire department that depended on him, a community. Yet over the last few days, none of it seemed as important in comparison to the woman at his side.

She was beautiful in ways he'd never known a person could be. Brooke was the epitome of the kind of woman he'd always wanted and never known how to explain. Mitch had never known until he met her what it was he needed, what his expectations in a woman in his life would be. Many times over the day, he'd been overcome with this new awareness in himself. It would strike out of nowhere and he'd have to sit or simply find her, to see for himself that she did exist. When his brother had fallen for Selene, Mitch had been thrilled for him but had vowed it wouldn't happen to him. Aware of the happiness he was willing to throw away on ignorance now, he called himself a fool for his brother, even if it was silently. No sense in letting Bram know how stupid Mitch had thought he'd been for going over the deep end or how humbled he'd become for his own feelings. Stealing a glance, her honey-blonde hair hung loosely, swaying with her easy gait across her shoulders. The shorts she loved were gone, replaced with a single long gown of a material he couldn't have named covered with a sheer gauze sheath similar to what Aunt Jerry had worn. The only difference was that Brooke's was startling white, almost glowing in its pure color. Studying her closely for a stolen heartbeat, it was possible it did glow considering who was wearing it.

Holding her in his arms that morning, he had wanted to make love to her with a depth of need that had knocked any previous perspective off the planet. He'd wanted her with a desire he couldn't remember ever feeling for a woman. It was the first time his control had been so thoroughly tested because with her, he didn't have any at all.

Mitch inhaled a deep breath and found her feminine allure in the night air, a sweet scent that immediately made his groin ache. She didn't rely on perfumes or expensive artifice of any manner. It was the same entrancing scent he'd found that morning, tasting her throat with licks that made his blood sizzle with electricity. The memory was enough to make his heart thud painfully and make his body crave more. The woman was driving him out of his mind with desire. But for the moment, he would wait until they both knew they could enjoy this passion between them. It was harder than any test he'd ever come across, but he was quickly discovering that this woman was worth it.

Brooke was pure and clean, good, and he meant it. He was going to help her. He would stay to see her through this challenge Aunt Jerry had given her. Brooke had taken on the fight with an air of grace that he wasn't so sure he himself could have maintained. Make no doubt, though, he had been honest when he'd told everyone he didn't like it.

He hated it. That was when he began to understand the depth of his feelings for the woman who walked with liquid grace next to him. When he understood she really didn't have any other choice. When he knew she might die. She was giving everyone a believable show of calm strength, including him. But he had seen the flickers of unease in her gaze, the small shadow of doubt as she'd began to prepare earlier in the day.

All he knew was that if it came down to it and him, she would not fail. He wanted to see her after the full moon. The alternative was too horrific to imagine.

Her steps slowed, and he focused out of his own thoughts ahead of them. She paused at the edge of a clearing, seeking upward. He followed her and found the glow of the nearly full moon rising. "I will need to be here sooner," she said. "It's farther than I had pictured."

He could see clearly in all directions from where they stood. "You knew where you were going?"

"Not really. I had a picture of it. I let the wind give me the direction." Her tone was completely serious, but her mouth curved in a teasing way. "I guess I'm still talking in Greek to you," she said as she released his hand and began to examine the edges of the clearing.

"No, I'm past Greek," he said. "I think I'm beginning to get it."

Her smile was lovely. "Good." Her bottomless eyes reflected the moonlight above them. She finished the first circle and paced another. She made one more, tighter still, until she stood in front of him. "This will work."

"How can you tell?" His eyes locked on her form bathed in the brilliant moonlight, and he pushed his hands into his pockets. They wanted to touch. A lot. Everywhere.

"Well, let's see how well-adjusted you are," she said with a kissable rise on her lips. "Do you know about spirits and souls? Ghosts?"

"What everyone else assumes, I guess. That they can become attached to a place or an object if something tragic separated them from their body."

"Very good." Her smile grew. "There aren't any here. It makes my job a little easier," she stated. "Something I did have to learn was how to displace a soul. It's tiring, especially when they don't want to leave."

"You evicted them?" he asked with a lightheartedness he had to fight to create. "You horrible landlady." Talking about battling ghosts was making this all too real suddenly.

"You are adjusting," she said, catching his gaze with a glimmer in hers that could only be laughter. Her voice deepened, and it hummed against his skin.

"Is that bad?"

"I hope not. It makes the future after the full moon very hopeful for me." Less than a few feet separated her from him. He closed the gap between them before he could tell himself not to. Before he could remind himself that they were on a schedule and had a reason for being there, he was kissing her.

His hands slid around her body, clasping her firmly into him, and her arms rose to his neck.

His lips drifted to her cheek, and he found her sweet scent. The one he wasn't supposed to be able to find, the same one which had almost driven him out of his mind that morning. His body reacted, aching and swift, crushing her to him with a shocked gasp escaping her parted lips. "I don't know who told you I can't smell your scent, but I can," he said, grinding out the words heatedly. "I can feel you on every inch of skin I have."

"You can?" she whispered in sensual shock. He looked to find that her eyes were closed. She was pliant in his embrace.

"You can be across the house, doors away, and I know where you are." He forced his body to obey. Tonight was not their night. Soon, but not yet. The level of restraint he was digging for was killing him. He brushed a kiss against her satiny skin instead of devouring her the way he truly hungered for. "You're beautiful tonight. I can barely stay away. I've never wanted like this before. I've never needed," he professed against her skin.

"We will have our night. I promise you."

"When?" He was having a hard time keeping the

depth of his desires out of his voice. He was on fire with his hunger, his desires growing in ways he'd never tasted. He fought it with a stiff control.

"Two nights, on the eve of the full moon. I need your help to purify this land."

His lips were tasting her, his mind already searching for arguments against waiting. "How?" It came out in a thick growl.

"With the blood of a virgin. I need you to love me," she whispered uncertainly. She quivered in his hold as much as he did, his hands holding her firm into his body.

It took a few minutes for her words to sink in. His movements slowed, and he caught his breath. "You're a virgin?" She nodded, still breathing heavily against him, her eyes closed. He held her tighter. "Oh Lord. Brooke." He was speechless.

Male pride ripped through him as the truth hit him. "You waited for the man who would be your mate."

Her warm breath seared his chest, where she pressed into him. "If he'll have me."

His hands shook as he cupped her face. "How could I turn away something as beautiful as you, as wonderful?" Her gaze was full and mesmerizing in the nighttime surrounding them, enigmatic depths drawing him into her in a way he was powerless to fight, and he didn't want to. His kiss was gentle and tender, savoring. She swayed on her feet but he held her, telling her everything he couldn't say in words. Her lips were lush and delicious beneath his. He groaned when he had no choice but to stop.

Or keep going.

He had to release her, and it felt like he was ripping out his own heart. He pressed his forehead to hers as he sucked in air. Breathy pants blew across his chest. Her eyes had drifted closed, and he kissed each lid. He kissed her skin.

"Show me," he whispered to her. His voice didn't want to work. His heart was beating too fast with everything he was feeling, with a raw anticipation. "Show me."

She nodded, and he convinced his hands to drop. She took two steps away, and he felt abandoned. He ignored it for what was about to happen, to see her with his own eyes.

He sank to his knees when she lifted her arms, and her tunic melted from her body to drop to the ground. She wore nothing between the sheer layers and her skin. Like a hued marble statue in the moonlight, she bared herself to his gaze. There was no shame in her expression, no embarrassment as material slithered against skin with a caressing sound.

Brooke stepped away from her clothing, and he watched the most amazing thing he could have ever dreamed. He watched the woman he loved become a wild animal of nature. It felt like an eternity that lasted no more than a few heartbeats of time. Her entire length shivered and shimmered in the darkness until she stood not on two, but on four feet. Unblinking eyes, onyx in color against her coat, stared at him.

Exactly like they had the night of his crash. "It was you," he croaked with a flash of acceptance. His heart squeezed at a memory. "The cat! Your shoulder! How... It hurt you! I saw it." He reached out to her, and she came willingly this time. His hand folded into her coat, silken and full on his fingers.

His hands roamed all over her, seeking the wounds he had seen and knew weren't there.

"You're beautiful," he told her reverently. Her golden-yellow coat glistened in the moonlight as she moved against him, in front of him. Her body was supple, lightweight, but utterly perfect. "Now I understand," he told her. "Bram wasn't crazy. He had it right all along." He felt a bubble of happiness inside and sought her gaze with his own, seeking her as the only woman he wanted. "Two brothers for two sisters. It works." He caressed her head with a gentle hand that adored her. "I wish you didn't have to do this." His voice cracked, but he fought past it. "I've finally hit the enlightened age, and I might lose you."

She shimmered beneath his fingertips. She was a goddess in all her glory, kneeling on the ground beneath his touch and nothing else. Those same fingers wound through the wayward strands of her hair, a little less perfect after her shift back to human. "I have to, Mitch, but I will be here when it is over. I want many more nights like this. I want a lifetime of this."

"Can you promise me that?" he asked her, sounding harsher than he'd intended. "Can you promise me you aren't going to come out here in three nights and disappear? That you won't die?" He lowered his head and shook himself. "I'm sorry. I'm the one who took too long to understand."

"No, I can't make that promise. You know I can't." Her fingers fluttered over his face. "But I have a deeper reason for success, a greater fear of failure to encourage me. I want to be here to see you after." She captured his wavering hand, and he felt his air freeze in his lungs. "I can't make you that promise, Mitch." She closed her eyes, but he had seen into her heart. Her lips were warm as she blessed him with her kiss. "But I can give you everything I am. I will offer myself to you as a woman does, as a lover, as a wife, as a mate. In two nights, you will know, and I will have your faith to keep me strong."

He crushed her against him. "I will!" he swore. "You know I will." His voice grew thick with emotion.

When he finally found the strength to let her free,

she said, "I can't change what must be done, but I can fudge it a little," she hedged.

"How?" Mitch waited as she picked up her sheath, pulling it over her head, letting it cover her where she knelt before him.

"Can I borrow your knife?" When he offered it, she took the sharp blade and, using it, made a small slice in her forearm.

"What are you doing? Give that back," he ordered, instantly confused and worried, grabbing for it to take it away.

She shook her head. "I'll heal quickly. Make a cut on your thumb." She handed it back. "Go on," she prompted. "A small one is fine." He took a breath and another leap of faith and did as she said, wincing at the sharp pain. "Perfect." She brought herself to her knees and steadily lifted his hand in her own once more. She blended two drops of his blood over the score in her arm. Then she moved her arm and he watched as the blood dripped from the slice she had made to rest on his thumb. It was warm. He didn't think blood stayed warm.

She began to speak, a melodic chanting voice that wound like silk over his ear.

"Of two hearts, two minds, two souls,

I offer me to you, I accept you into me."

She did the blood exchange again, purposefully blending their blood together on her skin over the neat slice in her forearm.

"Of one heart, one mind, one soul."

Again she allowed several drops to run and land on his sliced thumb. This time he felt a tingle, the warmth being very noticeable on his flesh.

"You take my life, I accept yours," she canted. "Life by life, age by age. Be thy bound, be thy strung. Between you and I, one." She licked his thumb clean, and he was surprised to note that it had ceased to hurt. The cut had healed. He blinked, shifting his thumb, searching where the noticeable slice had been.

"What was that?" he asked, mystified as he gaped at his thumb. His healed thumb.

"I have shared with you, connected us. You and I are mated where it counts," she explained with an aching tenderness. She raised her flat palm and formed it against his body. "Do you feel me?" she asked in her pure and gentle way that was Brooke and no one else.

His gaze widened. "I do! I can feel your heartbeat, I think," he said, his brows crossed, trying to understand. "But why did you do that?"

"It's an insurance policy," she said, almost too quietly to hear. "In case I don't make it. I want to find you again."

He cupped her chin. "You will make it, Brooke. I don't want to have to wait until my next life for you."

He was caught off his guard when she threw herself into him. "I don't either, Mitch, but I'm scared," she choked out, a shaky sound while she trembled against him. He felt her take a deep breath and somehow knew she wouldn't mention her doubts again.

The next three days were going to be hell, he thought. He held her tight in the clearing under the moonlight and tried not to think about what she was going to do on the last night.

Chapter Thirteen

Brooke wasn't at all surprised to find Roman waiting for her when they emerged from the tree line. His anger was pronounced in the arched tension of his body, a strung-tight, muscled form ready to strike, but no enemy to take his frustrations out on.

"Do you need me to stay?" Mitch asked, eyeing the bigger man with worried concern.

She shook her head. "I need to talk to him." Mitch squeezed her hand and left her to talk, striding toward the house.

"You had a choice!" he fired at her once Mitch was out of sight. "She had no right!" He paced like a caged animal in the darkness. Roman was massive, tall, strong, deadly, but in this, he was powerless. Infuriated, his brooding eyes flashed like a lava flow, dark and hot.

"No, she had no right to force the amulet on me," she agreed. "Aunt Jerry took that choice away from me."

"Then why do it?" he shouted. "She made the mistake." He whirled and slammed a fist into a tree, shaking it to its branches.

"Yes, she did, and she tried to correct it," she replied. His anger undulated off him in massive waves, making her just as determined to help him understand. "She failed."

"But why you, Brooke?" he said through clenched teeth. "Christ, you are not a slayer! You're a shifter."

She shrugged. "I never said I was, but I am capable. Do you want me to walk away and leave it alone to gather strength on this plane? Do you want Adrian to know he may be hunted because of what he will be? If the demon gets the amulet, we are all doomed." She pushed her hands firmly out in front of her, toward her brother, seeking his understanding. "I can't do that, Roman."

His head hung where he stood next to the tree he had just pummeled without restraint. "So do something with the amulet! Send it somewhere," he said, snarling. "You did not make this mistake." His fists clenched as he faced away, probably wanting to strike out again, but fighting the need. "This is not your problem."

She allowed her arms to drop. "Roman, this is not just my problem. It's all of ours." She cleared the few feet that separated them, halting at his shoulder. His chest heaved as he fought to not do what he instinctively wanted to do: protect the pack.

He snarled louder, in warning, when she rested a hand on his arm, pushing her away with an irate toss.

"She did take the choice away from me when she gave me the amulet, but she didn't force me to face her mistake. I could let it run rampant for centuries and nothing may happen, but think about what has happened since I've been here. Who has been hurt? Who has died? Can we afford a decade of that? Even a year?"

He remained immovable, silent, and menacing.

Brooke searched him, but he remained unbending, avoiding her at all costs. His face wore the cut strain of his pain.

She turned away several strained moments later, feeling his rejection keenly, knowing this was a battle she couldn't win. Her steps faltered when his anguish-filled words reached out to her.

"What if you die? What will happen to the pack?" He jerked around and faced her in the moonlight.

"The pack will be strong, Roman, and I will not die," she stated emphatically. "I have too much to live for."

"Mitch?" he asked her, not passing judgment.

"Yes, Roman."

He took a long soul-filling breath, his shoulders flexing under his shirt. "He better not swear at you anymore," he warned her gruffly.

She actually felt a commiserate smile and knew she had her brother's blessing, as much as it pained him to give it. "He won't. Not unless I start it," she assured him.

Roman stepped up and crushed her into his chest. "God, Brooke. I could kill her for this."

"But you won't. In truth, she was scared. That's why when I came home she gave it to me. If the demon tried to confront her, she would have been powerless to stop him. He would have taken it, and we'd have been following on a leash."

"I don't have to like it," his hoarse voice rumbled.

She stepped back, tipping to look deep into his midnight eyes, finding all the pain and anger at his inability to protect those he called his own. "I don't like it either, if you want the honest truth, but I want to be able to have that family I've been craving. Can't do it like this," she stated. She'd never risk having a child with this kind of a threat hanging over her head.

She waited for the outcome of the battle he raged internally until finally, he looped an arm over her shoulder. He gusted a long, tired sound when there was nothing more either could say. "Let's go show we've made up," he said with a straight face. "By the way, what is that on your skin? Did you roll in something out there?"

She shook her head, surprised he could tell anything at all. "I blood-bonded with Mitch."

His pace slowed, then halted completely. "You did? And it worked?" He twitched his head, his neck popping once, then said, "Well, it's going to get interesting, then."

"Why? It's only a melding spell," she explained as they both stepped up onto the porch.

"Babs, you're about to go take down a demon. Your ability has been growing for years, you're a trained witch and a shifter, and you bonded your mate with virgin blood. You should've studied more." He pushed open the door, and she walked through ahead of him, suddenly wondering if she'd done more to Mitch than she'd originally intentioned.

* * * *

Mitch was talking quietly with Bram when the two returned. Neither Brooke nor Roman were snarling or glaring at each other, even though neither appeared exactly thrilled, so he hoped they had come to an agreement. He hoped for her sake that they had. This was hard enough on her without one of her brothers turning his back on her.

Morgan was the first to speak up once they'd entered. "Well, it's been one of those days. I'm heading home." He shook hands and got hugs, then left.

"We're getting a room in town," Roman said as he curled an arm around Delilah. "We'll be here if you need us."

"Thank you, Roman. Delilah," Brooke offered, her voice a musical lightness that brought a smile to Mitch simply for hearing her. Lyrical and confident. Just like Brooke. Carrying a sleeping Adrian, Roman and Del left a few minutes later.

"You know, that little guy of theirs sure is something. Slept through everything." Mitch walked over to her and put his arm around her. It was a natural fit.

"That's what babies do," she joked, watching them through the window as they pulled out of sight. "They're cute now so you don't kill them when they turn sixteen and ask for the car."

He sensed a deeper hesitation in her, though, now that most everyone had left her in peace. Selene and Bram were in the kitchen putting away the mess of the evening. "You know, I love your shorts, but I think this is sexy." He tugged on the tunic. She didn't relax with his teasing.

"It won't be regular in the rotation. It helps the mindset." Her gaze drifted sightlessly to the world outside the window and when she neared the glass pane, he followed. He couldn't find a reason to let go of her. He didn't want to let her go, either.

"What's wrong, Brooke? Other than the obvious?" He bent close to whisper into her ear, "You're pale."

Her tongue darted out to her lower lip. "I think I may have done you wrong with the spell." She turned and faced him, her eyes wide, searching. Her cheeks were pale. "Do you feel anything?"

He shrugged. "Like what?"

"Different? When we were coming in, Roman mentioned that I smelled different. I told him what we did." She ducked her head, but he caught her evasive movement before she could completely hide from him. "I don't know. Maybe I'm just paranoid right now."

"No, I feel fine, and it doesn't matter." He tugged her against him, and he felt her relax in his hold. "I'm not going anywhere. We'll worry about what life is going to be like at the end of the week."

"That works for me," she agreed.

"Good night, guys. See you tomorrow," Bram called as he and Selene went to their room.

"I better get some sleep," she said into his chest. "I'm beat." It was late.

"Best thing I've heard all day," he told her as he scooped her up into his arms, tilting her into his chest. She gasped, and her eyes widened in surprise. He laughed. "I don't care what Selene says. You do not weigh one-twenty," he murmured as he carried her to the spare room. When she tensed within his arms, he told her, "Not tonight, sweetheart. I just need you with me." He kissed her mouth and almost dropped her as lightning flared over him brighter than any Fourth of July explosion. "Holy cow!"

"What was that?" Her eyes snapped open, staring at him, bright and wide with shock.

"I have no idea." He gazed at her in his hold. "I'm putting you on the bed before I hurt you." Her hair spilled around her in a golden cloud. "God, you're beautiful," he told her.

He stretched out along her length, holding her tenderly, and buried his nose in her hair. "Mmm, you do smell different. Sweeter, maybe," he said, considering the difference. "I don't know, but I can find it easier." She arched in his hold as he wrapped his arms around her. "Careful there, Brooke. I'm still only a man," he warned through a smile, fighting to keep the proof of his own arousal out of his voice. Just because she was killing him with wanting didn't mean she had to know it.

"Somehow, you are going to make sleep extremely difficult," she told him with a squeak of caution.

Mitch stretched to peer into her face. "I made my promise to you. I don't break my promises." He lowered himself to nip at her neck. "But I could use something to dream about," he crooned. She shivered like a delicate breeze in his hold as he found her skin.

He caressed her with his tongue. "What?" he groaned in astonishment, rearing over her as the contact sizzled over his lips. He dragged his tongue across his teeth to test the sensation. He licked her neck, in the same spot, testing what he'd experienced, and shuddered in reaction. "Oh man," he said breathily.

"What is it?" she asked, a concerned frown on her cute brow.

"It's better," he explained in a hoarse, subdued tone. "I don't know how to explain it." He dipped and gently suckled on her skin, almost coming unglued. Fire struck his limbs, burning a trail from his torso to his groin. His head reared up. "Oh boy. I think I better stop." He was panting like a freight train as the rush of desire seared his body.

"Mitch, what is it?" she whispered from beneath him. He found her dark, luscious gaze growing increasingly worried.

He lowered himself to the bed and rolled her above him until she hovered over him. "I can't explain it," he said, wondering when his voice had ever sounded so rough. "Just please, stop when I ask." He panted. "Taste me," he begged.

She cast him a disturbed frown but then he arched his neck, closed his eyes, and waited. He gripped the sheets in iron fists with the first brush of her breath, but they popped open as sensation after sensation ripped down his body when her lips found his skin. He growled deeply, lost in the ecstasy-filled feeling.

Her golden hair flew wildly when she whipped up from where she'd been skin to skin. He focused and found her staring at him in wide-eyed shock. "You... You smell different," she said on a choked yelp. "And you taste different."

"Different bad?" He forced it through a tight jaw.

He couldn't let go of the bed. He'd break his promise, then and there. All he could see was her beautiful face, wild and lost in passion beneath him as he loved her, filled her, and claimed her hungry little body for his own. It wasn't hard to imagine. The Brooke he envisioned was staring at him.

"No! It's...better." She licked her lips and his body leaped, demanding the feeling of her tongue. "Still like hot honey, but better." He hid the groan, not wanting to alarm her. He was enraptured beneath her. Moving was the last thing on his mind. Damn, he wanted her!

Brooke planted a hand on his chest, whether to hold him down or to hold her up, he couldn't say. He didn't care. Her weight was right over his racing heart. "Just one more time," she said next to his ear. It sounded like a plea to him.

"Please!" He ached everywhere. "Oh God," he said, grinding out the words when her hot little mouth found him.

Damp and wicked, her lips glided over his neck, drawing against his skin and nerves with delicate pulls of sensation as she tasted him and found the differences they were discovering in each other. Then the swirl of her tongue roamed over him and he arched, not caring if he groaned loud enough to wake the whole town. It was too much, the longing, the sensations, the erotic beat of his heart pulsing blood beneath her hot mouth. The heat enveloped him, tore through him, and for the first time since he'd been a kid, he lost himself. Completely. He threw his head and let the white-hot ecstasy of her mouth take him over the edge. And all she'd done was kiss his neck.

She lifted herself shakily from his side, trembling in shock. "I'm sorry! I had no idea!"

He couldn't think. He could barely breathe, so he just lay there for a long-winded moment, pulling his body in from parts unknown. He'd never done that! Talk about intense!

"Wow," he managed when he could speak at all. He was a mess and needed a shower, but for two more minutes, at least, he refused to care. He caught her when she tried to pull away from him and leave the bed. "Where do you think you're going?"

"I'm sorry, Mitch," she said, every syllable heavy with guilt.

"For what? I've never experienced anything like that in my life!" He sought her face with his fingers, not letting her escape. "That was incredible."

"Because of the spell. Roman was right," she muttered, avoiding him. "I had no idea it would change you."

"Wait just a second." He made himself move. He was liquid inside, but he somehow managed to make himself do it. "We did that together, remember? How did it feel for you?" He lifted his hand and captured her head, filling his fingers with the softness of her hair, refusing to let her escape.

Her body trembled harder. "I loved it," she admitted as her eyes slid closed, hiding them from him. "But it was fine before. The spell—"

Mitch used his other hand to cover her lips, but decided his mouth would be even better. He pulled her close and brushed his lips against hers, becoming blinded by the sparks. He was aching again within two solid beats of his heart. "If that is the spell, I don't care." He trailed his lips tenderly against her cheek. "You smell like a wonderful bouquet of flowers to me," he told her gently. "I can feel you on my skin, taste you on my tongue. Stronger. Sweeter." He wrapped his other hand into her hair, letting his fingers drive into the silk strands of heaven. "Tell me, do you see the light?" he whispered huskily just before their lips met.

He found the light and the sparks, letting them grow and fill him. His entire body rose to the occasion, craving her in any way he could have her. He drew her to him, surging into her to feel her breasts pushed deliriously into his chest, craving her skin to skin. She moaned when her hands fitted to his shoulders on their own. He'd never heard a more arousing sound.

Brooke whimpered when she slowly pulled away from him. He let her go. He knew when they'd reached the end of their endurance.

Her face was flushed, and her eyes were closed. He urged the swinging length of hair away to see her better. "Wow," she agreed. "I've never felt that."

"Me either." He caressed her face, memorizing everything with seeking fingertips. "Don't feel guilty. I didn't tell you not to do it."

"But it changed you," she persisted. "And I don't know how much."

That made him pause. "I see." He took a deep breath, wondering what surprises were now lying in wait for him because of the incredible woman in his arms. "Look, I'm going to shower. Don't let me find this bed empty when I get back." He kissed her gently, tenderly, and felt the flare of the electricity burn him. "We'll figure out the curves one day at a time," he told her honestly when he released her. He gave her a soft smile. "Hell, what am I talking about? Every day with you has curves, and I'm kind of liking it."

"Oh, Mitch," she groaned even as she grinned, blushing as she dipped her chin and her gaze.

It took monumental effort to leave her there in his bed but he managed it, gliding with quiet steps to the restroom. It was late, and he didn't want to wake the other two, if he hadn't already. He stripped and heated the water. He didn't waste time, showering quickly.

Mitch wasn't sure how he was going to get through

the night with her in his bed without having more of her. The only thing he was sure of was that she wouldn't be sleeping on the couch ever again. Finished in the shower, he shook his head and turned off the water.

He reached for a towel but overextended, blinded by the water in his eyes. His groping hand slid down the wall and hit the light switch as he wiped water out of his eyes. "Crap," he muttered. And blinked.

"Whoa."

He could see. There weren't any windows in this bathroom. It was pitch black, but he could see fine. He shrank into the shower and searched the room for any light. There wasn't even a hint under the door with the rest of the house asleep, but he could see everything in the bathroom in detail, as if it were high noon.

He impatiently grabbed the towel and dressed in clean sweats. When he stepped into the bedroom he noticed she had changed also, lying in a long T-shirt, and the sweet picture of her made him hard again. From the cute blonde swath of hair at her shoulder to the bend of her knee, it was the first time he'd seen her in absolute repose. Her curled shape took up a fraction of the bed, she was so tiny. He wondered if she was asleep. He wanted to ask her about the vision, but if she was already asleep, he didn't want to wake her either. He knew she was tired with how long she'd been preparing for the coming battle, then the family meeting. That had been draining on everyone.

Eventually, deciding to let her rest won over. He slid in next to her and pulled up the sheets, falling asleep wrapped around her, wondering what she had done to him, then realizing no matter what it accumulated to, he wasn't angry over it.

* * * *

When Mitch left for the shower, Brooke stripped and changed in a minute flat. What had she done? She'd never in her life experienced an orgasm and except for the sheer fact that they'd stopped, she was sure that was what would have happened. Even she knew why Mitch had to take a shower. She was innocent but not *that* innocent, and all because the spell had intensified everything beyond belief.

She had seen the light when he'd kissed her, and her whole body had hummed when he'd caressed her skin. She had shivered under the strength of the arousal pouring through her body at his slow discovery of the difference, a difference she hadn't picked up on because it wasn't as in her face until she was buried against his skin, until she was tasting him on her own tongue, becoming lost in the hunger he created within her. Then it exploded in her head, his taste, his heat, and she couldn't get enough.

What had she done? It was a simple melding spell, just a bond. Wasn't it? She sat on the edge of the bed until the water turned off, then she hurriedly stretched out and evened her breathing. He stood at the door for a minute, and she sensed him watching her. She found the aroma of the soap on his skin, could even smell the way his skin heated as he became aroused standing in the doorway. *What have I done?* she shrieked silently.

She heard the door close and he slid into bed with her, covering them both. He wrapped his arms over her, and she felt as he relaxed, cradled around her. With his body's warmth and the comfort of his touch, she drifted into a fitful sleep.

Chapter Fourteen

Alone at the cabin, Brooke was lost in her thoughts. It was quiet and peaceful as she strolled along the drive. She'd needed a relaxing stretch after the last few days. Bram and Mitch had gone into town for a little while, which was fine with her. She needed a spot of quiet to think.

The amulet rested underneath her shirt against her skin. She'd been searching for its power as she meandered. She knew it had adverse effects on male shape-shifters of her family, but how could she use it? Was she strong enough? Would it be enough to displace a demon? Would she be enough? Did she know enough?

She stuffed her hands into the pockets of her shorts. She'd used it on the two lesser demons, but not really. At least, she didn't think she had. She wished she knew what she had done, how she had tapped the power of the blood amulet. The truth spell had nothing to do with the stone. That was something she hadn't been able to admit to anyone.

She hadn't spoken to Mitch again about her doubts because in truth, she was terrified. Everyone thought she was going to win. Everyone thought she had this hands down. Except for her. She was putting up a good front if everyone was falling for it.

She kicked at a rock, following it as it bounced into the trees. The birds sang, and the sunshine was warm. It all seemed to be mocking her situation, being so bright and cheery. Oregon itself was a beautiful state if you could survive the winters and the rain. She'd always enjoyed it there. Bend was a cute little town.

She just hoped she was there to see it after the full moon.

"Don't fret so much, my child."

Brooke spun, and a smile lit her face. "Aunt Jerry!" She threw herself into her aunt's arms. "I'm glad to see you."

"I thought you might like a cheer or two," she said in her soothing voice. Silver bracelets flashed in the sunlight as she wrapped Brooke into a hug.

"It couldn't hurt, that's for sure," she agreed. She let her arms slide free and tried to step back, but Aunt Jerry held her tight.

"Okay, Aunt Jerry, you can let me go now. I'm happy to see you." Her nose twitched. "Phew! You've been doing your potions again, haven't you?" she teased her aunt.

"No, not potions." The voice deepened, sounding dry and gravelly. Brooke froze instantly. The arms wrapped around her tightened like a trap.

"You're not Jeralynna!" she cried in alarm, feeling a jolting stab of fear right between her shoulder blades. "Let me go!" She tried to move, but its hold was unbreakable.

The form morphed, growing taller and thinner, losing the visage of Jeralynna Aiza. The skull sunk in until it was worse than emaciated. "You have what the master wants," it said chillingly. The skin tightened until the teeth were a long snarling line of jaws and bone. Skin and clothing hung on it in torn strips. Hollow eye sockets mocked her. For being only bones, it was incredibly strong as Brooke tried to wrench herself free. Her skin crawled where it touched her.

"I don't have anything!" she shouted in

desperation. "I demand you let me go!" It remained silent and completely ignored her demands. She flinched when it raised bony fingers, fishing for the amulet around her throat.

Brooke did the only thing she could think of. She changed shape and landed on her feet, running when she squirreled her way out of the thing's hold. It hissed in rage and leaped after her.

Damn clothes! She needed to be human to speak a spell! It was gaining on her. Damn it! Where was the boundary? She didn't bother to see how close it was. She could hear it. She ran harder, fighting against the pull of the clothes with each stretched leap. It was too close to risk changing shape and trying a spell, and the house was coming into view. Why was it still following? It shouldn't be able to get this close!

She heard it scream in frustration and chanced a look behind her. It had stopped barely a hundred feet from the front porch, raging as it paced from side to side against an invisible wall.

Finally! She changed shapes again, which only seemed to enrage it more. It screamed a shrill cry that erupted birds from their nests. She tugged her clothes into place, glaring at it.

"I order you gone!" she shouted, lifting a commanding hand to the skeleton. It shrieked at her and forced a foot forward. "Crap! You would be dumb and deaf, wouldn't you?" she snapped at the lesser demon. She fought for strength as it forced another footstep forward. It was determined. Eventually the protections would block it completely, but she didn't want to know how close it could get before that happened. Demons like this one were programmed to fulfill their missions to the end or be destroyed trying. Can't kill something that's already dead.

"I can do this," she told herself. She shook out her

hands as she searched for the spell. It growled long and loud as it kept working its way toward her.

She opened her palms outward and breathed. The skeleton screamed when she began to speak. "I am the heart. I bleed the heart," she said. Warm sunlight streaked across her face, bolstering her courage. "I birth the heart. I slay the heart." The demon reared to its full height and cried out long and loud, a sharp penetrating sound that shook the glass of the cabin.

The heat of the magic she owned filled her, suffused her with the energy of goddesses and lifetimes. She opened her eyes and spoke again. Her voice was not raised at all, but it carried like a strong wind, a powerful force in itself. "I am the keeper of the heart. I control the heart."

The demon stopped moving, finger bones clenching and popping in hatred. "I am the daughter of the heart. I am the mother of the heart. I command you, be gone!"

The lesser demon shook in anger as it fought the spell, but she held the heat, absorbed the fight and rage of the creature, and used the energy it emanated to control it. When it started to fold in on itself, Brooke recognized the feeling from the two she had managed to truth-spell before. They had been kittens compared to this thing!

She clenched her teeth, keeping herself standing until it was dust on the ground. Then she allowed herself to collapse to a knee, huffing like she'd run to town and back.

"Brooke! Are you all right? God, what was that thing?" Mitch picked her up and held her close.

"A test," she breathed, panting. "A hunter."

His hand shook as he scooped her hair out of the way, running his fingers and hands all over her. "You used the amulet to get rid of it?" he asked, his finger tapping on the chain.

She shook her head. "No, that was all me. God, I'm pooped."

"That was you?" he said with a note of awe. "I promise, I will never piss you off."

"Why? What did you see?" She felt stronger just being held by him. It didn't matter that he was holding her up more than she was standing alone.

"That thing disintegrated. And honey, no matter how much you don't think you can, you were as bright as a lightbulb. You've got something going for you." He rubbed his chin on the top of her head in comfort.

She trembled against him. She didn't want to tell him how drained she felt. She was exhausted. He scooped her into his arms and carried her inside. Brooke couldn't tell him, couldn't say it, but she had to face it. She could die, and if she did that there was only one thing left for her to do. The demon had to go with her.

Mitch settled her on the couch and made her tea without being asked. He sat a few minutes later with her, with a cup for himself, and holding her. She sipped gratefully, absorbing his strength and comfort.

"What are you doing back? I thought you and Bram had stuff to do." She looked up at him from his chest when she felt strong enough to talk.

"Kind of weird that," he began, looking dazed. "We were talking in a store and all of a sudden the hair on my neck stood up." He gave her a lopsided grin. "I think I gave my brother a shock today." He sipped at his own mug, staring into the contents for a second. "I literally knew you were in trouble. I left him standing in town. He's going to be pissed when I see him again."

She arched to see him clearly. "You knew?" she asked him, stunned.

"Yeah, I said it was going to sound weird," he said,

shrugging.

"No, I think it's sweet," she told him, reaching up and kissing his jaw. "Mmm, good to the last kiss."

He studied her, and knew he didn't miss a single inch in his search. "Are you sure you're all right?"

"Yeah, I'm fine. Really." Even if she was shaking inside. That had been close.

"Then I better get back. I left him downtown. I hope I can find him."

"He's in the bookstore," she said without thinking about it. "And he's not mad. Not now."

"You can see him?" he asked her.

She sat up, staring at nothing, overwhelmed all over again. "Yeah, I can. I guess it's because you're worried about him." She rubbed a hand across her forehead. "Just what am I?"

"I don't know, but when you figure it out, could you tell me?" he teased her. He dropped a kiss to her lips. "I'll see you in a while, and no more dancing with demons."

"That I can promise," she quipped back. "I'm going to rest."

He walked her to the bedroom and made sure she was comfortable, then went to shut the door to let her sleep. "I'll wake you if you're still asleep when we get back," he said from the doorway.

"Sure," she said over a yawn, stretching out. The front door closed, and that was the last thing she heard.

* * * *

Driving into town, Mitch's grip twisted on the wheel of his rented Jeep. Bram was going to be upset, but he'd explain it. Bram would probably be the only one who would understand the statement, *My girlfriend is being attacked by a demon. I'm going to see if she's alive.*

He would have laughed himself if it hadn't been so damn true! He'd raced from town and slid to a stunned stop behind that thing, only to see it fall apart and turn to dust like the other two before it. He'd blinked and realized the sunlight blinding him wasn't sunlight, but Brooke. The sunburst went out like a switch had been hit, and he could only watch as she collapsed.

He'd never seen anything like it, and if seeing the demon turn to dust hadn't scared him, seeing her exhausted on the ground had. He pounded the wheel. "Damn it!"

He turned into downtown and found a space right in front of the bookstore. He slammed the door when he got out. He didn't want Brooke to do this! He fell against the fender and counted to ten. His insides were a knotted mess.

She was going to die! It was his greatest fear, and there wasn't anything he could do to help her.

Not one single thing. He ground his jaw in frustration, hearing Bram walk up to him.

"Thanks for coming back," Bram said, as if there had been a worry that he wouldn't.

Mitch didn't look up from the point he was glaring at between his toes. "I'm sorry. I had to make sure she was all right."

"Is she?" he asked, leaning against the vehicle with Mitch.

"Yeah, but it was close." Mitch looked in all directions and found they were alone on the block. "One of those things had cornered her!" He expelled out a rushed breath. "I just want this over," he said. His voice was quiet, a little nervous. "Bram, I'm scared she's going to die doing this. She was worn out after this one. What if she can't do what Aunt Jerry says she can? What if she's not strong enough? Do you even hear what I'm asking?" he said, a note of incredulity in his voice. "What the hell happened to a normal life?" He snorted derisively, then rubbed his eyes roughly with the heels of his palms, letting some of the tension pass.

"You fell for the wrong kind of woman to have normal anymore." His brother paused, staring out to the street. "Are you regretting it?" Bram asked seriously.

"No, I'm not. It took some getting used to. She's so," he waved a hand, "unexplainable, incredible, wonderful." He took a steadying breath. "Is that how you feel about Selene?"

"In a nutshell," he replied, nodding in understanding. "I never expected after what they'd told me about the quiet and demure Brooke that this would happen. I had a picture of a cute lady with a sunhat and trowel." He laughed. "This ain't her."

"No, she's not. That's for sure." Mitch grinned at his older brother. "But she is cute."

"So where is she now?" Bram asked.

"She's resting. How long before Selene is off shift?"

Bram twisted his wrist. "In about twenty minutes." Bram met his gaze with a calm smile. "Go home, Mitch, I'll ride home with her."

Mitch released a breath he didn't know he'd been holding. He couldn't forget what he'd seen outside the cabin. "Thanks." He reached for the Jeep door, but Bram spoke.

"By the way, she's probably going to wake up hungry. Beef tips go a long way."

Mitch nodded and slid behind the wheel. She was still passed out when he reached the bedroom, and it didn't look like she'd moved. He sat on the edge of the bed and watched her sleep. She didn't appear unusual in any way resting. She didn't look any different from any other woman on the planet, asleep or awake. So how did she get the job of stopping a demon? How was she born a witch? A shifter? He crossed his arms to keep himself from pulling her into his arms and not letting go. He'd never encountered this need to protect either, but he couldn't lie to himself. It was there, and it was huge, especially with this whole demon problem staring them all in the face.

He wanted to hold her, keep her safe. He hadn't thought about what they would do after the full moon. He hadn't wanted to think about it at all since Aunt Jerry's visit. Since then he'd come to those realizations about how much Brooke meant to him, but the questions were there, not to mention that he was still technically on medical leave from the station house.

He felt a stab of guilt realizing that he should have returned to St. Louis as soon as he was capable, but he hadn't. Brooke had become more important. She had surpassed every excuse, reason, and wall he had ever built for avoiding a relationship with a woman.

Janice had been a good woman, but he wouldn't have been happy. With Brooke, he just needed to be in the same room and every annoying problem he had disappeared. He realized he was happy, content to do nothing more than sleep beside her, like last night, no pressure to do anything more, nothing but hold her. He'd never felt that close to another woman because no one else was the right woman.

The last few days had been surreal, but when he put it all together, he couldn't argue with cold, hard facts. It didn't hurt that he'd witnessed most of them, and well, even a blind man could be made to see the truth.

She was what she said she was and then some. The problem was the *and then some* had him worried.

She sighed and rolled over. "Hi," she said,

brushing a hand over groggy eyes.

"Hi, how are you feeling?"

"Like I've been hit by a truck." She sat up, crossing her legs. "How long have you been there?"

"A while, I guess. I wasn't paying attention." He reached and wound fingers through her hair. It felt warm and smooth, and his heart tried to leap through his ribs at the contact. He felt the shock of her lips against his, unable to not at least steal a taste of her, and groaned at the slightest press of skin. He pulled back. "Do you still feel that?"

"Yes," she said thickly. "I think I need to undo the spell. All you have to do is touch me, and I fall apart."

"Don't you even think of it!" he argued immediately. "I love the way you feel, and I may sound like a jerk, but I'm looking forward to tomorrow like..." He stopped searching for the best explanation. He found her uncertain gaze again. He cradled her head in his palms, and her skin warmed against his with little flames. It took him a few minutes to put his thoughts into words. "I'm looking forward to tomorrow like my wedding night," he told her honestly. He brushed against her lips and soared, falling into the sensual heat she enflamed him with. "Brooke, I don't want for you to be hurt. I can't let you do this. There has to be another way."

"I have to, Mitch! I'm it," she pointed out. "I can't let my entire family live under this kind of a threat."

"But if you keep yourself protected, there has to be a way!" he argued.

"How can I keep myself protected, Mitch? I took a walk for the first time in days and was attacked!" She jumped from the bed but he caught her, stopping her from escaping.

"But you're wearing the amulet! It's safe here!" His gaze roamed her, feeling anxious and frightened for her in a way he'd never encountered. "Please, Brooke!"

"Mitch, you and I both know I need to do this." She cupped his chin with a firm assurance. "I can't just walk away from it because I'm scared. I can't let it go because I can't guarantee the outcome."

"I know. But I hate this!" he said fiercely.

"I know," she told him with a loving caress of her fingers. "I do too, but it doesn't change the need."

"Hell." He took a breath and tugged her onto his lap. He looped his arms around her waist and let her rest on his shoulder. "Hey, I just thought of something. Didn't you and Roman say that thing could be destroyed, the amulet? The maker could destroy it?"

"No, he can't destroy it. He's not alive any longer."

His shoulders sagged, his one good idea shot down. "Oh. Who made it?"

"Merlin."

"You're kidding? You have an amulet made by *the* Merlin? As in Arthur and the knights and Camelot?"

She chuckled against him. "Mmm-hmm. One and the same. So that also makes it very powerful. I haven't figured out how to make the power work yet."

He noticed she didn't say anything about how little time there was to figure it out. He tightened his hold and rested against her head. Her scent filled him with each breath. His voice wasn't the only thing that had gone thick by the time he spoke again. "Um, Bram had said you would probably be hungry. Are you?"

"Starving," she said.

"Yeah, me too, but not for food." Mitch nipped at her neck. "Sweet," he whispered against her skin, and she shivered. "I'm getting used to this, but I know I will never get enough."

She moaned as his tongue swirled over her and she let her head drop back.

"Just...glad...no...other...ahhhh!" Her fingers

clawed into his shoulders when he started to suck on the erratic beating of her pulse. She shouted his name, driving his hungers higher with the need in her cries.

He reached up and captured her head to claim her lips. He gasped at the shock, then plundered her sweet mouth. His tongue raked inside, thrusting hard, pushing against her. Wanting. He slipped away from her sweetness, then fought to not take her, to not be inside her. Her breathing was as hard and hot as his. His stomach wall clenched tighter than a fist when her breasts rubbed against him, her taut peaks burning him through two shirts. He let one of his hands drift in discovery over her back and groaned. "Do you ever wear a bra?"

"Not usually." She gasped.

"God, you're going to kill me," he whispered into her hair. "You better get up, slowly."

She nodded. "Just one thing."

"What?"

She planted a foot and shoved him over in a rush. "This," she told him in a husky drugging voice that made his blood boil with renewed need and lust.

"Brooke! No, I can't take it!" But her seducing mouth was already on him. He formed his hands to her shoulders and tried to slow her attacks, but he couldn't. It all felt too damn good. "You're playing with fire," he said in a raspy voice.

She wasn't listening. Her tongue was hot and wet on his already sensitive skin. He squirmed under her weight, and her breasts were rubbing into him again. He groaned when she bit his collarbone and laved her tongue over him. The heat of her crashed into his body like a high, rushing wave.

"I can't take it, Brooke! Please!" His eyes snapped open when she slid seeking fingernails under his shirt. "Ahhhhhhh!" He groaned. He shot off the bed when her tongue found ribs and skin.

"That's it!" he shouted. He grabbed her shoulders and tossed her off, bouncing them both to the bed, where he straddled her, holding her hands to pin her. "Either you stop this right now, or I make love to you for a week!"

She reached for him again, moaning.

"Brooke! Damn it! Look at me. Stop this!"

She raised her lashes. Her eyes were dark and glassy with lust. "Brooke! Stop right now!" Not a single sign in answer that she heard him.

"Brooke!" He shook her. "Brooke? Damn it!" She strained against him, pumping her hips in invitation. She was hot everywhere. "What is going on? Brooke, honey, come on! Snap out of it!" His own lust was quickly replaced by panic. He pinned her hands and dragged out the amulet. It was cool in his palm. He took it off her anyway. Nothing happened.

"Shit! Jeralynna! Jeralynna, help!" He sat on Brooke to keep her pinned. He had no idea if her aunt would show up, but whatever was going on wasn't normal. "Come on, baby. Snap out of it!" He brushed her hair away to see her face and she turned toward him, trying to reach any part of him, her pink tongue snaking out for his skin.

"What's going on?" a sharp voice responded.

"Thank God!" He choked the words out. "She's gone nuts." Daring to take his attention from Brooke, he found Aunt Jerry standing over them.

"She's been spelled," she stated with a note of worry. "Here, keep her still." He put his hands where she pointed and watched as she rested fingertips to Brooke's forehead.

Jeralynna murmured a phrase in a language Mitch knew he'd never heard, then she let out a breath. "Yuck, that one even tasted bad."

Brooke let out a rushed gasp, then blinked. "Mitch? Why are you sitting on me?"

He climbed off, still panting, his thoughts in turmoil.

"Aunt Jerry?" Her eyes widened, and she leaped off the bed too. "You are Jeralynna, right?" she asked, backing up.

"Yes, love. Mitch called me."

Brooke whipped around to him. "You called her? How did you do that?"

"I don't really know." He rubbed his neck. "Let's go sit a minute. I feel like hell." His entire being was a mass of tossed emotions. He opened the door, and they all filed out to the kitchen.

"Jeralynna, would you mind? Your tea is faster," he asked her, past feeling shocked by her ability as he pulled out a chair for Brooke. She wobbled a little when she planted herself into it. He rested a hand on her and she smiled up at him. He sat right next to her. It was going to take an ice pick to separate them as far as he was concerned.

"Happy to, love," she replied to his request. It took less than a minute before the cups were ready. He rubbed a hand over Brooke's arm. "How do you feel?"

"Shaky. What happened?"

He was glad to see that her gaze was clear again. "Aunt Jerry said you were under a spell," he said cautiously.

"It was a lust spell," Aunt Jerry clarified. "Big and bad tried to ruin things for you."

"Sheesh, that's twice today," she muttered. Brooke sipped at her tea.

"Twice?" Aunt Jerry shot a concerned frown between them.

Mitch explained what happened earlier to her.

"This isn't good, but then again..." Aunt Jerry said

with a satisfied smile.

"Want to explain that?" Mitch snapped. "She was attacked earlier! How can this be good?"

"He's scared, worried, concerned," Aunt Jerry said with a flippant ease, completely unruffled.

Brooke plunked her head onto the heel of a palm. "Aunt Jerry, I can't do this," she told them, sounding on the verge of tears. "I don't know how to use the amulet." Her other hand drifted up, seeking the root to all of their problems. "Where is it?" she cried in a panicked voice.

"It's on the nightstand. I didn't know what was happening and I took it off in elimination," Mitch said, wanting to calm her. Gradually, her face regained its natural pearl luster. "And how was she spelled? I thought the house was protected."

"The house is," Aunt Jerry replied. "All that is needed is a few strands of hair or something similarly personal."

"Which would have been easy when I hugged that *thing* thinking it was you." She growled with a shudder and a sharp gesture at her aunt. "Well, I don't care how you got here. Thank you."

Aunt Jerry waved off the thanks. "Happy I could help. Actually, Mitch was the one who thought of me. Smart man you have," she said with a congenial smile.

"Yeah, how did you do that anyway? I thought I was the only one linked to Aunt Jerry." She faced him, propped up on her palm.

He shrugged a shoulder. "I don't know. She was the only one I could think of who might even be able to help."

"The bond." Brooke groaned, her eyes sliding shut with deeper remorse. "A nice aftereffect, but what else? I hope I didn't do something stupid by doing that with you."

Aunt Jerry arched a well-shaped brow, her cup pausing halfway to her mouth. "You bonded?"

Brooke began to trace a pattern on the table, avoiding her aunt's stare, looking incredibly guilty in the process. "Yes. Last night. I have no excuse for doing it. I shouldn't have used magic on him," she said gravely. "I know the rules."

"Rules?" Mitch asked. "You didn't force me, Brooke, remember?"

Aunt Jerry made a dismissive flick with her hand. "Rules were made to be broken."

Brooke's head jerked up. "You're not mad?"

"No, of course not, love. Anyone else out there?"

She shook her head quickly. "No!"

"There you go," she teased her niece. "You knew what you were doing." Aunt Jerry turned to Mitch, and he blushed under the sharp, assessing gaze. "Any other effects?" she asked him in a cool, curious voice.

He cleared his throat. "Well, scent, taste..." He gripped his cup, avoiding Jeralynna's appraising stare. "Night vision, and I'm not a hundred percent sure because I haven't tried, but I think I may be stronger."

"Wow," Aunt Jerry murmured appreciatively. "All of that?" Mitch felt his face burn from his ears up.

He noticed Brooke's jaw drop out of the corner of his eye just as all three turned to see the front door swing open. "Aunt Jerry!" Selene cried, rushing to greet her aunt.

Standing from the table, she swept her up in a long, gauze-covered hug. "Hello, love. Let me get a look at you!" she said, stepping back. "You're pregnant!" she happily cried.

Selene nodded. "Just over two months."

She held out her hands to Bram. "Bram, darling," she said, getting kisses on both cheeks.

"Good to see you," he said with a welcoming smile.

"I have an idea," Selene said. "Let's call Roman in town and have them for dinner. Please stay, Aunt Jerry."

Mitch was surprised when she looked right at him, then faced Selene again. "I would love to," she replied.

Chapter Fifteen

Brooke balanced her cup of tea between her fingers and curled against Mitch's inviting chest in one of the chairs on the porch. She'd replaced the amulet around her neck before stepping outside. There was a certain relief of at least knowing where it was. Mitch had made sure she'd had a snack so she wouldn't be gnawing something off by dinnertime. He'd also stayed glued to her side. No more opportunities to be taken by surprise by anyone or anything.

With a tender sweep, he brushed her hair aside and gave her a gentle kiss. "Feeling better?"

"Much. Thank you," she said, glorying in the feeling of him on her skin. She was still a little shaken over the lust spell. She'd almost ruined everything. Mitch had done the right thing, calling for Aunt Jerry. She was proud of his quick thinking. She wasn't sure she would've had the same reaction if he had been the one under attack.

Yet even with all that had transpired, she couldn't restrain the guilt over the bonding spell. Night vision? She rubbed weary eyes. How did he get all of those benefits from bonding with her? Her senses had increased too, she guessed, if she took the time to think about it. They definitely had increased when it came to the man holding her and keeping her warm. Remembering the discoveries when she'd lain in his arms the night before sent a rush of longing through her.

Her body hummed, sitting quietly in his arms.

She startled when the door opened and Aunt Jerry stepped out. "All right, love, I need to talk to Mitch for a minute."

"Okay," he said. He lingered a kiss against her temple, squeezing out from behind her and following her aunt into the clearing that was essentially a front yard to the house. Brooke wished she were a fly on the proverbial wall to know what they were talking about.

Mitch was such a good man. A strong man. She watched his butt in his jeans and grew heated as he paced next to Aunt Jerry's lithe, delicate frame. Damn the man, anyway! He was gorgeous, and she was helplessly, hopelessly doomed, she thought with a sense of futility. She had two days to break the code of the amulet.

She filched the amulet from beneath her shirt. It was a simple red blob of a stone, a little larger than a nickel in size, but when you studied it just right, it resembled flowing blood. It was believed that Merlin had bled to make the stone and when the magician's blood had cooled, the stone itself had formed. If it was true, Brooke couldn't swear, but considering how much trouble it was causing, the amulet meant something important to whoever wanted it. She dangled it on its chain and watched the movement in the waning sunlight.

So how could she stop mean and nasty? Was she supposed to use the stone or simply keep it safe until she confronted him? She flattened her palm and levitated the amulet, the elegant gold chain going taut. She'd used it once and hadn't even known how. Brooke hadn't figured it out yet either. She'd thrown a projection of herself, which had stopped the hunters in the car. When they tried to nab the fake Brooke,

Roman had pounced with the gun. Somehow she had managed to remain invisible throughout the whole scenario. It seemed prudent under the circumstances.

But how? What had she done then to allow her to use it at all?

Her gaze flickered out and landed on Mitch. His hair soaked up the sunlight, and he had a playful, sensually sexy grin on his mouth like he was enjoying some private joke. She licked her bottom lip, unable to look away from that expression. Warmth, longing, and need made her breath quicken. The man was driving her insane, and he was yards away. She gasped, watching in wonder as the stone suddenly began to glow.

It hovered above her hand, and as she waited with bated breath for what would come, the glow cooled until it was a red stone sitting idly in her palm once more. "Damn!" she said, growling. How did she do that? She let it sink to her palm and fisted over it. How was she going to get this done in two days? How was she going to learn enough in two days?

She frowned at the pair talking in the clearing, then stood and marched out to her Aunt Jerry and Mitch. They stopped talking as she neared. "Aunt Jerry," she said sharply. "You told me I was strong enough to do this. How, damn it? I'm not a witch," she said, denying the implication, her mouth pinching into a grim line. "Do I even look like a witch?" She spread out her arms. "I look like a very scared woman who is about to be toast in forty-eight hours." She planted her hands on her hips and glared at her aunt. Mitch was speechless as well. "I've been attacked twice for this stupid rock. Just take it back! I don't want it. I never asked for this." She thrust her fist out, but Aunt Jerry didn't take it, watching her with a mildly amused stare.

"Brooke, I've asked Aunt Jerry to do a ceremony

tomorrow night for us," he said, his tone tender. "It won't be legal to make our parents happy, but I would be very happy if you said yes."

Brooke's head spun between them. "What? What ceremony?" Wait a minute... Wasn't she just screaming at her aunt?

He cupped her hands within his and told her, "I want to have a wife tomorrow night."

"Wh-what?" Brooke's legs trembled, and she locked her knees so as not to fall on her rear.

"I asked, and she said she could. A bonding ceremony. Only this time we won't need the knife," he said with a teasing grin. "Say yes, Brooke." The tender plea in his voice pricked her eyes with tears.

"But what about after? Mitchell! I can't do this!" Her chest hurt as emotions and fears battled inside. She tried to pull away, but she was captured firm within his grasp.

He closed the inches between them, winding sifting fingers through her hair. "I have faith in you, Brooke. I know you can." His thumbs rubbed against her where he held her immobile before him. "So does she. We all do, and no matter how loudly you deny it, you're a witch. A very sexy, beautiful witch." His gaze turned molten and luscious as he watched her. "I will get on a knee if you want, but the words won't change. I want you."

"But I'm going to die in two freaking days! Doesn't that matter? To anyone?" She blinked back hot, desperate tears. Why did she have to find him now? Why did Aunt Jerry have to do this to her? Didn't anyone understand?

"Listen with your heart, love," Aunt Jerry whispered into her ear, a sweet sound of faith. "You will find the secret."

Brooke whirled, but there wasn't anyone there.

"Where did she go?"

"She went to the house." Confusion contrasted with the tenderness in his gaze. "You didn't hear her?"

When she shook her head, she almost dislodged his fingers, hair whirling around her wildly. It was no less than how she felt inside: twisted, tossed, and unsure. "She just spoke in my ear. She was right here."

Mitch tugged her close, nearly body to body. "Brooke, honey. Did you hear me? I want to marry you."

"For one night? For one night of sex?" She snarled bitterly. "I'm going to die. It feels so hopeless."

"For eternity," he assured her gently. He tipped to her mouth and kissed her. "Say yes. I have faith in you. Believe me, I've seen what you can do. You're an absolutely remarkable woman, and not for one night of sex. I want you forever." Then, when she couldn't think past the lump in her chest and the tongue that wouldn't move, he lowered himself to one knee and asked her again.

"Please say yes, Brooke. We have an audience now," he warned her with that playful grin and flashing caramel eyes. She rolled her head on her neck and peeked.

"Oh!" Everyone was on the porch. As in *everyone*. "I can't guarantee anything," she repeated, forlornly. Desperation and defeat colored everything she felt and said.

His face sobered. "I know that. Commit to me, want me the same way I want you, and we'll make it. We'll watch the rise and the fall of that full moon. That is my promise to you." He squeezed her hands, and she felt the rounded shape of the amulet in the press of their joined hands. "Please, Brooke. I'm not above begging," he said with an easy grin, the lightness of his desires returning.

She caressed him with her gaze. He'd never mentioned love. He wanted her, and he adored her, but he'd never once said that he was in love with her. Maybe it was too much to ask. She was a triple whammy. Not exactly a mother's first choice. And he wanted her in spite of all of it. Mating didn't require feelings that deep. She also knew those same emotions could grow with time, as she knew without a doubt he would stand by her, protect her to the last breath he owned. Mitch, like Bram, was a man of deep honor.

Indecision and fear of her future and his filled her until she could taste it on her tongue, until she had to blink to block the tears that couldn't make up their mind if they were going to fall or not. The sweetest brown eyes gazed up at her. She knew she couldn't turn away from what she saw. She just wasn't strong enough.

"Yes," she finally whispered, unable and maybe even unwilling to not have at least this, refusing to let the fear of the coming days steal this little taste of happiness away from her. Mitch enfolded her clasped fist, gripping the amulet, and kissed it. A roar of power raced up her arm as his lips met her skin, and she gasped. His gaze was awed as she opened her palm. The stone glowed brighter than a flare. She buried it in her fist, and he picked her up easily. She cried out loud as he held her up and spun them crazily.

Why hadn't she seen it? Why had she ignored it? Brooke loved him! It was there, in front of her, and she'd never known it. She wanted him for thirty seconds or thirty millennia! He may not have feel as deeply, but he felt enough to commit to her. If he wanted her half as much as she wanted and needed him, then anything was possible. He still might grow to love her. Why throw away this one chance when he was asking her to take it?

She had two days to get through before she could

think of the future, but she would take each moment with Mitch as a special gift. If that was all she was meant to have, then she would do her best to make sure no one else would be forced to face this threat again. She owed him that for believing in her.

* * * *

The moon was rising high by the time the column completely entered the clearing in front of the house the following evening. Everyone was there. Aunt Jerry, then Brooke, Selene, and Delilah, followed by the men. Brooke and Aunt Jerry were the only women in the loose-flowing tunics, but Aunt Jerry didn't wear anything else anyway. Not that Brooke had ever seen. Her long hair flowed as she led the procession in front of Brooke, a long black waterfall that seemed to reflect the stars overhead.

Aunt Jerry strolled ahead until she found a spot where she was comfortable, then the others took their places to either side, facing her in a phalanx formation. Mitch's fingers reached for hers, twining them together, and she smiled but kept her gaze on her aunt. Together, they walked to stand before her aunt, and at her motion, knelt.

"This evening," Aunt Jerry began. "We bear witness to the joining of Brooke and Mitchell in bonding. This is a commitment they have made between themselves. They share in each other's destiny and future. We grant them our blessing to rise and be joined."

He rose first and helped her stand, then they faced each other, and Brooke knew she'd never seen a more handsome face in her life. He was breathtaking surrounded by the ambient lights of Mother Nature. Strong, secure in his place, with eyes only for her. His brown gaze sparkled with warmth while the curve of his mouth beckoned to her. That same gaze left her breathless with the depth of wanting, with the yearning she knew they both felt, the rightness of the moment. This was meant to be.

"Each family has granted their blessing with a gift for their bonding." Aunt Jerry paused as Morgan stepped forward. "As the eldest, Morgan has blessed this union with a gift of the earth." She opened the carved wood box Morgan offered her. "These are from the earth, from the sun, and from the elements of time." She held up the gold Byzantine intertwined bracelets, one of fair thickness, and offered it to Mitch.

"I accept your gift, brother," he said respectfully as Aunt Jerry clasped it on him.

She did the same with a lighter version for Brooke. "I accept your gift, brother," Brooke intoned, mesmerized as the gold circled her wrist, emulating the heavier one on Mitch. A tingle of awareness traveled up her arm as the weight of the bracelet settled to her skin. Knife or no, there was just as much magic in this bonding as there had been the night they'd promised themselves to each other with the help of a small carving knife.

Jeralynna spoke up again. "As the protector of this family, Roman has blessed this union with a gift of courage and strength."

Roman approached the pair. He sank to a knee before his sister first. "I offer my undying loyalty to the pack and to this family," he said in a rumbled voice. Roman rose and offered her a kiss on the forehead, and she whispered her acceptance, then shook Mitch's hand in a forearm clasp of brothers. He took his place next to Delilah, holding a sleeping Adrian.

"As the healer of the family, Selene has offered her compassion and ability." Selene stepped forward and repeated the pledge Roman had spoken. Instead of a hand clasp, she gave Mitch a kiss on either cheek. Then she took her place next to Bram.

"Have you each a cord to bind the other?" she asked.

Mitch handed his over. "I do."

Brooke did the same with a matching long, white silk cord.

Jeralynna twisted the two lengths together, creating a thick twined rope, and explained in a reverent, carrying tone, "With these cords you are willingly binding yourself to your mate." She began to wrap the lengths over their wrists. "You each agree to uphold this union, to remain bound by the laws of nature forever to each other?"

They responded in unison. "I do." Brooke felt weightless as the rope neared its end.

Aunt Jerry finished wrapping their wrists in an intricate pattern until only a few inches of cord remained. "Remember, the end of this twined bonding will always be enough to hang yourself if you break your vow," she stated for their ears only with a straight face.

When she was done, Jeralynna rested caring hands on their joined wrists. Mitch twined his fingers through Brooke's, and her heart skipped with a pounding thud. Their touching palms seemed to make a silent statement, bound together by cord, but so much more: body, heart, and soul. She blinked, breathing slowly to not burst into deliriously overwhelmed tears.

"Their union is bound and witnessed," Aunt Jerry announced. "They have accepted each other by the laws of nature, one mate. We may now give them a wish of welcome into this pack and into our family."

Jeralynna hugged Mitchell, then Brooke, stepping away to allow the others to wish them well. As each person did, they left until it was only the two of them alone, bound together, standing in the moonlit clearing, the lights of the house at their backs.

"Wow." Mitch breathed wondrously. His eyes sparkled under the starlight. Dressed in a dark green wrapped tunic over trousers and leather boots Aunt Jerry had supplied, he was the most handsome man she'd ever known. He hadn't even made a fuss about the wardrobe. They could do satin and tuxes later. Tonight, he was perfect.

"Do you feel married?" she asked him, subdued by the moment they'd shared.

"Not yet. I'm letting it soak in. That was incredible," he said with whispered awe. He raised their bound, clasped hands. His face sobered, but he still glowed with a happiness that beckoned like a gentle wave over her skin. "I wouldn't call it married, exactly," he said. "It feels deeper than that."

"I know, I feel it too," she agreed, completely awed by sensation.

He touched a hand to her cheek. "You are beautiful." Leaning down, he swept a tender kiss across her mouth and her legs threatened to buckle. "When you walked out, I couldn't believe I was the one who was getting you."

With an arm behind her knees, he cradled her against his chest. She reached around his neck, and he said with a devilish twinkle, "I hope you realize you may not be home before sunrise." He lowered his mouth to her neck, finding skin and nerves with lips and tongue, and he growled deep, sending a primal charge through her. The message was clear. Tonight, she would be his, completely, irrevocably. He marched through the trees, and she forgot what she was going to say.

Mitch carried her the entire way to the clearing

where she had deemed she would meet her fate, but tonight was theirs. He set her with the gentlest care to her feet.

"You must be stronger. You're not even winded," she pointed out.

He rocked on his heels. "You're right. I feel great." An unwavering hand hovered over the wrapped silk cords, tying them both together. "Are you ready to become unbound by your mate?"

"I am," she said breathlessly. Her heart raced as he reached for the end of the cords. His touch was the sweetest experience as he unwound the rope binding them together, as mates, as husband and wife. It slid free of its last circuit and fell to the ground in a small heap. He removed the tunic from his body, laying it on the cool grass, and helped her stretch out on it. "I know it's not a feather mattress," he joked as he laid down with her, but his laughter disappeared when she wandered her fingers over his chest. His eyes heated with a chocolaty glitter as he followed her touch, seemingly enthralled by the paleness of her skin.

"I have everything I need right here." She continued to caress him. "You're beautiful," she told him, lifting up on an elbow and kissing his jaw. He groaned.

He filled his fingers with her hair, and she melted from the hungry heat in his gaze. "I have to do this," he warned her as he hovered over her. Her eyes shut like slammed windows when his tongue crawled up her neck. "This was the longest day of my life, not having that." He purred, hot breath washing over her. "Not being able to taste you, touch you, kiss you." She moaned when his teeth hit nerves and flesh.

She reached for him and dug into muscle and warm skin. Her body awoke with a raging flame of desire as he moved across her neck to nip at her chin.

"Mmm, still the sweetest candy for me," he murmured against her. She shivered as his hand grazed her through her tunic with a learning touch.

Rising over her on an elbow, he covered her mouth with his and she trembled at the electric shock of his kiss. Her hands locked behind him, gripping him tightly as the only stable point in her universe. His tongue danced over her lips, tasting and licking, then he thrust between them, claiming her to her last thought. She whimpered and moaned as flames scorched her from the inside out.

"Oh lord," he said, groaning against her lips.

She couldn't think enough to blink. A delicate stroke teased at her breast, and she jumped. He curved a palm to her flesh, warming her even as she shivered. She moaned like a dark wind, deep and endless. She became enraptured by the bombardment of new sensations.

"Brooke," he said with a voice rich in desire. "I want to see you."

Shifting backward, he knelt in front of her and helped her sit up to shimmy out of the shift and tunic. He dropped it away and caressed from her shoulders to her calves. She felt electric beneath his touch. Tenderly, he settled onto the tunic. She cried out endlessly on gasps of wondered passion as his mouth delivered sensual shocks all over her body, light heated sips and decadent kisses that devoured her.

He traveled from shoulder to breast to stomach to thigh. She swirled in a maelstrom of feeling, tossed and tumbled without purchase as his mouth, teeth, and tongue invaded and conquered her. When she couldn't find him at her finger's ends, she gripped the tunic and begged for mercy.

"Not a chance," he said from somewhere, the tremor of his needs deepening his voice, making her body ache and burn. "I've waited forever to do this." His tongue traced a wet path along her ribs and she squirmed, dipping into her belly button. Tight, controlling fingers massaged and kneaded her body, leaving no part of her untouched. "God, I can smell how wet you are!" The raw ache in his words sent a pulsing shiver through her.

"Is that bad?" she managed through dry lips, then cried out as he found one hot peak with the same tongue that had been traveling along her body in blatant enjoyment.

"It's the biggest turn-on of my life," he said, groaning against her. "I had no idea all those times. You've been as hot and achy as I have." He encased her breast between his burning lips, and she cried out in vivid pleasure. She felt the grass beneath her pull up in tufts as wave after wave of ecstasy coursed over her.

Rushed gasps were all she could manage when he finally released her from the sweet torture of his lips. She quivered on every nerve, ached in every cell as he continued to adore her body. She moaned in shock when he touched her center with delving fingers. A blast of naked demanding heat, unlike anything she'd ever experienced, overtook her as his fingers opened her further. He murmured in appreciation, gliding his fingers through her tight curls.

She cried into the night, and her legs snapped closed in reaction to the intensity of his touch, unprepared for the shock. "It's all right, sweet. You know I won't hurt you." He caressed her again, and she melted like snow under the gentleness of his palm. She trembled in wanting, passion arching through her system with his hand touching, his fingers delving into her slick body.

Her entire body shattered when his tongue flicked into her. She screamed as endless ripples of pleasure washed over her. His tongue danced across hot damp flesh. Shock after shock coursed over her, centered beneath the gentle tug and sip of lips on aching skin. Brooke screamed as the ecstasy boiled over, sweeping her away on a river of bliss and passion.

Her limbs shook as her body floated to the tunic. Literally. She'd forced herself inches off the ground.

"Easy, sweet. Come back to me," he coaxed her. "I guess it's a good thing we are all the way out here." He chuckled lightly. "I'd have a hard time explaining that one. Not without sounding conceited."

She licked her lips, feeling her heart fall into place. She gradually recognized the loving meandering of fingers on skin when she opened her eyes again. She found him propped over her, caressing her tenderly, watching her with an adoring, if slightly concerned, expression.

"You still alive?" Mitch asked with a quirky smile.

"I have no idea," she replied breathily. "Kiss me."

"Your wish, my sweet." He set his lips to hers, and Brooke shuddered with the shock. Her hands roamed over him again. She didn't move as she felt his weight rise over her. She was a liquid pool of desire inside. The weight wasn't unwelcome as he paused, his engorged shaft between her trembling thighs. "Are you ready? I'll try not to hurt you," he said as he cradled her.

"I won't feel it, not now." She sighed, full of passionate wonder.

Her eyes popped open as bliss sparked over her again with brilliant explosions when he pressed into her. She groaned, feeling the heat of his body as he filled hers, so slowly.

"God, you're tight." He hissed as he pushed further, taking care to not hurt her, letting her body accept him.

All Brooke wanted was more. He was driving her insane! He kissed her passionately as he let her adjust, gliding slowly back and forth over her. She felt the vibration of his growl deep in his chest as he rocked back and forth. She raked her nails over his in crazed need. He moved once more, and the sharp pain was a mere flash of discomfort.

They shuddered as one, and he froze. "Shh, it will pass," he said, soothing her. He groaned, tightening all over with a tight jaw when she flexed her hips, gripping around the heat of his length deep inside her.

"Easy, sweet. I don't want to hurt you."

She bit his shoulder. "Then you better finish this, Mitch! I'm coming apart at the edges!" she told him in a throaty whimper. Flames of hunger licked at her from the inside out. She twitched, arching into him, and he moaned, sucking a hard kiss to her neck.

"Oh man. A woman who knows what she wants," he said as he started to thrust again, both becoming lost in their passions.

Brooke cried out and moaned wildly as he filled her. She hooked her legs around his thighs, urging him to go deep, needing him to complete her. She threw her head and cried out a lusty wail.

"Again!" she cried when he answered her pleas, driving into her fiercely. "Oh God, oh God," she shouted, oblivious to anything but the man in her arms.

Her release hit her like a lightning strike and flowed from her hair to her toes. It was a primal surge unlike anything she'd ever imagined as she detonated. He roared a heartbeat later, a male possessive sound that melted her into a satisfied puddle under his weight.

She embraced him as his body collapsed forward, his breathing deep and rasping against her ear. She couldn't think, only feel as her body absorbed his heartbeat, returning to some semblance of reality.

"Um, Brooke. I don't want to alarm you, but could you put us back on the ground?" he asked her warily a few seconds later.

She brought her mind nearly online and realized she was feeling a draft on her skin. She smiled into his neck. "Sorry." She giggled and focused on the tunic until it rubbed beneath her again.

"We need to work on keeping you grounded," he said with a released breath. He tightened his arms around her and tucked his face into her. She squealed when he rolled, landing her on top of his chest.

"Hello, beautiful," he whispered with dreamy eyes. He reached up and tucked her hair away from her face. "So, are you going to put screamer on your next job application?"

Brooke felt her face flare. "I had no idea." She searched his face. "I did it wrong, didn't I?" She collapsed against him, mortified. He began to shake beneath her, and she realized a second later that he was laughing at her. "What's so funny?" she demanded.

"Brooke, you couldn't do anything wrong if you tried." He pulled her up until she rested on a shoulder, her body half on and half off his. "No, you didn't do anything wrong. I just wasn't expecting it." He gave her a stare and a wink. "To be honest, I loved it. But if we ever have neighbors," he said with a shrug, his grin tucked away while his eyes sparkled with mischief, "I could get into a lot of trouble. People thinking I'm murdering you or something."

"You weren't exactly the epitome of a vow of silence either," she shot back, punching his shoulder with a small fist.

"Want to make me do it again?" he challenged lowly. His mouth had curved into a delicious dare of a smile.

She didn't wait to argue but tugged his hair,

arching him to her exploration. "We'll see who screams," she threatened. But instead of attacking him blindly she started small and slow, making circles with her tongue and sucking on nerves until his hands were gripping the tunic like hers had been just moments before.

His taste had intensified with the heat of passion, and Brooke reveled in it, licking and sucking and biting with little nips until Mitch was the one panting and groaning through his teeth. She raked her nails over his ribs, and his entire chest quaked. "I'm liking that," she told him as she lowered her lips to his skin. "Let's see how well I learn," she said right before she found one of his nipples and stroked it with a tongue.

His entire body surged with desire as she rolled him between her lips. She felt the growl against her tongue when he arched against her teasing mouth. She bathed his body with her tongue, feeling his reaction through every pore.

She drifted over his chest and dipped her tongue into his navel. His air left him with a hissed exclamation. She roamed fingers down his thigh, imitating his earlier caresses, and watched as his body reacted and pulsed. "Holy cow!" she cried. "It's a good thing we already know it fits," she said with a wry twist of her lips. "I might have been scared otherwise."

"Is that a compliment?" he asked through a gasping moan.

"Let's just say fair is fair," she taunted throatily, then licked her tongue up his length and thrilled at the pure animalistic groan he released.

"Oh man, Brooke," he said, sucking in air. He tossed his head and groaned louder when she did it again.

It was a powerful feeling having a man lying so welcoming under her. She gloried in it. She followed his heaving chest for a second until she had the courage to go a step further.

He shouted a deep bellow when she met his length with lips and light dragging teeth, his entire body quivering like a live wire beneath her. She closed her eyes and took him between her lips, her tongue savoring the heat of his skin, of his desire. He filled her mouth, letting the natural craving guide her, and he shouted her name for her efforts. Her whole body responded, igniting.

His hands grasped for her, raising her above him, his eyes luscious with need and hunger. "Ride me, sweet," he begged. With his hands controlling her hips, he pulled her high, guided her to slide over him, settling her to sink completely over his flesh. New sensations rocketed over her with a ferocious feeling.

His fingers held her, urged her, dug into her thighs and waist as she rocked over him. Her nails scraped across his chest as the energy flowed, as the climax rolled up her spine. It rushed through her with the velocity of a comet, spiraling to where they were joined.

He thrust upward, urging her to come apart with a taut, hungry pace. She screamed when her body shattered. He thrust once, twice, and bellowed, shouting her name. Ripples electrified her nerves as her release overwhelmed her into a sublime state of bliss.

Exhausted, she fell forward across his chest. His arms looped over her, and all she could do was breathe.

Chapter Sixteen

It was time. Brooke had done everything she could think of, had prepared as much as she knew how. In her arms she carried a linen cloth and candles, and she would make one plea for surcease. If it was not answered, then she would have to take care of it herself. She was prepared regardless of the answer.

Brooke had rested for the day and bathed using the oil-scented water Aunt Jerry had given her. She wore the simple linen sheath and gauze tunic of her status, but she didn't wear the white. Now she wore the crimson. The only jewelry she wore was the woven bracelet she had received from her brother the night before and the amulet. It rested against her skin beneath the sheath, safe.

The sun would be setting soon, and she needed to leave. She paused at the edge of the porch and listened to the breeze, finding the smells of life around her. She was at peace with her decision.

She had experienced real love. Without looking, she knew he was right behind her, a solid wall of support and devotion, absolute belief in her. He had kissed her passionately for endless moments before she had walked through the door. He believed in her, even though he was scared for her, without saying the words. He knew as well as she did that if she didn't face this, whether it had been her problem or not, they had no future. And after last night and this morning, she would give every breath she had to guarantee a future for them.

She wanted him, adored him. Loved him. Brooke would die if only to know that Mitch could live and the family would not be threatened. She was calm with her decision.

She didn't turn around. She cherished him close to her heart already. Taking that final look would be like making a final goodbye, admitting that this was the end of their time, and she refused to believe that was the case. Feeling the setting sun on her skin, she took the first step toward her destiny.

Brooke found the clearing when the shadows were at their longest, moments before the crest of the sun would begin its final, elusive disappearance. She set the bundle she carried on the ground and spread the cloth, setting out the candles to mark the edges. She lit them, invoking the passages of the goddesses where her power originated from. Diana, Aphrodite, Andrasta, Selene, Luna, Nimue. She asked each one for the strength to persevere, to grant her the courage to stay with her decision and to not falter in her moment of need.

Her voice was quiet but strong as she chanted, moving with easy grace around the cloth, lighting the candles one by one as shadows floated and melded into the dusk before the dark. She felt strong, welcomed the blessing of her power as it filled her. She warmed with the light of that strength as it grew inside of her.

Her voice rose in cadence as she repeated the chant again, as full night draped over her and the world around her, dancing purposefully until she was breathless, when she collapsed to her knees, her head bowed, and waited for their answer.

A single breeze trickled over her patient body, and she shivered. The candle flames flickered but didn't die. The power wrapping around her was warm and kept her from losing all hope.

They could not stop him, but she had their support. It was more than she had hoped for.

She spoke reverently. "I accept your decision, and I am thankful. I will abide by your choice and defend my pack to my fullest ability."

Brooke rolled to her feet and swept her palm midair across the cloth, the candles dying instantly. She folded the cloth and gathered the candles. She peered over her shoulder. The sun had set.

She made a circuit of the clearing, chanting a protection spell four times, granting each of the four winds to come to her aid to help her. Standing firm, searching the sky, she knew she was as prepared as she could be, as strong as she physically knew how to be. The glow of the blood moon was rising. It was time.

She stepped to the side, the full moon filling the sky behind her as a large, red, spherical sentinel, and she raised her arms, chanting the summoning spell.

"Belphegor, Asmodeus, Satan, Lucifer, Beelzebub, Leviathan, Mammon. I call on the seven princes of hell in the name of Belphegor." The names flowed off her tongue, her voice lyrical, riding into the night to carry her wish.

"I summon you to face my challenge."

"Hear my voice and obey my summons."

A drop of sweat rolled between her shoulder blades, but she ignored it. She repeated the summons, then let her hands sink to her sides to wait. It didn't take long. Whether that was a good sign or not, she couldn't know.

An arrogant, graveled snarl filled the clearing. She fought off the feeling of dread it brought to her. "Who dares to summon me?" it thundered, leaves shaking in its wake, in horror. "Mortal witch, thee try me." The voice growled, a demonic vibration that left a heinous, bitter taste on her tongue and a darker cloud on her mind.

"I am the keeper of the blood heart. You and I have a word to share," she informed it coolly.

"Ah, yes," it replied in a purr, the voice rolling between the trees. A wind whipped through the branches overhead, blowing her tunic and hair into a swirling mass. A man appeared from the tree line as it died down. He was easily as tall as Roman but wiry with midnight hair and moss-green eyes that flashed with fire in the moonlight. "Thee have made quite a bit of sport, daughter of the moon," the imposter said with a menacing snarl. "But I think it is time." Its hand lifted between them with a confident sneer on its thin face but when she resisted the pull of his demand, it bellowed its anger into the night.

"How dare you resist me?" it shouted as the wind blew again.

"I have come to ask you to leave this quest, Belphegor. The amulet does you no good, does not encourage greed, avarice, or sloth. Be gone, Belphegor, and let the curse of your name be heard no more!" she cried in challenge.

Her face remained expressionless when its pale skin split, cracking the face before her like a giant egg. Her heart jumped. The sweat drop grew a family. Brooke didn't dare blink.

Bony brown, scaly fingers knifed through the skull of the body and split the form apart with a horrible sound of ripping flesh. Daggerlike, pointed nails covered in blood glinted red in the distorted moonlight. She fought the impulse to flee at the horror of the sight, knowing her revulsion was the intended reaction.

She pinched her mouth tight to lock the gasp behind her lips as the stench of death and putrid odor pummeled her. The demon stepped out of the fake human body, throwing aside the shell as easily as clothing and with about as much concern. Brooke didn't know if that form had been of an actual person, possessed, or if it was an illusion of the creature before her. There wasn't room to allow for the distraction.

The creature's jaws were elongated into points, teeth that ground together like stone as it moved its jaw. Leathery wings unfurled from its back, whipping the ground debris into a cyclone as it stretched to its full size. Its legs were long and gaunt. Bones pressed against the scaly skin of its horrid body, thin ribs countable as it flexed.

It arched its length and cried a shattering scream, a wind rising to mock her power. It shook in rage at her.

"Feel thee no fear, daughter of the moon?" it said in a thundering voice. "Dare thee not quake in my presence?" It blinked at her with a dark malevolent stare of pure hatred and evil.

"I feel no fear in the presence of a bug," she said, keeping her voice calm and even. The demon would feed on fear and would be incensed by her lassitude.

It threw its head to the heavens and screamed again. It took a step toward her, and she shivered. "I demand you leave this quest, Belphegor. You have fed on the souls of two innocents for your purpose. No more shall die in your name!" She thrust up a hand as a sharp light appeared. She launched the fireball and watched as it splintered against him. The demon barely flinched.

It laughed a mocking, pitying sound. "Is that the best thee have? Insults and weakness?" it taunted, but even then, its voice sounded like a roar of death.

"I am a daughter of the moon, a daughter of the blood, a daughter of nature, and a daughter of Wicca," she stated back, keeping her sights on the being before her. *No fear,* she silently said. *No fear.* It took another step at her.

She raised her hands and called on the power of her being to hurl a shock wave at it. The impact made it stagger. Its teeth ground together in fury as it balanced, its flaming eyes savage in the light of the red moon.

"I have played enough! Thee shall pay for thy insolence, daughter of hell!" It screamed as it lunged at her. "Give me the amulet!" It raised its claws, and she deflected, letting it pass by her to crash to the ground in an enraged mass.

"Be thy gone!" she commanded. She was starting to feel the strain as she leaped away. It was wearing on her to deflect the creature and fight back at the same time. It rose with a whip of its wings, hefting itself to its feet with a snarl of hatred.

Finger bones popped and crunched as it flexed and fisted its hands. It tilted its head, and the bones snapped with a loud sound. "Thee will pay, daughter of hell," it said in an ominous voice. It stepped forward again.

* * * *

Mitch followed her with his heart in his gaze as she walked away from him, fighting with every cell of his being and soul to not leap after her, carry her away, and keep her safe. She was peaceful, holding an ethereal beauty in the late-day sunlight. She glowed; that was the best way to explain it.

He gripped the rail of the porch to restrain himself from flying after her. He needed her, he wanted her. He loved her! He couldn't let her do this!

He heard a crunch and sought the source, feeling a wave of shock. He had split the wood, a long crack beneath his hands, and felt the sharp split as if it were inside, as if his soul had shattered in two with fear. His head tumbled forward, desperate for control. When he sought her in the clearing again, she was gone.

He searched the trees, but there was nothing of her. His soul chilled with bleak despair. Helpless had nothing on how he felt.

He didn't look up when a hand found his shoulder. He didn't have to. He knew who it was. Roman's deep voice proved him right.

"Have faith in her," he said quietly.

Mitch could barely talk; his tongue was swollen and dry, a dead weight. "Why did it have to be her?" he finally managed. It sounded bitter to his ears.

"If anyone else had a chance, it would not have been," Roman stated calmly. "You love her?"

"To my last breath," Mitch said without a single hesitation or doubt. "She can't die, Roman!" He bit out the words through clenched teeth. "Not now! Hell."

"Does she know?" Roman asked.

Mitch shook his head. "I never told her. I knew why she felt she needed to do this. I couldn't be selfish." Even though he wanted to be with the last fiber of his being, he thought. Mitch ached as the rough edge of his fear seared his throat. "Everyone's life is at stake." He jerked his hands from the rail, rolling his shoulders. After a moment he rested on his arms, his hands clenched in front of him as he bowed over clasped fists.

He blinked as the shadows disappeared and night swooped in on them. "It won't be long now, will it?" Mitch asked with a sense of dread.

"No." Roman's supporting hand fell free, but he didn't leave.

"She's your favorite, isn't she? That's why you're so hard on her," Mitch asked.

"You can't breathe a word to Selene," he said on a lowered growl. When Mitch agreed, Roman continued. "Yes. She's always been impulsive, tender, kindhearted." Roman sighed. "Selene is sensible. Bram was the first and only impulsive thing she ever attempted. She's been laid out like a road map since she was born. Brooke is different."

Mitch heard Roman's affection for his sister, losing some of the gruff, worried weight. "Brooke isn't the baby, but she feels like it. When she would spend her summers with Aunt Jerry, I would get worried, seeing so much of her change. I knew she was going to be like Aunt Jerry, but I didn't like it."

Roman settled against the rail with Mitch, avoiding the split. He didn't say anything about it, only shooting Mitch a questioning glance. "Morgan and I have always kept the girls close, but you can only do that for so long," he said on an exhalation. "Until they grow up."

"And she's all grown up now," Mitch said.

"Yes, she is. And she's even stronger than any of us could have imagined." There was pride in that, but it only added more worry to Mitch's concerns.

Mitch kicked at the porch. "Jeralynna said she was this generation's her. Is that supposed to be a good thing?" He caught Roman's shocked expression.

"I guess it depends on who you ask. I don't think Dad is going to be thrilled, but he's male. The women of his life are more important than precious gems." Roman chuckled knowingly. "Do you know that you're the only one who calls Aunt Jerry by her name and doesn't get destroyed for it?" Roman clapped him on the shoulder again. "I guess we didn't hit it off right away, but you're all right."

"Yeah, you too," Mitch agreed. He looked up with his heart in his throat and found the red nimbus of the moon. "I guess she was right. Brooke knows what she's doing. I just couldn't take it if she lost." His heart pinched all over again, and his breathing shortened. He fought off the dread clamoring at him at the thought. He knew she could do this. The knowledge did little to ease his terror for her.

"What was she right about?" Roman asked curiously.

Mitch gestured out across the clearing in the direction they had gone last night, the way he knew she had disappeared tonight. Last night and this morning had been very special, even for a regular guy like him. He would forever hold those memories deep inside, where she'd touched him the most.

He cleared his throat.

"Brooke told me a few things this morning before we returned for her to prepare," he said solemnly. "She knew the moon would be a blood moon, for one thing," he told Roman carefully. A sudden chill rocked his spine, seeing the red sphere for himself just above the trees. "Hey, isn't that like an omen or something? Didn't sailors have a saying about the red moon?"

When Roman didn't answer right away, Mitch turned toward him and his stomach fell straight to his shoes. Roman never paled, but he had, his gaze staring unblinking at the same red moon right in front of both of them.

"Roman, talk to me, damn it!" Mitch shook his arm, and Roman blinked. "Tell me!" Mitch demanded.

Roman cursed on a low hiss.

"I'm not liking the sound of that," Mitch said.

"It's not good," Roman finally admitted between tight teeth. "Christ! She should have said something!"

Mitch's chest began to hurt painfully again. "Why? What does it mean?"

Their heads snapped collectively as a howl that

wasn't human ripped through the forest with a chill of death in its wake. "Oh, God!" Mitch's skin crawled as the sound disappeared. Every hair on his body stood up. He couldn't stay there and do nothing! Brooke was in danger!

He shot off the porch, barely hearing Roman's order to not follow after her. Mitch was not going to let her do this alone. *God, how stupid can a guy get,* he berated himself as he ran, ducking branches and jumping over fallen debris. Letting her face whatever this was alone! *Idiot, coward. A mate does not allow his own to fight alone.* He knew that! He'd witnessed how tight this family was, and he had let her just walk away. Hell, no man worth his skin would ever allow a woman to fight a battle alone.

He heard another screeching scream and fought the urge to cover his ears. It rang through his head, sending a sharp pain between his eyes. He blinked and forced it out of his thoughts. His heart pounded forcefully against his ribs, but he allowed nothing to slow him down.

The clearing was almost a mile from the cabin. He had to make it! She couldn't die! He raced through the thick trees, ignoring the scratches whipping branches left on his arms. He barreled through it all without caring, without thought of anything but reaching her. He had to be there! He had to help! Somehow, some way, he would help her. He knew he was getting close when the smell of putrid flesh and blood barreled over him. He took a deep breath and found Brooke beneath the stench. "Thank God," he whispered, praying she was still safe and alive.

A few minutes later, he skidded to fall hard against a tree at the edge of the clearing. He could see her, glowing in the moonlight, her crimson tunic swirling around her body. It didn't take long to spot the form on the ground with his improved vision.

Mitch turned his head and stifled the gag the sight of that thing had prompted. It was a creature of nightmares. Tall, skinny, bony, covered in a dark, leathery skin that crackled when it moved. His eyes widened when, with a burst, the beast flapped those awful wings and rose from the ground to stand again. The stench was unbelievable, worse than any burning thing he could name. He heard it in his head when it talked, a cackling grinding sound that was unlike any voice Mitch had ever heard. Bone grated against bone, leather snapped and popped as it stalked around Brooke. Its wings flared in anger as it moved.

A high-pitched wind flared from nowhere and forced Brooke to stumble, but she stayed on her feet. She glared at the beast and raised her arms. "Belphagor," she said, her voice crying above the wind, "I will end this now!"

Mitch stared in stunned shock as a flare flew from her hands and wrapped around the creature like a rope. It struggled within the coiled bonds and screamed. Mitch closed his eyes, fighting off the nausea the scream of hatred created in him. It screamed again, and Mitch couldn't hold back. He propped himself against the tree with a shoulder and lost everything in his stomach, retching violently in reaction to the ear-splitting decibels.

He gasped and spit, running a shaking hand across his mouth. Momentarily weakened, he sagged helplessly against the tree. He blinked, fighting the remnants of his tortured stomach.

"Damn!" He breathed deeply. He could only watch as the creature tossed its head and laughed, pushing against the bonds Brooke had placed on it. She stumbled when it broke free of her control.

The creature's voice rolled again, death and

thunder. "Witch, thee are no match for a son of hell!" it crowed. "I will own thee!"

"I have not even begun!" she challenged. "Your name is a curse heard nevermore!"

The creature stalked forward, and she reached inside her tunic. Mitch saw the creature freeze like a wall of ice when it realized what Brooke was holding. Mitch caught his breath, his heart pounding.

"Please, baby," he whispered. *Please be safe!*

Mitch froze as the creature's head swiveled completely around on neck bones. Empty holes for eyes stared right at him. Clear through him.

"You!" it shouted gleefully. Its gaze flared instantly into twin pyres of red, volcanic hatred.

Mitch shouted in agony as a claw of sharp knives gripped him around his lungs and dragged him forward, forcing him to his knees on the cool grass only a few feet away from the stench of the creature and Brooke's alarmed gaze. Sweat broke out instantly on Mitch's forehead as he fought to stay coherent, to not black out from the pain ravaging his insides. He blinked, squaring his double vision.

"Mitch," Brooke cried in an anguished voice.

"Thy mate?" the creature purred in a seductive, silky voice. "He will die!"

Mitch screamed as the claw of knives twisted his insides, rending his lungs to shreds. Stars imploded on his eyelids, blood red and agonizing.

"No!" she yelled. The hand released him, and he could breathe. He shuddered in violent waves as the pain receded, but he felt like he'd been sliced from the inside out without anesthesia.

"Daughter of hell," the creature roared, making Mitch's ears ring. "Give me the amulet!"

Mitch fought the rising spots, the agony from the demon attacks numbing him. He took a deep breath and groaned as pain racked him anew. "Brooke!" he tried to shout. "Don't do it!" It was no more than a croak, but somehow he knew she heard him. Mitch noticed the creature stalk up to her, glaring from overhead. Brooke clutched the amulet in her fist, her fearful gaze locked on him. He shook his head, feeling pain everywhere. "Don't, Brooke!"

"Will he live or die?" the creature asked in a rumbled, disinterested tone, the sound harsher than tumbling boulders.

Her terrified gaze was glued on him. He licked his lips, tasting bile and blood. He didn't know if it was from his bitten tongue or if his insides were on their way to being on his outside. "Brooke, don't give it to him!" He snarled at the creature, gathering enough strength to shout at it. "Take me, you asshole! Leave them alone!"

Brooke screamed as he shouted in blistering agony.

"Thee dare to speak to me, human filth?"

Mitch lived on short breaths for several minutes. His shirt was soaked with sweat as he weakly rested on his calves. His hands hung limply at his sides. He didn't care; he was half dead already.

"I said, leave them alone," he said, grinding out the words.

It took Mitch several seconds to realize he wasn't in renewed pain. He looked up and focused, feeling a glacial chill wrap around his very being.

Brooke was speaking, the creature listening with avid intensity. Her head dipped, as if in defeat, and she faced Mitch, taking one long, loving look. He knew with a sinking feeling what she was doing. It froze him to his bones. She'd made a bargain with the devil himself.

"Brooke! No! I love you!" he cried as loudly as he could, uncaring if it earned him the wrath of hell.

Mitch watched as a tear trekked from her eye, cutting a shimmered path down her pale cheek. "And I love you," she whispered.

The next few seconds happened so fast, he would never be able to put the whole scene together. He followed her every motion as she dropped the stone from her grip, crying out in shocked surprise when the amulet lit up like a skylight, the shine of its power enveloping her with a ruby-red glow as she thrust her hands at the creature's body.

It wrapped those hideously bony fingers around her neck and screamed in victory just as she found its chest with her fingers. The following explosion and burst of light knocked him out cold.

Chapter Seventeen

Mitch frowned when his carving blade slipped, glancing at the knick on his knuckle. He wiped away the line of blood, swiping it on his blue trousers. He wasn't worried about the cut. It would heal in a few minutes, as small as it was. He stared at the shape in his hands with a hollow feeling. It was the cedar block he had started at Bram's. Only it wasn't a bear. It was something that meant far more to him.

Three months had passed since the red blood moon. Three long months without Brooke. After the battle, Roman had found him incapacitated and unconscious at the clearing, bringing him to the cabin to be with family as they all came to grips with what had happened.

Mitch stayed with Bram for more than a week until his chest had stopped aching with every breath he drew. Yet the agonizing pain the demon had inflicted on him hadn't lasted near as long as the pain he still carried.

His chest ached from the shattered pain of a broken heart. It would likely never end, a constant reminder of the woman he loved.

Brooke was gone. She'd sacrificed herself for him. For all of them. He had no idea where the amulet was, but it had ceased to matter without her there.

Jeralynna contacted him at least once a week and told him she couldn't feel its powers being used in any way, which told her it was safe. Mitch was glad of that at least. The pack would remain safe and unharmed because of Brooke's sacrifice.

Today was his last day with Tory in St. Louis. He was returning to the pack. They were his family now, all of them, and his brother. If she had lived, he would have wanted to be close. It was what Brooke would have wanted too. The family was like that, all of them, including his brother. They stood next to each other through all their individual trials.

He just learned that fact a little too late.

Bram and Selene were doing great, and their baby was doing fine. As much as it killed him, he refused to turn his back twice, to walk away from his brother and the family he now had through him, through Brooke. His nephew Adrian—he almost managed a smile at the thought that he now had a nephew—was a little charmer. He was going to kill the ladies when he grew up. He had Roman's straight black hair and Del's blue eyes. The kid had it going on for him, that was for sure.

Mitch sighed as he sculpted the shape of the wood with the knife's sharp edge. God, he missed her. Life just wasn't the same without her. He had come home, hoping to find a reprieve of some sort with his old life, but it hadn't happened.

There was no life at his apartment, nothing worth living for in St. Louis. His old life was gone. Without Brooke, his future was bleak, but he would go on. Brooke had given everything for the family.

He refused to disgrace her sacrifice.

Jeralynna was having a hard time admitting the truth, not that he could blame her. Brooke was her protégé. She never once mentioned Brooke as gone either, almost as if saying the words out loud made it reality.

He worked his throat and blinked, keeping the tears of pain from becoming real. Three months later it still stabbed worse than a hot, twisting knife. To have found a woman like her, who could be every reason he could live for, then to lose her, because he'd loved her enough to offer himself, and she couldn't let that happen. He grimaced and then began cutting into the wood again.

He carved the toes and the teeth, taking loving care with the tail and ears. And he knew for a fact that they could smile.

He guessed things had settled as he'd tried to regain the world he had. He'd done his shifts, made the emergency calls without thinking about it, just like he always had, but he'd felt a place apart from everything since he'd returned.

Like the day he'd come on duty, and walking past the pumper truck had pointed out a gas leak to Mack, a pinprick of a drip that wouldn't have damaged anything, provided they'd never been close to a flame. It would have been found during maintenance, but that wasn't for another month. Or when they'd had to paint and needed to move the cabinets, which he did, alone. He'd just shrugged and claimed he'd been taking vitamins. And that was nothing to say of Jeralynna's assessment of his knowledge of a flame, of what direction it would feed on, of where the hotspots were without being in the inferno, feeling the waves and hunger of the flames. Sensing them was easier now, following them instinctively. After the first time, he'd kept his mouth shut. It was too hard to explain, and he didn't want to try.

He didn't fit in anymore. He had no idea if he would fit in in Oregon either, but he had to try. He was more like them now anyway.

The bonding was still there. He never took off the bracelet, even though it broke dress code to wear loose jewelry on duty. He couldn't bring himself to care. He knew nothing would happen to it, knew he would never be in jeopardy because of it.

Mitch rubbed his eyes, pushing the misery away with purpose. His chest tightened painfully when he found her lingering scent on his next breath. Like a distant memory, it filled him, and he wanted to scream with rage at the unfairness of it all. It flowed over him and caressed him, and he closed his eyes and reveled in it.

He didn't care that it was his imagination. He didn't care that mourning like this qualified him for a straitjacket. Her essence and touch were the only memories he had, the only memories he could think of without falling apart. If he was going to fall apart, he did that at home, alone.

He breathed again and smiled in poignant memory. Flowers, just like her. Sweet. He moved the blade again and tucked an eye on the wood figure.

"What ya working on?" Tory asked as he came in for a cup of coffee. Tory was used to his carving after so many years. He even had a piece or two himself.

"My latest project," he said without inflection. He held it up and Tory whistled.

"Beautiful," he said.

He scraped another curve and blew away the dust. *Yes, she was,* he thought to himself.

Mitch heard Big's shoes on the landing and a second later he popped through the door, getting his attention when he found Mitch. "Hey, Benedetti, there's some blonde downstairs. Says she's your wife? Mack's talking to her... Hey!"

Mitch shoved clear of the table, his chair crashing with an unholy ring when it hit cement. He was out the door and leaping past the big man, over the second-floor rail, falling to the cement floor fifteen feet below, without a thought of hesitation. He landed in a crouch, every muscle tensed as he sniffed.

"Brooke?" he whispered in aching incredulity and disbelief. He rose cautiously, a stealthy, silent fluid movement, until he stood to his full height. Mack's back was to him and blocking whoever he was talking to, but he recognized her SUV and felt a glaring ball of hope. Irrational as it was, he didn't care.

He staggered forward, fully finding her scent, and almost collapsed. Men didn't faint, he hoped, as he began to believe in the unbelievable all over again.

"Mitch? Yeah, he's a great guy, but if you want, we could go out," Mack was saying, trying to ply his way into something with Brooke.

"Back off, Mack." Mitch growled with a dark primal possessiveness spearing him at his best friend's words.

Mack spun, startled at the tone and the voice. "Yeah, sure, whatever, Mitch." Mack shoved his hands into his pockets and edged out of the way.

Mitch sank, stunned, to his knees in front of her. She was gorgeous, a lovely smile and whimsical laugh that he'd believed he'd never get to hear again. "Brooke?" He swore he was hallucinating, nearly speechless as his head swam. Sunlight brightened her honey-blonde hair, drawing the bottomless darkness of her eyes up until he felt staked to the ground by her stare. "But I thought you died," he said hoarsely, rocketing emotions bombarding him all at once. He dropped the knife that he'd forgotten he clutched in his hand from numb fingers, oblivious to the sound of steel on asphalt.

Her hand formed to his face and lifted him with hardly an ounce of effort. Angel's wings could have lifted him, for all he cared. "I did, and I didn't," she started to explain. "The explosion happened and I went—" She paused, looking over, and found they had an audience.

Mitch glared at all of them, growling low in his throat. The whole group spun and disappeared. He cupped her hand to his cheek and felt the shock of her heated skin all the way to his toes. His eyes slid shut for a brief moment of discovery. "You're alive!" he finally managed to say, reaching beyond his disbelief to say it, to really feel her hand on his skin.

She nodded. "I went into a dimension for a little while. Belphegor is gone. I just needed to get home, but I was wounded, and it took time. I didn't heal as quickly as I would have if I had been here."

"He's gone?" he asked. She nodded. "And the amulet?"

"Tucked away, safe," she assured him. "It's so protected Fort Knox looks like a corner store." His hands shook when he lifted them to touch her, tenderly cradling her face.

"I can't believe this!" he whispered. His brows drew together. "Jeralynna never said."

She pressed a finger to his lips, and he almost folded over. "She couldn't find me until I was strong enough to call to her. She didn't know if I had lived or not either. She didn't mislead you by not saying anything."

He crushed her into his arms, holding her as tight as he could against his body. "You're alive!" he cried. "Oh, God! Never leave me again!" He collapsed against the fender of the vehicle, tucking her in front of him. He scooped his hand through her hair, relearning the sensation.

"I love you," he said firmly, without hesitation.

Her smile grew, and his chest swelled. "I love you, too." Her lips were pink and lush as she looked up at him through her golden lashes. "So am I going to have to actually ask for a kiss, or what?"

Barking a quick laugh, he swooped down and claimed her. He groaned the instant he touched her, the light of their bond nearly blinding him as he caressed her mouth. He savored every little touch, locking her shaking body within his hold. He released her mouth and slid to her ear, unable to make his own shakes go away with her in his arms. "I hope you know that we're going home in about two minutes, and if you see daylight, it's going to be to answer the door for takeout."

"Who needs takeout?" she teased him. He groaned like a starving man as her tongue snaked across his flesh, expressing the lack of need for food, at least right then.

"God, I've missed that," he said.

"Me, too." She was trembling deliciously, proof of her own reactions, her own needs. He closed his eyes, thankful and nearly delirious with happiness.

He took a breath, resting his hands on her shoulders. "I'm still in shock, I think," he said as he played through her hair again. He knew he was smiling like a fool, but he just couldn't make himself care.

"I would have given you a warning, but I needed to get to you," she said with a warming, beautiful blush. "I missed you too much to wait."

He pulled her against his chest, pressing her tight to his pounding heart. "I'll get over this shock." He chuckled. "Just another one of your curves," he told her, laughing, overjoyed, too happy to care who was watching. He looked into her adoring gaze. "So now what?"

"Is today still your last day?"

"How'd...?" he asked, confused.

"Aunt Jerry. How do you think I found you on my first try?" she quipped, walking her fingers up his chest.

He gripped her hand. He was already hard as a

rock all over. He nodded, finding it difficult to talk, finding it hard to breathe.

"How do you feel about spending some time in Belgium? At Aunt Jerry's?"

He rolled his tongue, considering. "I think I could take it. No more demons or car chases or..." He watched her smile brighten her entire face.

She swept a finger to his mouth again. "No, just some plain old family, and maybe a few potions." She shifted her fingers and caressed his face. "She'd be happy to have you. She's claimed you as her favorite."

"Oh lord," he said, groaning. "Is that good?"

"Very," she assured him. "Then we come home and settle down and harass your brother and my sister about who can have the largest family."

He rocked his head and laughed. "I like that!" He wrapped his arms around her waist and lifted her up. He buried his nose in her neck and inhaled, swearing it felt as though he was flying. "Um, honey, are we on the ground?" he asked.

"Oops. Sorry."

He chuckled again.

* * * *

It was several hours later and very dark before he remembered the carving. He had tucked it inside his duffel when he'd rushed from the firehouse after saying goodbye to Tory. His chief only laughed and made a joke about how Mitch had found a wife while on vacation, but he hadn't put himself in Mitch's way from leaving early on the shift either.

Mitch slipped from bed where she slept peacefully, going to the living room and unzipping the duffel. Moonlight shined through the blinds and flashed on his bracelet, stilling his motions. As far as Mitch was concerned, it was as good as a ring, and it meant more to him. Even through her ordeal, Brooke still wore hers. They were bound. Period.

Lord, but he loved that woman.

His hand folded over the wood carving. He heard her in the bedroom as she slid from the bed and joined him. He licked his lips, remembering every nuance of her taste on his tongue. He would never take her for granted. She meant too much to him.

She caressed him as she joined him, and he stood. They'd returned to his place in her SUV, and he'd had to leave his car at the firehouse. He peeked through the blinds, and there was his car. He shook his head. Loving a witch was interesting at the very least.

"What are you hiding?" she asked.

"Something I've been working on," he admitted shyly. "But I want you to have it." He unfurled his hand, and the sharp detail of the carved wolf rested against his palm.

She sucked in an awed gasp. "It's beautiful." Her fingers traced the carving delicately. "You are talented. This is incredible."

He shrugged. "I do it to pass time. I had a lot of that until today." He caught her gaze. "It's you."

"I can tell," she replied with delighted admiration. "You even got the little fluff right there," she said, pointing behind the ear. "How did you do that?"

"I was afraid this would be my only memory. I wanted it to be perfect. You deserved that." He watched as two fat tears rolled from her eyes. "Honey, don't cry." He wrapped an arm over her shoulder, tugging her close.

She shook her head and tried to talk. It took her a moment between hard, shuddering breaths to start. "No, I understand. I was terrified. I really thought I was gone, especially when it took so long to start to heal. And all I wanted was to come back. It was the worst kind of not knowing." She held him tightly, as if she didn't want to ever let him go.

He placed the carving down on the windowsill. A moonbeam fell to wash over it. He scooped her up into his embrace and whispered, "We have the rest of our lives. Let's go to bed. We'll figure out the rest after I've kissed you another thousand times."

She sighed in teary contentment. "I love you," she murmured once more as he laid her out.

"I know, sweet. I love you, too." He stretched out next to her and set out to make her float with happiness.

* * * *

"So the family knows you're all right?" Mitch was stretched alongside her, running his hand up and down her stomach in a leisurely erotic enticement. After almost a solid day of being with each other, filling each other's hearts, lazy in bed, other concerns were starting to filter through.

Brooke lifted her arms and stretched in pure relaxed enjoyment. "Yes, I did make sure they knew, but my first priority was finding you." She locked on to his adoring gaze and blushed. "In truth, I've only been back for barely two days," she told him.

His brow arched, pain and surprise darkening his brown eyes. "You were on the other side for the whole three months?"

She nodded and shivered, not wanting to remember too vividly how it had felt, being completely devoid of sensation, of action. "It was like living in a vacuum. I never got hungry, never slept. That's probably why it took so long for me to find the energy to heal. I needed food for it to happen." She covered his hand where he rested it, flattened against her abdomen, as if offering his strength. "For all I know, it might have been less time or longer. I had no way of knowing."

"Believe me, it was the worst three months of my life," he told her in a hoarse voice, his gaze sliding closed, hiding the tortures of the past three months from her. "I died on that night," he said, his agony relived. "Today," he licked his lips and took a shaky breath, "you... I can't even put it into words." He laid his head on her abdomen, unable to put distance between them.

With a wandering finger, she traced the wrist and hand that spanned her. "I see you didn't forget." She slid a fingertip down the length of his bracelet. Her voice cracked on the lumped feeling in her throat, aware of the statement he made by still wearing it.

"And I never would have," he said, solemn in his voice and gaze. "I had plans to return to the pack. That was why I was leaving. I was going home."

"You're still happy with everything? With me?" she asked, quietly stunned but overjoyed at the same time. "After all of that? After what you know?"

He twined hands with her, their bracelets sliding on their skin. "I made a vow. 'Between you and I, one.' I haven't forgotten and I never would have, and I will never for the rest of my life let you walk away again. For anything."

His possessive tone made her smile. "You didn't last time. Even though you tried. You were still there for me." She caressed his shoulder, thrilling in the way his body shivered and tightened for her. "That was when I knew you really loved me. You were willing to face the worst thing imaginable."

"And I knew, when you sacrificed everything to keep him from killing me or anyone else." His lashes lay in gentle repose against stubble-rough cheeks as he rested against her. "So, why are we going to Aunt Jerry's?"

She smiled when he used her title instead of her name. She knew Aunt Jerry and Mitch had become close friends. "Mostly time for ourselves. We'll stay in touch with everyone and probably come back in a few months. If that's all right?"

He nodded in easy agreement. "I guess I need a passport. I've never left the States."

Brooke waved a hand. "Nah, we'll go the short way."

He cracked an eye. "Two questions. You know how to do that? And does it hurt?"

She felt a laugh tickle from the inside. "Now I do, yes. And no. Not at all." Mitch let out a relieved breath, his cracked eye closing again, and the laughter escaped. Her fingers played through his short hair. "One thing, Mitch." He murmured in contentment against her stomach. "How do you feel about kids?"

His eyes snapped open. "I don't know. I haven't even thought of it."

"Are you against trying?" she asked. Her heart was beating heavily, concerned he might be completely against children.

"Against trying, never." He grinned with a wicked smile. "But with you," he dropped a kiss where he rested, "I think you'd make a great mom." He shifted to a more serious expression. "Do you think you are?"

She shook her head. "No, but I've wanted a family and my mate for so long, I had an ache right here." She pressed a small fist against her chest. "I have you and I'm gloriously happy, but if you can handle it, I'd like to start soon."

"The old-fashioned way?" he asked with a meaningful chuckle. "I know I can handle that." He kissed her again and made leisurely tracks across her skin.

Her body surged and pulsed under his touch. She moaned hungrily when he released her hand and started warming her body to an aching simmer.

He stopped and peered at her with a sudden, surprised expression. "You know, this just occurred to me, but you realize our children and Bram's children are going to practically be siblings. Double relations."

She nodded as her lips curved. "You're right. But you do know they are five months ahead of us now," she teased him.

He dipped his head again. She moaned as his tongue lit sparks across her body. "Not for long." And he was right.

About the Author

With more than fifty e-books currently to her credit and several books in print, Diana Castilleja has kept busy since she started writing professionally in late 2004.

Diana currently resides in central Texas with her husband and son. When not focusing her energy on her family and her writing, she loves to travel and haunt bookstores. She's lived in several states across the south and midwest, as well as traveling to Mexico. With moving every year or changing schools since the fourth grade to her sophomore year, she learned that reading was a fast escape. The freedom to read about anything and everything has fueled her adult imagination. She also enjoys romance, horses, and yes, still loves to read.

Visit her online at www.DianaCastilleja.com

PURPLE SWORD PUBLICATIONS
Romance and Speculative Fiction
www.purplesword.com